THE MEDUSA HAD ARRIVED . . .

Sharon Brevix squatted on the dry part of a stony stream bed, dying. It was the second night, and she hadn't come to the ocean or a city or any people at all. Billy had told her that lost people just have to find a river and go downstream and they'll be all right, because all the rivers flow into the sea and there's always a town or people there. She had started downstream as soon as it was light on the first morning. It never occurred to her to stay where she was until she heard a car, because she must certainly still be near the road, and a car had to come by eventually. She did not reason that when she traveled the stream bed for the first hour and it did not bring her to the road, it must therefore be leading her away from it.

She was, after all, only four years old.

She heard a sound, she raised her head. She saw what at first she thought was a Christmas tree ornament, a silver ball with a dangle of gewgaws under it, in midair a few inches from her face. She blinked and resolved it into something much larger, much farther away, coming down out of the night sky. She heard a snarling howl. . . .

THEODORE STURGEON

TO MARRY MEDUSA

The two parts of this book were originally published as follows: *To Marry Medusa*, © 1958 by Theodore Sturgeon; "Killdozer," *Astounding Science Fiction*, © 1944 by Street & Smith Publications.

A Baen Book

Baen Publishing Enterprises
260 Fifth Avenue
New York, N.Y. 10001

First printing, December 1987

ISBN: 0-671-65370-9

Cover art by Armand Cabrera

Printed in the United States of America

Distributed by
SIMON & SCHUSTER
1230 Avenue of the Americas
New York, N.Y. 10020

TO MARRY MEDUSA

CHAPTER 1

"I'll bus' your face, Al," said Gurlick. "I gon' break your back. I gon' blow up your place, an' you with it, an' all your rotgut likker, who wants it? You hear me, Al?"

Al didn't hear him. Al was back of the bar in his saloon, three blocks away, probably still indignantly red, still twitching his long bald head at the empty doorway through which Gurlick had fled, still repeating what all his customers had just witnessed: Gurlick cringing in from the slick raw night, fawning at Al, stretching his stubble in a ragged brown grin, tilting his head, half-closing his sick-green, muddy-whited eyes. "Walkin' in here," Al would be reporting for the fourth time in nine minutes, "all full of good-ol'-Al this an' hiya-buddy that, an' you-know-me-Al, and how's about a little, *you*-know'; an all I says is I know you all right, Gurlick, shuck on out o' here, I wouldn't give you sand if I met you on the beach; an' him spittin' like that, right on the bar, an' runnin' out, an' stickin' his head back in an' callin' me a—" Sanctimoniously, Al would not sully his lips with the word. And the rye-and-ginger by the door would be nodding wisely and saying, "Man shouldn't mention a feller's mother, whatever," while the long-term would be clasping his glass, warm as pablum and headless as Ann Boleyn, and intoning, "You was right, Al, dead right."

Gurlick, four blocks away now, glanced back over his shoulder and saw no pursuit. He slowed his scamper to a trot and then a soggy shuffle, hunching his shoulders against the blowing mist. He kept on cursing Al, and the beer, and the rye-and-ginger, announcing that he could take 'em one at a time or all together one-handed.

He could do nothing of the kind, of course. It wasn't in him. It would have been success of a sort, and it was too late in life for Gurlick, unassisted, to start anything as new and different as success. His very first breath had been ill-timed and poorly done, and from then on he had done nothing right. He begged badly and stole when it was absolutely safe, which was seldom, and he rolled drunks providing they were totally blacked out, alone, and concealed. He slept in warehouses, box-cars, parked trucks. He worked only in the most extreme circumstances, and had yet to last through the second week. "I'll cut 'em," he muttered. "Smash their face for them, I'll . . ."

He sidled into an alley and felt along the wall to a garbage can he knew about. It was a restaurant garbage can and sometimes . . . He lifted the lid, and as he did so saw something pale slide away and fall to the ground. It looked like a bun, and he snatched at it and missed. He stooped for it, and part of the misted wall beside him seemed to detach itself and become solid and hairy; it scrabbled past his legs. He gasped in terror and kicked out, a vicious, ratlike motion, a hysterical spasm.

His foot connected solidly and the creature rose in the air and fell heavily at the base of the fence, in the dim wet light from the street. It was a small white dog, three-quarters starved. It yipped twice, faintly, tried to rise and could not.

When Gurlick saw it was helpless he laughed aloud and ran to it and kicked it and stamped on it until it was dead, and with each blow his vengeance became more mighty. There went Al, and there the two barflies and one for the cops, and one for all judges and jailers, and a good one for everyone in the world who owned anything, and to top it, one for the rain. He was a pretty big man by the time he was finished.

Out of breath, he wheezed back to the garbage can and felt around until he found the bun. It was sodden and slippery, but it was half a hamburger which some profligate had tossed into the alley, and that was all that mattered. He wiped it on his sleeve, which made no appreciable difference to sleeve or bun, and crammed the doughy, greasy mass into his mouth.

He stepped out into the light and looked up through the mist at the square shoulders of the buildings that stood around to watch him. He was a man who had fought for, killed for what was rightfully his. "Don't mess with me," he growled at the city.

A kind of intoxication flooded him. He felt the way he did at the beginning of that dream he was always having, where he would walk down a dirt path beside a lake, feeling good, feeling strong and expectant, knowing he was about to come to the pile of clothes on the bank. He wasn't having the dream just then, he knew; he was too cold and too wet, but he squared his shoulders anyway. He began to walk, looking up. He told the world to look out. He said he was going to shake it up and dump it and stamp on its fat face. "You going to know Dan Gurlick passed this way," he said.

He was perfectly right this time, because it was in him now. It had been in the hamburger and before that in the horse from which most of the hamburger had been made, and before that in two birds, one after the other, which had mistaken it for a berry. Before that . . . it's hard to say. It had fallen into a field, that's all. It was patient, and quite content to wait. When the first bird ate it, it sensed it was in the wrong place, and did nothing, and the same thing with the second. When the horse's blunt club of a tongue scooped it up with a clutch of meadow-grass, it had hopes for a while. It straightened itself out after the horse's teeth flattened it, and left the digestive tract early, to shoulder its way between cells and fibers until it rested in a ganglion. There it sensed another disappointment, and high time too— once it penetrated into the neurone-chains, its nature would be irreversibly changed, and it would have been with the horse for the rest of its life. As, in fact, it was. But after the butcher's blade missed it, and the meat-grinder wrung it, pinched it, stretched it (but in no way separated any part of it from any other), it could still go on about its job when the time came. Eight months in the deepfreeze affected it not at all, nor did hot fat. It was sold from a pushcart with a bag full of other hamburgers, and wound up in the bottom of the bag. The boy who bit into this particular hamburger was the only human being who ever saw it. It looked like a boiled raisin, or worse. The boy had had enough by then, anyway. He threw it into the alley.

The rain began in earnest. Gurlick's exaltation faded, his shoulders hunched, his head went down. He slogged through the wet, and soon sank to his usual level of feral misery. And there he stayed for a while.

CHAPTER 2

This girl's name was Charlotte Dunsay and she worked in Accounting. She was open and sunny and she was a dish. She had rich brown hair with ruby lights in it, and the kind of topaz eyes that usually belong to a special kind of blonde. She had a figure that Paul Sanders, who was in Pharmaceuticals, considered a waste on an office job, and an outright deprivation when viewed in the light of the information that her husband was a Merchant Marine officer on the Australia run. It was a matter of hours after she caught the attention of the entire plant (which was a matter of minutes after she got there) that news went around of her cheerful but unshakable "Thanks, but no thanks."

Paul considered this an outright challenge, but he kept his distance and bided his time. When the water-cooler reported that her husband's ship had come off second best in a bout with the Great Barrier Reef, and had limped to Hobart, Tasmania, for repairs, Paul decided that the day was upon him. He stated as much in the locker room and got good odds—11 to 2—and somebody to hold the money. It was, as a matter of fact, one of the suckers who gave him the cue for the single strategic detail which so far escaped him. He had the time (Saturday night), the place (obviously her apartment, since she wouldn't go out) and the girl. All he had to figure out was how to put himself on the scene, and when one of the suckers said, "Nobody gets into that place but a for-real husband or a sick kitten," he had the answer. This girl had cried when one of the boss's tropical fish was found belly-up one morning. She had rescued a praying mantis from an accountant who was flailing it against the window with the morning *Times*, and after she let the little green monster out, she had then rescued the accountant's opinion of himself with a comforting word and a smile that put dazzle-spots all over his work for the rest of the afternoon. Let her be sorry for you, and . . .

So on Saturday night, late enough so he would meet few people in the halls, but early enough so she wouldn't be in bed yet, Paul Sanders stopped for a moment by a mirror in the hallway of her apartment house, regarded his rather startling appearance approvingly, winked at it, and then went to her door and began rapping softly and excitedly. He heard soft hurrying footsteps behind the door and began to breathe noisily, like someone trying not to sob.

"Who is it? What's the matter?"

"Please," he moaned against the panel, "please, please, Mrs. Dunsay, help me!"

She immediately opened the door a peering inch. "Oh, thank God," he breathed and pushed hard. She sprang back with her hands on her mouth and he slid in and closed the door with his back. She was indeed ready for bed, as he had hardly dared to hope. The robe was a little on the sensible side, but what he could see of the gown was fine, just fine. He said hoarsely, "Don't let them get me. Don't let them get me!"

"Mr. *Sanders!*" Then she came closer, comforting,

cheering. "No one's going to get you. You come on in and sit down until it's safe for you. Oh," she cried as he let his coat fall open, to reveal the shaggy rip and the bloodstain, "you're hurt!"

He gazed dully at the scarlet stain. Then he flung up his head and set his features in an approximation of those of the Spartan boy who denied all knowledge of a stolen fox while the fox, hidden under his toga, ate his entrails until he dropped dead. He pulled his coat straight and buttoned it and smiled and said, "Just a scratch." Then he sagged, caught the doorknob behind him, straightened up, and again smiled. It was devastating.

"Oh, oh, come and sit down," she cried. He leaned heavily on her but kept his hands decent, and she got him to the sofa. She helped him off with his coat and the shirt. It was indeed only a scratch, laboriously applied with the tips of his nail scissors, but it was real, and she didn't seem to find the amount of blood too remarkable. A couple of cc's swiped from the plasma lab goes a long way on a white sport shirt.

He lay back limp and breathing shallowly while she flew to get scissors and bandages and warm water in a bowl, and averted his face from the light until she considerately turned it out in favor of a dim end-table lamp, and then he started the routine of not telling her his story because it was too bad . . . he was not fit to be here . . . she shouldn't know about such things, he'd been such a fool . . . and so on until she insisted that he could tell her anything, anything at all if it made him feel better. So he asked her to drink with him before he told her because she surely wouldn't afterward, and she didn't have anything but some sherry, and he said that was fine. He emptied a vial from his pocket into his drink and managed to switch glasses with her, and when she tasted it she frowned slightly and looked down into the glass, but by then he was talking a blue streak, a subdued, dark blue, convoluted streak that she must strain to hear and puzzle to follow. In twenty minutes he let it dwindle away to silence. She said nothing, but sat with slightly glazed eyes on her glass, which she held with both hands like a child afraid of spilling. He took it away from her and set it on the end table and took her pulse. He looked at the glass. It wasn't empty, but she'd had enough. He moved over close to her.

"How do you feel?"

She took seconds to answer, and then said slowly, "I feel . . ." Her lips opened and closed twice, and she shook her head slightly and was silent, staring out at him from topaz eyes gone all black.

"Charlotte . . . Lottie . . . lonely little Lottie. You're lonesome. You've been so alone. You need me, li'l Lottie," he crooned, watching her carefully. When she did not move or speak, he took the sleeve of her robe in one hand and, moving steadily and slowly, tugged at it until her hand slipped inside. He untied the sash with his free hand and took her arm and drew it out of the robe. "You don't need this now," he murmured. "You are warm, so warm . . ." He dropped the robe behind her and freed her other hand. She seemed not to understand what he was doing. The gown was nylon tricot, as sheer as they come.

He drew her slowly into his arms. She raised her hands to his chest as if to push him away but there seemed to be no strength in them. Her hand came forward until her cheek rested softly against his. She spoke into his ear quietly, without any particular force or expression. "I mustn't do this with you, Paul. Don't let me. Harry is the . . . there's never been anyone but him, there never must be. I'm . . . something's happened to me. Help me, Paul. Help me. If I do it with you I can't live any move; I'm going to have to die if you don't help me now." She didn't accuse him in any way. Not once.

Paul Sanders sat quite still and silent. It wasn't easy. But sometimes when you rush things they snap out of it, groggy, even sick, but nonetheless out of it, and then that's all, brother. . . . After a silent time he felt what he had been waiting for, the slow, subsiding shiver, and the sigh. He waited for it again and it came.

The blood pounded in his ears. Well, boy, if it isn't now it never will be.

CHAPTER 3

The carcass of the old trunk stood forgotten in the never-visited back edge of a junk-yard. Gurlick didn't visit it; he lived in it, more often than not. Sometimes the weather was too bitterly cold for it to serve him, and in the hottest part of the summer he stayed away from it for weeks at a time. But most of the time it served him well. It broke the wind and it kept out most of the rain; it was dirty and dark and cost-free, which three items made it pure Gurlick.

It was in this truck, two days after his encounter with the dog and the hamburger, that he was awakened from a deep sleep by . . . call it the Medusa.

He had not been having his dream of the pile of clothes by the bank of the pool, and of how he would sit by them and wait, and then of how *she* would appear out there in the water, splashing and humming and not knowing he was there. Yet. This morning there seemed not to be room in his head for the dream nor for anything else, including its usual contents. He made some grunts and a moan, and ground his stubby yellow teeth together, and rolled up to a sitting position and tried to squeeze his pressured head back into shape from the outside. It didn't seem to help. He bent double and used his knees against his temples to squeeze even harder, and that didn't help either.

The head didn't hurt exactly. And it wasn't what Gurlick occasionally called a "crazy" head. On the contrary, it seemed to contain a spacious, frigid, and meticulous balance, a thing lying like a metrical lesion on the inner surface of his mind. He felt himself capable of looking at the thing, but, for all that it was in his head, it existed in a frightening *direction*, and at first he couldn't bring himself to look that way. But then the thing began to spread and grow, and in a few rocking, groaning moments there wasn't anything in his head *but* the new illumination, this opening casement which looked out upon two galaxies and part of a third, through the eyes and minds of countless billions of individuals, cultures, hives, gaggles, prides, bevies, braces, herds, races, flocks and other kinds and quantities of sets and groupings, complexes, systems and pairings for which the language has as yet no terms; living in states liquid, solid, gaseous and a good many others with combinations and permutations among and between: swimming, flying, crawling, burrowing, pelagic, rooted, awash; and variously belegged, ciliated and bewinged; with consciousness which could be called the skulk-mind, the crash-mind, the paddle-, exaltation-, spring-, or murmuration-mind, and other minds too numerous, too difficult or too outrageous to mention. And over all, the central consciousness of the creature itself (though "central" is misleading; the hive-mind is permeative)—the Medusa, the galactic man o' war, the superconscious of the illimitable beast, of which the people of a planet were here a nerve and there an organ, where entire cultures were specialized ganglia; the creature of which Gurlick was now a member and a part, for all he was a minor atom in a simple molecule of a primitive cell—this mighty consciousness became aware of Gurlick and he of it. He let himself regard it just long enough to know it was there, and then blanked ten elevenths of his mind away from the very idea. If you set before Gurlick a page of the writings of Immanuel Kant, he would see it; he might even be able to read a number of the words. But he wouldn't spend any time or effort over it. He would see it and discard it from his attention, and if you left it in front of him, or held it there, he would see without looking and wait for it to go away.

Now, in its seedings, the Medusa had dropped its wrinkled milt into many a fantastic fossa. And if one of those scattered spores survived at all, it survived in, and linked with, the person and the species in which it found itself. If the host-integer were a fish, then a fish it would remain, acting as a fish, thinking as a fish; and when it became a "person" (which is what biologists call the individual polyps which make up the incredible colonies we call hydromedusae), it would *not* put away fishly things. On the contrary, it was to the interest of the Medusa that it keep its manifold parts specialized in the media in which they had evolved; the fish not only remained a fish, but in many cases might become much more so. Therefore in inducting Gurlick into itself, he remained—just Gurlick. What Gurlick saw of the Medusa's environment(s) he would not look at. What the Medusa sensed was only what Gurlick could sense, and (regrettably for our pride of species) Gurlick himself. It could not, as might be supposed, snatch out every particle of Gurlick's information and experience, nor could it observe Gurlick's world in any other way than through the man's own eye and mind. Answers there might be, in that rotted repository, to the questions the Medusa asked, but they were unavailable until Gurlick himself formulated them. This had always been a slow process with him. He thought verbally, and his constructions were put together at approximately oral speed. The end effect was extraordinary; the irresistible demands came arrowing into him from immensity, crossing light-years with considerably less difficulty than it found in traversing Gurlick's thin tough layer of subjective soft-focus, of not-caring, not-understanding-not-wanting-to-understand. But reach him they did, the mighty union of voice with which the super-creature conveyed ideas . . . and were answered in Gurlick's own time, in his own way, and aloud in his own words.

And so it was that this scrubby, greasy, rotten-toothed near-illiterate in the filthy clothes raised his face to the dim light, and responded to the demand-for-audience of the most mamestic, complex, resourceful and potent intellect in all the known universe: "Okay, *okay*. So whaddaya want?"

He was not afraid. Incredible as this might seem, it must be realized that he was now a member, a person of the creature; part of it. It no more occurred to him to fear it than a finger might fear a rib. But at the same time his essential Gurlickness was intact—or, as has been pointed out, possibly more so. So he knew that something he could not comprehend wanted to do something through him of which he was incapable, and would unquestionably berate him because it had not been done. . . .

But this was Gurlick! This kind of thing could hold no fears and no surprises for Gurlick. Bosses, cops, young drunks and barkeeps had done just this to Gurlick all his life! And "Okay, *okay!* So whaddaya want?" was his invariable response not only to a simple call but also, and infuriatingly, to detailed orders. They had then to repeat their orders, or perhaps they would throw up their hands and walk away, or kick him and walk away. More often than not the demand was disposed of, whatever it was, at this point, and that was worth a kick any time.

The Medusa would not give up. Gurlick would not listen, and would not listen, and . . . had to listen, and took the easiest way out, and subsided to resentful seething—as always, as ever for him. It is doubtful that anyone else on earth could have found himself so quickly at home with the invader. In this very moment of initial contact, he was aware of the old familiar response of anyone to a first encounter with him—a disgusted astonishment, a surge of unbelief, annoyance, and dawning frustration.

"So whaddaya want?"

The Medusa told him what it wanted, incredulously, as one explaining the utter and absolute obvious, and drew a blank from Gurlick. There was a moment of disbelief, and then a forceful repetition of the demand.

And Gurlick still did not understand.

CHAPTER 4

I am Guido, seventeen. I . . . think; nearly seventeen. There is always doubt about us who crawled out of the bones of Anzio and Cassini as infants, as . . . maggots out of the bones when the meat is gone. I never look back, never look back. Today the belly is full, tomorrow it must be filled. Yesterday's empty belly is nothing to fear, yesterday's full belly is meaningless today; so never look back, never look back . . .

And I am looking back because of Massoni, what he has done. Massoni who will never catch me, has locked me into his house, never knowing I am here. While he goes to all the places I live, all the places I hide, I come straight here to his own house because he is not so clever as I am and will never dream I am here. Perhaps I shall steal from him and perhaps I shall kill him. Massoni's house was part of a fortification in the war, so they say, concrete walls and an iron door and little slits for windows on two sides of the single room. But at the back, where the house is buried in the hill, is plywood, and a panel is loose. Behind is space to climb. Above the room is a flat ceiling; above that a slanted roof, so there is a small space that I, Guido, would think of and he, the clever (but not clever enough) Massoni could live with for years and never suspect. I come here. I find the iron door unlocked. I slip in. I find the loose panel, the climbing space, the dark high hole to hide in, the crack to look through at the room of Massoni. There is time. It is I, Guido, he is looking for and will look in many places before he comes back tired.

And he comes, and he is tired indeed, falling onto his bed with his overcoat on. It is nearly dark and I can see him staring up and I know he is thinking, *Where is that Guido?* And I know he is also thinking (because he talks this way), *If I could understand that Guido I could be there before he breaks the legs of another beggar, smashes the stained glass of another church, sets another fire in another print shop. . . .* If Massoni says this aloud I shall laugh aloud, because Massoni does not understand Guido and never will; because what Guido does once, Guido will never do again, so that nobody knows where Guido strikes next.

He sighs, he tightens his lips in the dimness, shakes his head hard. He is thinking. *And though he must make a mistake some day, that is not good enough. If one knew, if one could understand why, one could predict, one could be there at the time—before the time, waiting for him.*

He will never understand, never predict, and never, never be there when Guido strikes. Because Massoni cannot understand anything as simple as this: that I am Guido, and I hate because I am Guido, and I break and maim and destroy because I am Guido—because that is reason enough. Massoni is afraid because Massoni is a policeman. His life is studying things as they are, and making them into what they should be. But . . . he is not like other policemen. He is a detective policeman, without the bright buttons and the stick. The other policemen catch breakers of laws so they may be punished. Some catch them and punish them too. Massoni likes to say he stops the criminal before there is a crime. Massoni is indeed not like the other police. They understand, as I understand, that a crime without witnesses and without clues is not the affair of the police, and that is why they shrug and try to forget the things Guido does. Massoni does not forget. Worse, Massoni knows which are Guido's acts and which are not. When the acid was put in the compressor tank at the bus garage and caused the ruin of sixty-one tires, everyone thought it was Guido's work. Massoni knew it was not; four different people told me what he said. He said it was not the kind of ruin Guido would make. This is why I hide. I never hid before. Eleven times I am arrested and set free, for no clues, no witnesses. I walk in the daytime and I laugh. But now Massoni knows which things I do and which I do not. I do not know how he knows that, so I hide. They are all enemies, every one, but this Massoni, he is my first and greatest enemy. They all want to catch me, *after*; Massoni wants to stop me, *before*. All the rest are making me a plague, a legend, capable of anything; Massoni credits me only with what I do, and says—and says—that I did not do this, I could not do that. Massoni makes me small. Massoni follows everywhere, is behind me; he is beginning to be at my side too often; he will be ahead of me waiting soon, if I do not take care . . . by himself he will surround me. I am Guido and I do not underestimate real danger. I am Guido, who looks and talks and behaves like any other seventeen (I think) year old, who fills the belly yesterday and today, and possibly tomorrow, any way he can, like all the others . . . but who knows there is more in life than the belly; there is the hating to be done and too short a life to do it all if I live to be a hundred and ten; there is ruin to do, breaking hurting silencing most of all silencing . . . silencing their honks and scrapes and everlasting singing.

Massoni, lying on his bed in his overcoat, sighs and rolls over and sits up. From there he can reach the little kerosene stove to light it. When the flame is blue, he sighs, yawns, lifts the kettle to shake it and put it back on the fire. He gets up slowly, walks as if his shoes are too heavy, opens the cabinet, lifts out a—

No! Oh . . . *no!*

—lifts out a portable phonograph, sets it on the table, strokes it like a cat, opens it, takes out crank, fits it in, winds it up. Goes to cabinet again, takes a record, looks, another, another, finds one and brings it to the machine—

Not now, not now, Massoni, or you will die in a slow way Guido will plan for you.

—puts it on, puts the needle down, and again it begins, oh why, why, why is everyone in this accursed country forever making music, hearing music, walking from one music to another and humming music while they walk? Why can Massoni not make a pot of coffee without this? It is the one thing I, Guido, cannot bear . . . and I must bear it now . . . and I cannot . . . Ah, look at the fool, swinging his hand, nodding his head, he who was too tired to move not ninety seconds ago; it is as if he drew some substitute for sleep from it, and I do believe all these fools can do it, with their dancing half the night and singing the rest . . . Why, why must they have music? Why must Massoni make it now, when I am trapped up here hiding and cannot stop it and *cannot stand it* . . .

Oh look, look at him now, what is he taking from under the bed . . . surely not a . . . Oh it is, it is, it's a violin, it's that horror of shingles and catgut and the hair of horses' tails, and he, and he . . .

I will not listen, I will wrap my arms around my

head, I . . . He goes now, sawing at the thing, and the caterwauling starts and I can't keep him out of my head! . . .

He plays a lot of notes, this policeman. A lot of notes. He plays with the record, note for note with the swift fall of notes from the machine.

I look at last. His feet are apart, his chin couched on the ebony rest, his eyes half asleep, face quiet, left fingers running like an insect. His whole body . . . not sways . . . turns a little, turns back, turned by the music. His right hand with the bow is very . . . wide, and free. His whole body is . . . free in a way, like . . . flying . . . But this *I cannot stand!* I will—

He has stopped.

The record is finished. He turns it over, sets down the violin on the table, winds the crank, puts on the needle again. I hold my breath, I will roar, I will scream if . . . But he is looking at the kettle, he is at the cabinet, he is fetching a cookpot, a big can with a cover. Opens. Empty. He is sighing. He goes to phonograph (*stop it, stop it*), he stops it—only to start it over again at the beginning. He takes the big can, he—

He goes out.

Locking the door.

I am alone with this shriek of music, the violin staring up at me from its two long twisted slits.

I can run away now. Can I . . . ?

He has locked the door. Iron door in concrete wall.

And he has left his overcoat. He has left the record playing. He has left the fire in the little stove, the water about to boil on it.

He will be right back then. No time for me to pick that lock and go. I must stay here hidden and hear that gabble of music and look down at that violin, and wait, oh my God, and wait.

This country has music through its blood and bones like a disease, and a man cannot draw in a breath of air that isn't a-thrum with it. You can break the legs of a singing beggar and stop his music, you can burn the printing presses and the stacks of finished paper bearing the fly-specks and chicken-tracks by which men read the music, and still it does not stop; you can throw a brick through the shining window of a shrine and the choir practicing inside will stop, but even as you slip away in the dark you hear a woman singing to a brat, and around the corner some brainless fumbler is tinkling a mandolin. . . .

Ah, God curse that screeching record! What madness could possess what gibbering lunatic to set down such a series of squeaks and stutters? I do not know. (I will not know.) Once he did it, it should have killed him, that mish-mash of noises, but they are all mad, the Frenchmen, all lunatics to begin with, and can be excused for calling it a good Italian name. Massoni, Massoni, come back and quiet this bellowing box of yours or I shall surely come down in spite of all safety and good sense and smash it along with that grinning fiddle! To be caught, to be caught at last . . . it might be worth it, for a moment's peace and a breath of air undrenched by the *Rondo Capriccioso*.

I bite my tongue until I grunt from the pain.

I do not know what they call it, that music; cannot, will not know!

Someone laughs.

I open my throat, to be silent, breathing like this, breathing like running up a kilometer of steps . . . the door moves. It is Massoni. I will kill him very soon now. It may be that for one man to dry up the music in this country is like drying up the River Po with a spoon, but oh, this one drop of music, this Massoni, surely I will scoop him up and scatter him on the bank; for if I hate (and I do), and if I hate the gurgling men call music (and I do), and if I hate policemen (and before God I do that) then in all the world I hate this maestro-detective most of all, aside and apart and above all other things. Now I know I have been a child, with my breaking here, wrecking there. Guido will be *Guido* after this killing, so now—

But the door swings open and I see Massoni is not alone, and I sink down again quiet, and watch.

He is bringing a child, an eight-year-old boy with a dirty pale face and eyes shiny-black as that damned record. They both stop as the door swings shut and listen to it, both their silly mouths agape as if they each tried to make another ear of it to hear better. And now Massoni puts down the covered can and snatches up the violin; now again he makes the chatter and yammer of notes fly up at me, along with the violin on the record, and the boy watches, slowly moving his hands together until they hold each other, slowly making his eyes round. Massoni's face sleeps while the one hand swoops, the other crawls, then for a moment he looks down at the boy and winks at him and smiles a little and lets the face doze off again, playing notes the way a hose throws water-drops.

Then like slipping into warmth out of the snow, like the sudden taste of new bread to the starving, a silence falls over the room and I slump, weak and wet with sweat.

The boy whispers, "Ah-h-h, Signor Massoni, ah-h-h . . ."

Massoni puts down the violin and touches it with his fingertips, as if it were the hair of a beloved instead of a twisted box with a long handle on it, says, "But Vicente, it's easy you know."

"Easy for you, Signor . . ."

Massoni laughs. He gets covered can, opens. Puts ground coffee into cookpot, pours in boiling water, sets kettle aside, puts cookpot on stove, lowers flame, stirs with long spoon, talks.

I lie limp, wet in the dark, smelling the coffee, watching them.

Massoni says, smiling, "Yes if you like, easy for me, impossible for you. But it will be easy for you, Vicente. You have two lessons now—tonight, three, and already what you do is easy for you. When you have been playing for as many years as I have, you will not play as well as I; you will play better; you will not be good, you will be great."

"No, Signor, I could never—"

Massoni laughs and sweeps away the black bubbles on his coffee with his spoon. He lifts it off the burner and turns out the flame, and sets the pot on the table to settle. Says, "I tell you, small one, I know what is good and what is great and what is hopeless. I know better than anybody. I am a policeman, glad of what I do, and not a good violinist eating out my heart wanting greatness, because I know what greatness is. Take up the violin, Vicente. Go on, take it."

The boy takes the violin from the table and sets the ebony under his cheek and chin. He is afraid of it and he is past speech, and on him the violin looks the size of a 'cello.

"There," Massoni says, "there before you play a note, it is to be seen. Your feet placed so, to balance you when your music tilts the world. Your chest full like the beginning of a great voice which will be heard all over the earth. Throat, chin, belonging to the violin and it grown to you. . . . Put up the bow, Vicente, but don't play yet. Ah . . . there is what the violinist calls the Auer arm, and you in your eighth year, your third lesson! Now put the violin down again, boy, and sit, and we will talk while I have my coffee. I have embarrassed you."

I, Guido, watch from above with the bitter black

wonder of the coffee smell pressing deep in the bridge of my nose, watch the child put down the violin exquisitely, like some delicate thing sleeping lightly. He sits before Massoni, who has poured a little coffee and much milk for him in a large cup, and is ladling in sugar like an American.

Massoni drinks his black and looks through the steam at the boy, says, "Vincente, such a gift as yours is a natural thing and you must never feel you are different because of it . . . there are those who will try to make it so; pity them if you like, but do not listen to them. A man with talent eats, sweats, and cares for his children like any other. And if talent is a natural thing, remember that water is also, and fire, and wind; therefore flood and holocaust and hurricane are as natural as talent, and can consume and destroy you. . . . You do not understand me, Vicente? Then . . . I shall tell you a story. . . .

"There was a boy who had talent such as yours, or greater . . . oh, almost certainly greater. But he had no kind mother and father like yours, Vicente, no home, no sisters and brother. He was one of the wild ones who used to roam the hills after the war like dogs. Where he was born I cannot tell you, nor how he lived at all; perhaps some of the girls cared for him when he was a small baby. He was a year and a half old when he turned up at one of the UNRRA centers, starved, ragged, filthy.

"But you know what that baby could do, at a year and a half? He could whistle. Yes, he could. He would lie in his bundle of blankets and whistle, and people would stop and come and cluster around him.

"Perhaps if this happened today he would be cared for just for this one thing. But then, all was confusion; he was put with one family where the man died, and then into an orphanage which burned: these were unhappy accidents, but purely accidents. They could not quench the thing that was in him.

Before he was three he knew a thousand melodies; he could sing words he did not understand, before he could speak; he could whistle the themes of any music he had once heard. He was full of music, that boy, full to bursting."

(Above, listening, I, Guido, thought, now Massoni, who is filling you with such fairy-tales as this?)

Massoni puts his hands around the big cup as if to warm them, searches down into the black liquid as if to find more of his story, says, "Now a natural thing like talent, like pure cool mountain water, if you put it in a closed place, cover it tight, set a fire under it, nothing happens, and nothing happens, and nothing . . . until *blam!* it breaks the prison and comes out. But what comes out is no longer pure cool kind water, but a blistering devil ready to scald, soak, smash whatever is near enough. You have changed it, you see, by what you have done to it.

"So. There is this small boy, three or four years old, with more music than blood in his body. And then something happens. He is taken into the family of a Corfu shepherd and not seen for six years. When we next hear of him he is a devil, just such a blistering devil as that gout of tortured mountain water. But he is not a jet of water, he is a human being; his explosion is not over in a second, but is to go on for years.

"Something has happened to him in the shepherd's house in those six years, something which put the cover down tight over what was in him, and heated it up."

Vicente, the boy, asks, "What was it?"

Massoni says nothing for a long time, and then says he doesn't know. Says, "I mean to find out some day . . . if I can. The shepherd is dead now, the wife disappeared, the other children gone, perhaps dead too. They lived alone in a rocky place, without neighbors, fishing and herding sheep and perhaps other things . . . anyway, they are gone. All but this unhappy demon of a boy."

(I, Guido, feel a flash of rage. Who's unhappy?)

Massoni says, "So you see what can happen if a talent big enough is held back hard enough."

Vicente, the boy, says, "You mean to live apart from all music did such a thing to this child?"

Massoni shakes his head, says, "No, that would not be enough by itself. It must have been something more—something that was done to him, and done so thoroughly that this has happened."

"What things does he do?"

"Cruel, vicious things. They say meaningless things; but they are not meaningless. He beat an old beggar one night and broke his legs. He set fire to a print shop. He cut the hydraulic brake tube on a parked bus. He threw a big building-stone through the stained glass of St. Anthony's. He destroyed the big loud-speaker over the door of a phonograph shop with the handle of a broom. And there are dozens of small things, meaningless until one realizes the single thread that runs through them all. Knowing that, one can understand why he does these things (though not why he wants to). One can also know, in the long list of small crimes, cruelties and ruinations a city like this must write each day, each week, which are done by this unfortunate boy and which are not."

"Has no one seen him?" asks Vicente.

"Hardly. He took a toy from a child and smashed it under his foot, and we got a description; but it was a five-year-old child, it was after dark, it happened very quickly; it was not evidence enough to hold him. There was a witness when he wrecked the loud-speaker, and when he pushed a porter's luggage-truck on to the tracks at the railroad station, but again it was dark, fast, confused; the witnesses argued with one another and he went free. He moves like the night wind, appears everywhere, strikes when he is safe and the act is unexpected."

(Ah now, Massoni, you are beginning to tell the truth.)

The boy Vincente wants to know how one may be sure all these things are really the work of this one boy.

Massoni says, "It is the thread that runs through all his acts. In the shrine, St. Anthony's, a choir was practicing. The toy he smashed was a harmonica. On the luggage truck were instrument cases, a trombone and a flügelhorn. The damaged bus carried members of an orchestra and their instruments (and a driver who had his wits about him, tried his brakes even as he began to move, or all might have been killed). The destruction of the loud-speaker speaks for itself. Always something about music, something against music."

"The beggar?"

"A mad old man who sang all the time. You see?"

"Ah," says the boy Vicente sadly.

"Yes, it is a sad thing. If music angers him so, his days and his nights must be a furnace of fury, living as he does in the most musical land on earth, with every voice, whistle, bell, each humming, singing, plunking, tinkling man, woman and child reaching him with music . . . music reaches him, you see, as nothing can reach you and me, Vicente; it reaches him more than rain; it splashes on his heart and bones. . . . Ah, forgive me, forgive me, boy; I am using your lesson time on a matter of police business. Yet—it is not time wasted, if you gain from it something about the nature of talent, and how so natural a thing can break a block of stone to thrust one tender shoot into the sun, as you have seen a grass-blade do. And remember, too, that a great talent is not a substitute for work. A man of small skill, or even good skill like mine, must practice until his fingers bleed to bring his talent to flower; but if your talent is great, why then you must work even harder. The stronger the growth, the more tangled it can become; we want you to make a tall tree and not a great wide bramble-patch. Now enough of talk. Take up the violin."

. . . So again I Guido descended into hell, while Massoni coaxes and goads the boy who goads and coaxes the instrument to scratch, squawk, squeak and weep. In between noises is advice and learning: "A little higher with the bow arm, Vicente—so; now if there is a board resting on wrist, elbow, shoulder, I may set a brimming glass there and never spill. And to this level you must always return." . . . "Na, na, get the left elbow away from the body, Vicente. Nobody scrunches up arm and fingers that way to play . . . except Joseph Szigeti of course, and you are not going to be the second Szigeti but the first Vicente Pandori."

From my hole in the ceiling I Guido watch, and then strangely cease to watch . . . as if watching was a thing to do, to try to do and a thing I could do or not do . . . and as if I ceased trying to do this thing and became instead something not-alive, like a great gaping street-sewer, letting everything pour into me. A few minutes ago I am ready to shout, to come out, to kill—anything to stop this agony. Now I am past that. I am beaten into a kind of unconsciousness . . . no; a sleep of the will; the consciousness is open and awake as never before. Along with it a kind of blindness with the eyes seeing. I see, but I am past seeing, past understanding what I see. I do not see them finish. I do not see them go. I am, after a long time, aware of what seems to be the sound of the violin, when the big low G string is touched by one single soft bounce of the bow, scraping a little under the boy's fledgling fingers. Hearing this, over and over, I begin to see normally again and see only the dark room with a single band of light across it from a street-lamp outside the wide slit of window. Massoni is gone. Vicente is gone. The violin is gone. Yet I hear it, the soft scraping *staccato*, over and over.

It hurts my throat.

Hcoo . . . hcoo . . .

It hurts each time, the quiet sound, as if I am the violin being struck softly, and being so tender, hurting so easily, I softly cry out. . . .

And then I understand that it is not a violin I hear; I am sobbing up there in the dark. Enraged, I swallow a mouthful of sour, and stop the noise.

CHAPTER 5

"So—whaddaya want?"

The Medusa told him what it wanted, incredulously, as one explaining the utter and absolute obvious, and drew a blank from Gurlick. There was a moment of disbelief, and then a forceful repetition of the demand.

And Gurlick still did not understand. Few humans would, for not many have made the effort to comprehend the nature of the hive-mind—what it must be like to have such a mind, and further, to be totally ignorant of the fact that any other kind of mind could exist.

For in all its eons of being, across and back and through and through the immensities of space it occupied, the Medusa had never encountered intelligence except as a phenomenon of the group. It was aware of the almost infinite variations in kind and quality of the *gestalt* psyche, but so fused in its experience and comprehension were the concepts "intelligence" and "group" that it was genuinely incapable of regarding them as separable things. That a single entity of any species was capable of so much as lucid thought without the operation of group mechanisms, was outside its experience and beyond its otherwise near-omniscience. To contact any individual of a species was—or had been until now—to contact the entire species. Now, it pressed against Gurlick, changed its angle and pressed again, paused to ponder, came back again and, puzzling, yet again to do the exploratory, bewildered things a man might do faced with the opening of, and penetration through, some artifact he did not understand. There were tappings and listenings, and (analogously) pressures this way and that as if to find a left-hand thread. There were scrapings as for samples to analyze, proddings and pricks as for hardness tests, polarized rayings as if to determine lattice structures. And in the end there was a—call it a pressure test, the procedure one applies to clogged tubing or to oxide-shorts on shielded wire: blow it out. Take what's supposed to be going through and cram an excess down it.

Gurlick sat on the floor of the abandoned truck, disinterestedly aware of the distant cerebration, computation, discussion and conjecture. A lot of gabble by someone who knew more than he did about things he didn't understand. Like always.

Uh!

It had been a thing without sight or sound or touch, but it struck like all three, suffused him for a moment with some unbearable tension, and then receded and left him limp and shaken. Some mighty generator somewhere had shunted in and poured its product to him, and it did a great many things inside him somehow; and all of them hurt, and none was what was wanted.

He was simply not the right conduit for such a force. He was a solid bar fitted into a plumbing system, a jet of air tied into an electrical circuit; he was the wrong material in the wrong place and the output end wasn't hooked up to anything at all.

Spectacular, the degree of mystification which now suffused the Medusa. For ages untold there had always been some segment somewhere which could come up with an answer to anything; now there was not. That particular jolt of that particular force ought to have exploded into the psyche of every rational being on earth, forming a network of intangible, unbreakable threads leading to Gurlick and through him to Medusa itself. It had *always* happened that way—not almost always, but always. This was how the creature expanded. Not by campaign, attack, siege, consolidation, conquest, but by contact and influx. Its "spores," if they encountered any life-form which the Medusa could not control, simply did not function. If they functioned, the Medusa flowed in. *Always*.

From methane swamp to airless rock, from sun to sun through two galaxies and part of a third flickered the messages, sorting, combining, test-hypothesizing, calculating, extrapolating. And these flickerings began to take on the hue of fear. The Medusa had never known fear before.

To be thus checked meant that the irresistible force was resisted, the indefensible was guarded. Earth had a shield, and a shield is the very next thing to a weapon. It *was* a weapon, in the Medusa's lexicon; for expansion was a factor as basic to its existence as Deity to the religious, as breath or heart beat to a single animal; such a factor may not, must not be checked.

Earth suddenly became a good deal more than just another berry for the mammoth to sweep in. Humanity now had to be absorbed, by every measure of principle, of gross ethic, of life.

And it must be done through Gurlick, for the action of the "spore" within him was irreversible, and no other human could be affected by it. The chances of another being in the same sector at the same time were too remote to justify waiting, and Earth was physically too far from the nearest Medusa-dominated planet to allow for an attack in force or even an exploratory expedition, whereby expert mind might put expert hands (or palps or claws or tentacles or cilia or mandibles) to work in the field. No, it had to be done through Gurlick, who might be—must be—manipulated by thought emanations, which are nonphysical and thereby exempt from physical laws, capable of skipping across a galaxy and back before a light-ray can travel a hundred yards.

Even while, after that blast of force, Gurlick slumped and scrabbled dazedly after his staggering consciousness, and as he slowly rolled over and got to his knees, grunting and pressing his head, the Medusa was making a thousand simultaneous computations and setting up ten thousand more. From the considerations of a space-traveling culture deep in the nebula came a thought in the form of an analogy: as a defense against thick concentrations of cosmic dust, these creatures had designed spaceships which, on approaching a cloud, broke up into hundreds of small streamlined parts which would come together and reunite when the danger was past. Could that be what humanity had done? Had they a built-in mechanism, like the chipmunk's tail, the seacucumber's ejectible intestines, which would fragment the hive-mind on contact from outside, break it up into two and a half billion specimens like this Gurlick?

It seemed reasonable. In its isolation as the only logical hypothesis conceivable by the Medusa, it seemed so reasonable as to be a certainty.

How could it be undone, then, and humanity's total mind restored? Therein lay the Medusa's answer. Unify humanity (it thought, reunify humanity) and the only problem left would be that of influx. If that influx could not be done through Gurlick directly, other ways might be found: it had never met a hive-mind yet that it couldn't enter.

Gasping, Gurlick grated, "Try that again, you gon' kill me, you hear?"

Coldly examining what it could of the mists of his mind, the Medusa weighed that statement. It doubted it. On the other hand, Gurlick was, at the moment, infinitely valuable. It now knew that he could be hurt, and organisms which can be hurt can be driven. It realized also that Gurlick might be more useful, however, if he could be enlisted.

To enlist an organism, you find out what it wants, and give it a little in a way that indicates promise of more. It asked Gurlick then what he wanted.

"Lea' me lone," Gurlick said.

The response to that was a flat negative, with a faint stirring of that wrenching, explosive force it had already used. Gurlick whimpered, and the Medusa asked him again what he wanted.

"What do I want?" whispered Gurlick. He ceased, for the moment to use words, but the concepts were there. They were hate and smashed faces, and the taste of good liquor, and a pile of clothes by the bank of a pond: she saw him sitting there and was startled for a moment; then she smiled and said, "Hello, Handsome." What did he want? . . . Thoughts of Gurlick striding down the street, with the people scurrying away before him in terror and the bartenders standing in their open doors, holding shot-glasses out to him, calling, pleading. And all along South Main Street, where the fancy restaurants and clubs are, with the soft-handed hard-eyed big shots who never in their lives had an empty belly, them and their clean sweet-smelling women, Gurlick wanted them lined up and he would go down the line and slit their bellies and take out their dinners by the handful and throw it in their faces.

The Medusa at this point had some considerable

trouble interrupting. Gurlick, on the subject of what Gurlick wanted, could go on with surprising force for a very long time. The Medusa found it possible to understand this resentment, surely the tropistic flailing of something amputated, something denied full function, robbed, deprived. And of course, insane.

Deftly, the Medusa began making promises. The rewards described were described vividly indeed, and in detail that enchanted Gurlick. They were subtly implanted feedback circuits from his own imaginings, and they dazzled him. And from time to time there was a faint prod from that which had hurt him, just to remind him that it was still there.

At last, "Oh, sure, sure," Gurlick said. "I'll find out about that, about how people can get put together again. An' then, boy, I gon' step on their face."

So it was, chuckling, that Daniel Gurlick went forth from his wrecked truck to conquer the world.

CHAPTER 6

Dimity Carmichael sat back and smiled at the weeping girl. "Sex," she told Caroline, "is, after all, so *unnecessary*."

Caroline knelt on the rug with her face hidden in the couch cushion, her nape bright red from her weeping, the end strands of her hair wet with tears.

She had come unexpectedly, in mid-afternoon, and Dimity Carmichael had opened the door and almost screamed. She had caught the girl before she could fall, led her to the couch. When Caroline could speak, she muttered about a dentist, about how it had hurt, how she had been so sure she could make it home but was just too sick, and, finding herself here, had hoped Dimity would let her lie down for a few minutes. . . . Dimity had made her comfortable and then, with a few sharp unanswerable questions ("What dentist: What is his name? Why couldn't you lie down in his office? He wanted you out of there as soon as he'd finished, didn't he? In fact, he wasn't a dentist and he didn't do the kind of operations dentists do, isn't that so?"), she had reduced the pale girl to this sodden sobbing thing huddled against the couch. "I've known for a long time how you were carrying on. And you finally got caught."

It was at that point, after thinking it out in grim, self-satisfied silence, that Dimity Carmichael said sex was after all so unnecessary. "It certainly has done you no good. Why do you give in, Caroline? You don't *have* to."

"I did, I did . . ." came the girl's muffled voice.

"Nonsense. Say you wanted to, and we'd be closer to the truth. No one *has* to."

Caroline said something—*I love* (or *loved*) *him so*, or some such. Dimity sniffed. "Love, Caroline, isn't . . . *that*. Love is everything else that can be between a man and a woman, without *that*."

Caroline sobbed.

"That's your test, you see," explained Dimity Carmichael. "We are human beings because there are communions between us which are not experienced by—by rabbits, we'll say. If a man is willing to make some great sacrifice for a woman, it might be a proof of love. Considerateness, chivalry, kindness, patience, the sharing of great books and fine music—these are the things that prove a *man*. It is hardly a demonstration of manhood for a man to prove that he wants what a rabbit wants as badly as a rabbit wants it."

Caroline shuddered. Dimity Carmichael smiled tightly. Caroline spoke.

"What? What's that?"

Caroline turned her cheek to rest it in her clenching hand. Her eyes were squeezed closed. "I said . . . I just can't see it the way you do. I can't."

"You'd be a lot happier if you did."

"I know, I know . . ." Caroline sobbed.

Dimity Carmichael leaned forward. "You can, if you like. Even after the kind of life you've lived—oh, I know how you were playing with the boys from the time you were twelve years old—but that can all be wiped away, and this will never bother you again. If you'll let me help you."

Caroline shook her head exhaustedly. It was not a refusal, but instead, doubt, despair.

"Of course I can," said Dimity, as if Caroline had spoken her doubts aloud. "You just do as I say." She waited until the girl's shoulders were still, and until she lifted her head away from the couch, turned to sit on her calves, look sideways up at Dimity from the corners of her long eyes.

"Do what?" Caroline asked forlornly.

"Tell me what happened—everything."

"You know what happened."

"You don't understand. I don't mean this afternoon—that was a consequence, and we needn't dwell on it. I want the cause. I want to know exactly what happened to get you into this."

"I won't tell you his name," she said sullenly.

"His name," said Dimity Carmichael, "is legion, from what I've heard. I don't care about that. What I want you to do is to describe to me exactly what happened, in every last detail, to bring you to *this*," and she waved a hand at the girl, and her "dentist," and all the parts of her predicament.

"Oh," said Caroline faintly. Suddenly she blushed. "I—I can't be sure just wh-which time it was," she whispered.

"That doesn't matter either," said Dimity flatly. "Pick your own. For example the first time with this latest one. All right? Now tell me what happened—every last little detail, from second to second."

Caroline turned her face into the upholstery again. "Oh . . . why?"

"You'll see." She waited for a time, and then said, "Well?" and again, "Look, Caroline; we'll peel away the sentiment, the bad judgment, the illusions and delusions and leave you free. As I am free. You will see for yourself what it is to be that free."

Caroline closed her eyes, making two red welts where the lids met. "I don't know where to begin . . ."

"At the beginning. You had been somewhere—a dance, a club . . . ?"

"A . . . a drive-in."

"And then he took you . . ."

"Home. His house."

"Go on."

"We got there and had another drink, and—and it happened, that's all."

"*What* happened?"

"Oh, I can't, I can't talk about it! Not to you! Don't you see?"

"I don't see. This is an emergency, Caroline. You do as I tell you. Forget I'm me. Just talk." She paused and then said quietly, "You got to his house."

The girl looked up at her with one searching, pleading look, and staring down at her hands, began speaking rapidly. Dimity Carmichael bent close to listen, and let her go on for a minute, then stopped her. "You have to say exactly how it was. Now—this was in the parlor."

"L-Living room."

"Living room. You have to see it all again—drapes, pictures, everything. The sofa was in front of the fireplace, is that right?"

Caroline haltingly described the room, with Dimity repeating, expanding, insisting. Sofa here, fireplace there, table with drinks, window, door, easychair. How warm, how large, what do you mean red, *what* red were the drapes? "Begin again so I can see it."

More swift and soft speech, more interruption. "You wore what?"

"The black faille, with the velvet trim and that neckline, you know . . ."

"Which has the zipper—"

"In the back."

"Go on."

She went on. After a time Dimity stopped her with a hand on her back. "Get up off the floor. I can't hear you. Get up, girl." Caroline rose and sat on the couch. "No, no; lie down. Lie down," Dimity whispered.

Caroline lay down and put her forearms across her eyes. It took a while to get started again, but at last she did. Dimity drew up an ottoman and sat on it, close, watching the girl's mouth.

"Don't say *it*," she said at one point. "There are names for these things. Use them."

"Oh, I . . . just *couldn't.*"

"Use them."

Caroline used them. Dimity listened.

"But what were you feeling all this time?"

"F-Feeling?"

"Exactly."

Caroline tried.

"And did you say anything while this was going on?"

"No, nothing. Except—"

"Well?"

"Just at first," whispered the girl. She moved and was still again, and her concealing arms clamped visibly tighter against her eyes. "I think I went . . ." and her teeth met, her lips curled back, her breath hissed in sharply.

Dimity Carmichael's lips curled back and she clenched her teeth and sharply drew in her breath. "Like that?"

"Yes."

"Go on. Did he say anything?"

"No. Yes. Yes, he said, 'Caroline. Caroline. Caroline,' " she crooned softly.

"Go on."

She went on. Dimity listened, watching. She saw the girl smiling and the tears that pressed out through the juncture of forearm and cheek. She watched the faint flickering of white-edged nostrils. She watched the breast in its rapid motion, not quite like that which would result from running up stairs, because of the shallow shiver each long inhalation carried, the second's catch and hold, the gasping release. "Ah-h-h-h!" Caroline screamed suddenly, softly. "Ahh . . . I thought he loved me, I did think he loved me!" She wept, and then said, "That's all."

"No, it isn't. You had to leave. Get ready. Hm? What did he say? What did you say?"

Finally, when Caroline said, ". . . and that's all," there were no questions to ask. Dimity Carmichael rose and picked up the ottoman and placed it carefully where it belonged by the easy-chair, and sat down. The girl had not moved.

"Now how do you feel?"

Slowly the girl took down her arms and lay looking at the ceiling. She wet her lips and let her head fall to the side so she could look at Dimity Carmichael, composed in the easy-chair—a chair not too easy, but comfortable for one who liked a flat seat and a straight back. The girl searched Dimity Carmichael's face, looking apparently for shock, confusion, anger, disgust. She found none of these, nothing but thin lips, dry skin, cool eyes. Answering at last, she said, "I feel . . . awful." She waited, but Dimity Carmichael had nothing to say. She sat up painfully and covered her face with her hands. She said, "Telling it was making it happen all over again, almost real. But—"

Again a silence.

"—but it was like . . . doing it in front of somebody else. In front of—"

"In front of me?"

"Yes, but not exactly."

"I can explain that," said Dimity. "You did it in front of someone—*yourself. You were watched.* After this, every time, every single time, Caroline, you will always be watched. You will never be in such a situation again," she intoned, her voice returning and returning to the same note like some soft insistent buzzer, "without hearing yourself tell it, every detail, every sight and sound of it, to someone else. Except that the happening and the telling won't be weeks apart, like this time. They'll be simultaneous."

"But the telling makes it all so . . . cheap, almost . . . funny!"

"It isn't the telling that makes it that way. The act is itself ridiculous, ungraceful, and altogether too trivial for the terrible price one pays for it. Now you can see it as I see it; now you will be unable to see it any other way. Go wash your face."

She did, and came back looking much better, with her hair combed and the furrows gone from her brows and the corners of her long eyes. With the last of her makeup gone, she looked even younger than usual; to think she was actually two years older than Dimity Carmichael was incredible, incredible. . . . She slipped on her jacket and took up her top coat and handbag. "I'm going. I . . . feel a lot better. I mean about . . . things."

"It's just that you're beginning to feel as I do about . . . things."

"Oh!" Caroline cried from the door, from the depths of her troubles, her physical and mental agonies, the hopeless complexity of simply trying to live through what life presented. "Oh," she cried, "I wish I were like you. I wish I'd always been like you!" And she went out.

Dimity Carmichael sat for a long time in the not-quite-easy chair with her eyes closed. Then she rose and and went into the bedroom and began to take off her clothes. She needed a bath; she felt proud. She had a sudden recollection of her father's face showing a pride like this. He had gone down into the cesspool to remove a blockage when nobody else would do it.

It had made him quite sick, but when he came up, unspeakably filthy and every nerve screaming for a scalding bath, it had been with that kind of pride. Mama had not understood that nor liked it. She would have borne the unmentionable discomforts of the blocked sewer indefinitely rather than have it known even within the family that Daddy had been so soiled. Well, that's the way Daddy was. That's the way Mama was. The episode somehow crystallized the great difference between them, and why Mama had been so glad when he died, and how it was that Dimity's given name—given by him—was one which reflected all the luminance of wickedness and sin, and why Salomé Carmichael came to be known as Dimity from the day he died. No cesspools for her. Clean, cute, crisp was little Dimity, decent, pleated, skirted and cosy all her life.

To get from her bedroom into the adjoining bath—seven steps—she bundled up in the long robe. Once the shower was adjusted to her liking, she hung up the robe and stepped under the cleansing flood. She kept her gaze, like her thoughts, directed upward as she soaped. The detailed revelation she had extracted from Caroline flashed through her mind, all of it, in a second, but with no detail missing. She smiled at the whole disgusting affair with a cool detachment. In the glass door of the shower-stall she saw the ghost-reflection of her face, the coarse-fleshed, broad nose, the heavy chin with its random scattering of thick curled hairs, the strong square clean yellow teeth. *I wish I were like you, I wish I'd always been like you!* Caroline had said that, slim-waisted, full-breasted Caroline, Caroline with the mouth which, in relaxation, pouted to *kiss me*, Caroline with the skin of a peach, whose eyes were long jewels of a rare cut, whose hair was fine and glossy and inwardly ember-radiant. *I wish I were like you* . . . Could Caroline have known that Dimity Carmichael had yearned all her life for those words spoken that way by Caroline's kind of woman? For were they not the words Dimity herself repressed as she turned the pages of magazines, watched the phantoms on the stereophonic, technicolored, wide deep unbearable screen?

It was time now for the best part of the shower, the part Dimity looked forward to most. She put her hand on the control and let it rest there, ecstatically delaying the transcendent moment.

. . . *Be like you* . . . perhaps Caroline would, one day, with luck. How good not to *need* all that, how fine and clear everything was without it! How laughingly revolting, to have a man prove the power of a rabbit's preoccupations with his animal strugglings and his breathy croonings of one's name, "Salomé, Salomé, Salomé . . ." (I mean, she corrected herself suddenly and with a shade of panic, "Caroline-Caroline-Caroline.")

In part because it was time, and partly because of a swift suspicion that her thoughts were gaining a momentum beyond her control and a direction past her choice, she threw the control hard over to *Cold*, and braced her whole mind and body for that clean (surely sexless) moment of total sensation by which she punctuated her entire inner existence.

As the liquid fire of cold enveloped her, the lips of Dimity Carmichael turned back, the teeth met, the breath was drawn in with a sharp, explosive sibilance.

CHAPTER 7

Gurlick sank his chin into his collarbones, hunched his shoulders, and shuffled. "I'll find out," he promised, muttering. "You jus' let me know what you want, I'll find out f'ya. Then, boy, look out."

At the corner, sprawled out on the steps of an abandoned candy store, he encountered what at first glance seemed to be an odorous bundle of rags. He was about to pass it when he stopped. Or was stopped.

"It's on'y Freddy," he said disgustedly. "He don't know nothin' hardly."

"Gah dime, bo?" asked the bundle, stirring feebly, and extending a filthy hand which flowered on the stem of an impossibly thin wrist.

"Well, sure I said somebody oughta know," growled Gurlick, "but not him, f'godsakes."

"Gah dime, bo? Oh . . . it's Danny. Got a dime on ya, Danny?"

"All right, all right, I'll ast 'im!" said Gurlick angrily, and at last turned to Freddy. "Shut up, Freddy. You know I ain't got no dime. Listen, I wanna ast you somethin'. How could we get all put together again?"

Freddy made an effort which he had apparently

not considered worth while until now. He focused his eyes. "Who—you and me? What you mean, put together?"

"I *tole* you!" said Gurlick, not speaking to Freddy; then at the mingled pressure of threat and promise, he whimpered in exasperation and said, "Just tell me can we do it or not, Freddy."

"What's the matter with you, Danny?"

"You gon' tell me or aincha?"

Freddy blinked palely and seemed on the verge of making a mental effort. Finally he said, "I'm cold. I been cold for three years. You got a drink on you, Danny?"

There wasn't anybody around, so Gurlick kicked him. "Stoopid," he said, tucked his chin down, and shuffled away. Freddy watched him for a while, until his gritty lids got too heavy to hold up.

Two blocks farther, Gurlick saw somebody else, and immediately tried to cross the street. He was not permitted to. "No!" he begged. "No, no, no! You can't ast every single one you see." Whatever he was told, it was said in no uncertain terms, because he whined, "You gon' get me in big trouble, jus' you wait."

Ask he must: ask he did. The plumber's wife, who stood a head taller than he and weighed twice as much, stopped sweeping her stone steps as he shuffled toward her, head still down but eyes up, and obviously not going to scuttle past as he and his kind usually did.

He stopped before her, looking up. She would tower over him if he stood on a box; as it was, he was on the sidewalk and she on the second step. He regarded her like a country cousin examining a monument. She looked down at him with the nauseated avidity of a witness to an automobile accident.

He wet his lips, and for a moment the moment held them. Then he put a hand on the side of his head and screwed up his eyes. The hand fell away; he gazed at her and croaked, "How can we get together again?"

She kept looking at him, expressionless, unmoving. Then, with a movement and a blare of sound abrupt as a film-splice, she threw back her head and laughed. It seemed a long noisy while before the immense capacity of her lungs was exhausted by that first great ring of laughter, but when it was over it brought her face down again, which served only to grant her another glimpse of Gurlick's anxious filthy face, and caused another paroxysm.

Gurlick left her laughing and headed for the park. Numbly he cursed the woman and all women, and all their husbands, and all their forebears.

Into the park, the young spring had brought slim grass, tree buds, dogs, children, old people and a hopeful ice-cream vendor. The peace of these beings was leavened by a scattering of adolescents who had found the park on such a day more attractive than school, and it was three of these who swarmed into Gurlick's irresolution as he stood just inside the park, trying to find an easy way to still the demand inside his head.

"Dig the creep," said the one with *Heroes* on the back of his jacket, and another: "Or-*bit*!" and the three began to circle Gurlick, capering like stage Indians, holding fingers out from their heads and shrilling, "Bee-beep! bee-beep" satellite signals.

Gurlick turned back and forth for a moment like a weathervane in a williwaw, trying to sort them out. "Giddada year," he growled.

"Bee-beep!" cried one of the satellites. "Stand by fer re-*yentry!*'" The capering became a gallop as the orbits closed, swirled around him in a shouting blur, and at the signal, "Burnout!" they stopped abruptly and the one behind Gurlick dropped to his hands and knees while the other two pushed. Gurlick hit the ground with a *whoosh*, flat on his back with his arms and legs in the air. Around the scene, one woman cried out indignantly, one old man's mouth popped open with shock, and everyone else, everyone else, laughed and laughed.

"Giddada year," gasped Gurlick, trying to roll over and get his knees under him.

One of the boys solicitously helped him to his feet, saying to another, "Now, Rocky, ya shoonta. Ya shoonta." When the trembling Gurlick was upright and the second of the trio—the "Hero"—down on his hands and knees behind him again, the solicitous one gave another push and down went Gurlick again. Gurlick, now dropping his muffled pretenses of threat and counterattack, lay whimpering without trying to rise. Everybody laughed and laughed, all but two, and they didn't do anything. Except move closer, which attracted more laughters.

"Space Patrol! Space Patrol," yelled Rocky, pointing at the approaching blue uniform. "Four o'clock high!"

"Esss-*cape* velocity!" one of them barked; and with their antenna-fingers clamped to their heads and a chorus of shrill *beep-beeps* they snaked through the crowd and were gone.

"Bastits. Lousy bastits. I'll killum, the lousy bastits," Gurlick wept.

"Ah right. *Ah* right! Break it up. Move it along. Ah right," said the policeman. The crowd broke it up immediately ahead of him and moved along sufficiently to close the gap behind, craning in gap-mouthed anticipation of another laugh . . . laughter makes folks feel good.

The policeman found Gurlick on all fours and jerked him to his feet, a good deal more roughly than Rocky had done. "Ah right, you, what's the matter with you?"

The indignant lady pushed through and said something about hoodlums. "Oh," said the policeman, "hoodlum, are ye?"

"Lousy bastits," Gurlick sobbed.

The policeman quelled the indignant lady in mid-protest with a bland, "Ah right, don't get excited, lady; I'll handle this. What you got to say about it?" he demanded of Gurlick.

Gurlick, half suspended from the policeman's hard hand, whimpered and put his hands to his head. Suddenly nothing around him, no sound, no face, pressed upon him more than that insistence inside. "I don't care there *is* lotsa people, don't make me ast now!"

"What'd you say!" demanded the policeman truculently.

"A'right! A'right!" Gurlick cried to the Medusa, and to the policeman. "All I want is, tell me how we c'n get together again."

"*What?*"

"All of us," said Gurlick. "Everybody in the world."

"He's talking about world peace," said the indignant woman. There was laughter. Someone explained to someone else that the bum was afraid of the Communists. Someone else heard that and explained to the man behind him that Gurlick was a Communist. The policeman heard part of that and shook Gurlick. "Don't you go shootin' your mouth off around here no more, or it's the cooler for you. Get me?"

Gurlick sniveled and mumbled, "Yessir. Yessir," and sidled, scuttled, cringed away.

"Ah right. Move it along. Show's over. Ah right, there. . . ."

When he could, Gurlick ran. He was out of breath before he began to run, so his wind lasted him only to the edge of the park, where he reeled against the railing and clung there to whimper his breath back again. He stood with his hands over his face, his fingers trying to press back at that thing inside him, his mouth open and noisy with self-pity and anoxia. A hand fell on his shoulder and he jumped wildly.

"It's all right," said the indignant woman. "I just wanted to let you know, everybody in the whole world isn't cruel and mean and—and—mean and cruel."

Gurlick looked at her, working his mouth. She was in her fifties, round-shouldered, bespectacled, and most earnest. She said, "You go right on thinking about world peace. Talking about it too."

He was not yet capable of speaking. He gulped air, it was like sobbing.

"You poor man." She fumbled in an edge-flaked patent leather pocketbook and found a quarter. She held it and sighed as if it were an heirloom, and handed it to him. He took it unnoticing and put it away. He did not thank her. He asked, "Do you know?" He pressed his temples in that newly developed compulsive gesture. "I got to find out, see? I got to."

"Find out what?"

"How people can get put back together again?"

"Oh," she said. "Oh, dear." She mulled it over. "I'm afraid I don't know just what you mean."

"Y'see?" he informed his inner tormentor, agonized. "Ain't nobody knows—nobody!"

"Please explain it a little," the woman begged. "Maybe there's *some*one who can help you, if I can't."

Gurlick said hopelessly, "It's about people's brains, see what I mean, how to make all the brains go together again."

"Oh, you poor man . . ." She looked at him pityingly clearly certain that his brains indeed needed putting together again, and *Well, at least he realizes it, which is a sight more than most of us do.* "I know!" she cried. "Dr. Langley's the man for you. I clean for him once a week, and believe me, if you want to know somebody who knows about the brain, he's the one. He has a machine that draws wiggly lines and he can read them and tell what you're thinking."

Gurlick's vague visualization of such a device flashed out to the stars, where it had an electrifying effect. "Where's it at?"

"The machine? Right there in his office. He'll tell you all about it; he's such a dear kind man. He told *me* all about it, though I'm afraid I didn't quite—"

"Where's it at?" Gurlick barked.

"Why, in his office. Oh, you mean, where. Well, it's 13 Deak Street, on the second floor; look, you can almost see it from here. Right there where the house with the—"

Without another word Gurlick put down his chin and hunched his shoulders and scuttled off.

"Oh, dear," murmured the woman, worriedly. "I do hope he doesn't bother Dr. Langley too much. But then, he wouldn't; he *does* believe in peace." She turned away from her good deed and started home.

Gurlick did not bother Dr. Langley for long, and he did indeed bring him peace.

CHAPTER 8

Mbala slipped through the night, terrified. The night was for sleep, for drowsing in the kraal with one of one's wives snoring on the floor and the goats shifting and munching by the door. Let the jungle mutter and squeak then, shriek and clatter and be still, rustle and rush and roar; it was proper that it should do all these things. It was full of devils, as everyone knew, and that was proper too. They never came into the kraal, and Mbala never went into the dark. Not until now.

I am walking upside down, he thought. The devils had done that. The top of him had forgotten how to see, and his eyes stretched round and protuberant against the blackness. But his feet knew the trail, every root and rock of it. He sidled, because somehow his feet saw better that way, and his assegai, poised against—what?—was more on the ready.

His assegai, blooded, honorable, bladed now for half its length . . . he remembered the day he had become a man and had stood stonily to receive it, bleeding from the ceremony, sick from the potions which had been poured into him and which, though they bloated his stomach, did nothing to kill the fire-ants of hunger that crawled biting inside him. He had not slept for two nights and a day, he had not eaten for nearly a week, and yet he could remember none of these feelings save as detached facts, like parts of a story told of someone else. The single thing that came to him fine and clear was his pride when they pressed his assegai into his hand and called him man. His slender little assegai, with its tiny pointed tip, its long unmarked shaft. He thought of it now with the same faint leap of glory it always brought him, but there was a sadness mixed with it now, and an undertone of primal horror; for although the weapon which slanted by his neck now was heavy steel, beautiful with carvings, it was useless . . . useless . . . and he was less of a man than that young warrior with his smooth tipped stick, he was less of a man than a boy was. In the man's world the assegai was never useless. It might be used well or ill, that was all. But this was the devil's world, and the assegai had no place or purpose here save to comfort his practiced hand and the tight-strung cords of his ready shoulder and back. It became small comfort, and by the moment smaller, as he realized its uselessness. His very manhood became a foolishness like that of old Nugubwa, whose forearm was severed in a raid, who for once did not die but mended, and who carried the lost limb about with him until there was nothing left of it but a twisted bundle like white sticks.

A demon uttered a chattering shriek by his very ear and scampered up into the darkness; the fright was like a blaze of white light in his face, so that for long seconds the night was full of floating flashes inside his eyeballs. In the daytime such a sound and scamper meant only the flight of a monkey; but here in the dark it meant that a demon had taken the guise of a monkey. And it broke him.

Mbala was frozen in the spot, in the pose of his

fright, down on one knee, body arched back and to the side, head up, assegai drawn back and ready to throw at the source of his terror. And then—

He slumped, wagged his head foolishly, and climbed to his feet like an old old man, both hands on the staff of the spear and its butt in the ground. He began to trudge forward, balanced no longer on the springs of his toes, no longer sidewise and alert, but walking flat-footed and dragging his assegai behind him like a child with a stick. His eyes had ceased to serve him so he closed them. His feet knew the way. Beside him something screamed and died, and he shuffled past as if he had heard nothing. He dimly realized that he was in some way past fear. It was not any kind of courage. It was instead a stupidity marching with him like a ring of men, a guard and a barrier against everything. In reality it was a guard against nothing, and a gnat or a centipede would penetrate it quite as readily as a lion. But through such a cordon of stupidity, Mbala could not know that, and so he found a dim content. He walked on to his yam patch.

With Mbala's people, the yam patch was a good deal more than a kitchen garden. It was his treasure, his honor. His women worked it; and when it yielded well and the bellies of his kin were full, a man could pile his surplus by his door and sit and contemplate it, and accept the company of the less fortunate who would come to chat, and speak of anything but yams while the yearning spittle ran down their chins; until at last he deigned to give them one or two and send them away praising him; or perhaps he would give them nothing, and at length they would leave, and he could sense the bitter curses hiding in the somber folds of their impassive faces, knowing they could sense the laughter in his own.

Tribal law protecting a man's yam patch was specific and horrifying in its penalties, and the tabus were mighty. It was believed that if a man cleared a patch and cultivated it and passed it on to his son, the father's spirit remained to watch and guard the patch. But if a man broke some tabu, even unknowingly, a devil would drive away the guardian spirit and take its place. That was the time when the patch wouldn't yield, when the worms and maggots attacked, when the elephant broke down the thorn trees . . . and when the grown yams began to disappear during the night. Obviously no one but a demon could steal yams at night.

And so it was that misfortune, grown tall, would mount the shoulders of misfortune. A man who lost yams at night was to be avoided until he had cleansed himself and propitiated the offended being. So when Mbala began to lose yams at night, he consulted the witch doctor, who at considerable cost—three links of a brass chain and two goats—killed a bird and a kid and did many mumbling things with stinking smokes and bitter potions and spittings to the several winds, and packed up his armamentarium and hunkered down to meditate and at last inform Mbala that no demon was offended, except possibly the shade of his father, who must be furious in his impotence to guard the yams from, not a devil, but a man. And this man must be exorcised not by devil's weapons but by man's. At news of this, Mbala took a great ribbing from Nuyu, his uncle's second son. Nuyu had traveled far to the east and had sat in the compound of an Arab trader, and had seen many wonders and had come back with a lot less respect than a man should have for the old ways. And Nuyu said among howls of laughter that a man was a fool to pay a doctor for the doctor's opinion that the doctor could not help him; he said that he, Nuyu, could have told him the same thing for a third the price, and any unspoiled child would have said it for nothing. Others did not—dared not—laugh aloud like

Nuyu, but Mbala knew well what went on behind their faces.

Well, if a man stole his yams at night, he must hunt the man at night. He failed completely to round up a party, for though they all believed the doctor's diagnosis, still night marches and dealings with demon's work—even men doing demon's work—were not trifles. It was decided after much talk that this exorcism would bring great honors to anyone so brave as to undertake it, so everyone in the prospective hunting party graciously withdrew and generously left the acquisition of such honors to the injured party, Mbala. Mbala was thereby pressured not only into going, but also into thanking gravely each and every one of his warrior friends and kinsmen for the opportunity. This he did with some difficulty, girded himself for battle, and was escorted to the jungle margin at evening by all the warriors in the kraal, while his wives stood apart and wept. The first three nights he spent huddled in terror in the tallest solid crotch he could find in the nearest tree out of sight of the kraal, returning each day to sit and glower so fiercely that no one dared ask him anything. He let them think he had gone each night to the patch. Or hoped they thought that. On the fourth morning he climbed down and turned away from the tree to be greeted by the smiling face of his cousin Nuyu, who waved his assegai and walked off laughing. And so at last Mbala had to undertake his quest in earnest. And this was the night during which the demons scared him at last into the numbness of impenetrable stupidity.

He reached his patch in the blackest part of the night, and slipped through the thorns with the practiced irregular steps of a modern dancer. Well into the thickest part of the bush which surrounded his yams—a bush his people called *makuyu* and others astralagus vetch—he hunkered down, rested his hands on his upright spear and his chin on his forearms. So he was here—splendid. Bad luck, thievery, shame and stupidity had brought him to this pinnacle, and now what? Man or devil, if the thief came now he would not see him.

He dozed, hoping for some lightening of the leaden sky, for a suspicious sound, for anything that would give him a suggestion of what to do next. He hoped the demons could not see him crouched there in the vetch, though he knew perfectly well they could. He was stripped of his faith and his courage; he was helpless and he did not care. His helplessness commanded this new trick of stupidity. He hid in it, vulnerable to anything but happily unable to see out. He slept.

His fingers slipped on the shaft of the assegia. He jolted awake, peered numbly around, yawned and let the weapon down to lie across his feet. He hooked his wide chin over his bony updrawn knees and slept again.

CHAPTER 9

"You Doctor Langley?"

The doctor said, "Good God."

Dear kind man he might be to his cleaning lady, but to Gurlick he was just another clean man full of knowledges and affairs which Gurlick wouldn't understand, plus the usual foreseeable anger, disgust and intolerance Gurlick stimulated wherever he went. In short, just another one of the bastits to hate.

Gurlick said, "You know about brains?"

The doctor said, "Who sent you here?"

"You know what to do to put people's brains together again?"

"What? Who are you? What do you want anyway?"

"Look," said Gurlick, "I got to find this out, see. You know how to do it, or not?"

"I'm afraid," said the doctor icily, "that I can't answer a question I don't understand."

"So ya *don't* know anything about brains."

The doctor sat tall behind a wide desk. His face was smooth and narrow, and in repose fell naturally into an expression of arrogance. No better example in all the world could have been found of the epitome of everything Gurlick hated in his fellow-man.

The doctor was archetype, coda, essence; and in his presence Gurlick was so unreasonably angry as almost to forget how to cringe.

"I didn't say that," said Langley. He looked at Gurlick steadily for a moment, openly selecting a course of action: Throw him out? Humor him? Or study him? He observed the glaring eyes, the trembling mouth, the posture of fear-driven aggressiveness. He said, "Let's get something straight. I'm not a psychiatrist." Aware that this creature didn't know a psychiatrist from a CPA, he explained, "I mean, I don't treat people who have problems. I'm a physiologist, specializing on the brain. I'm just interested in how brains do what they do. If the brain was a motor, you might say I am the man who writes the manual that the mechanic studies before he goes to work. That's all I am, so before you waste your own time and mine, get that straight. If you want me to recommend somebody who can help you with whatev—"

"You tell me," Gurlick barked, "you just tell me that one thing and that's all you got to do."

"What one thing?"

Exasperated, adding his impatience with all his previous failures to his intense dislike of this new enemy, Gurlick growled, "I tole ya." When this got no response, and when he understood from the doctor's expression that it would get no response, he blew angrily from his nostrils and explained, "Once everybody in the world had just the one brain, see what I mean. Now they's all took apart. All you got to tell me is how to stick 'em together again."

"You seem to be pretty sure that everybody—how's that again?—had the same brain once."

Gurlick listened to something inside him. Then, "Had to be like that," he said.

"Why did it have to be?"

Gurlick waved a vague hand. "All this. Buildin's.

Cars, cloe's, tools, 'lectric, all like that. This don't git done without the people all think with like one head."

"It did get done that way, though. People can work together without—thinking together. That is what you mean, isn't it—all thinking at once, like a hive of bees?"

"Bees, yeah."

"It didn't happen that way with people, believe me. What made you think it did?"

"Well, it did, thass all," said Gurlick positively.

A startled computation was made among the stars, and, given the axiom which had proved unalterably and invariably true heretofore, namely, that a species did not reach this high a level of technology without the hive-mind to organize it, there was only one way to account for the doctor's incredible statement—providing he did not lie—and Gurlick, informed of this conclusion, did his best to phrase it. "I guess what happened was, everybody broke all apart, they on their own now, they just don't remember no more. I don't remember it, you don't remember it, that one time you and me and everybody was part of one great big brain."

"I wouldn't believe that," said the doctor, "even if it were true."

"Sure not," Gurlick agreed, obviously and irritatingly taking the doctor's statement as a proof of his own. "Well . . . I still got to find out how to stick 'em all together again."

"You won't find it out from me. I don't know. So why don't you just go and—"

"You got a machine, it knows what you're thinkin'," said Gurlick suddenly.

"I have a machine which does nothing of the kind. Who told you about me, anyway?"

"You show me that machine."

"Certainly not. Look, this has been very interesting, but I'm busy and I can't talk to you any more. Now be a good—"

"You got to show it to me," said Gurlick in a terrifying whisper; for through his fogbound mind had shot his visions (she's in the water up to her neck, saying, *Hello, Handsome*, and he just grins, and she says, *I'm coming out*, and he says, *Come on then*, and slowly she starts up toward him, the water down to her collarbone, to her chest, to—) and a smoky curl of his new agony; he had to get this information, he *must*.

The doctor pressed himself away from his desk a few inches in alarm. "That's the machine over there. It won't make the slightest sense to you. I'm not trying to hide anything from you—it's just that you wouldn't understand it."

Gurlick sidled over to the equipment the doctor had pointed to. He stood looking at it for a moment, flashing a cautious ratlike glance toward the doctor from time to time, and pulling at his mouth. "What you call this thing?"

"An electroencephalograph. Are you satisfied?"

"How's it know what you're thinkin'?"

"It doesn't. It picks up electrical impulses from a brain and turns them into wavy lines on a strip of paper."

Watching Gurlick, the doctor saw clearly that in some strange way his visitor was not thinking of the next question; he was waiting for it. He could see it arrive.

"Open it up," said Gurlick.

"What?"

"Open it. I got to look at the stuff inside it."

Again that frightening hiss: "I got to see it."

The doctor sighed in exasperation and pulled open the file drawer of his desk. He located a manual, slapped it down on the desk, leafed through it and opened it. "There's a picture of it. It's a wiring diagram. If it makes any sense to you it'll tell you more than a look inside would tell you. I hope it tells you that the thing's far too complicated for a man without train— "

Gurlick snatched up the manual and stared at it. His eyes glazed and cleared. He put the manual down and pointed. "These here lines is wires?"

"Yes."

"This here?"

"A rectifier. It's a tube. You know what a tube is."

"Like radio tubes. Electric is in these here wires?"

"This can't mean anyth— "

"What's this here?"

"Those little lines? Ground. Here, and here, and over here the current goes to ground."

Gurlick placed a filthy fingertip on the transformer symbol. "This changes the electric. Right?"

Dumbfounded, Langley nodded. Gurlick said, "Regular electric comes in here. Some other kind comes in here. What?"

"That's the detector. The input. The electrodes mean whatever brain the machine is hooked up to feeds current in there."

"It ain't very much."

"It ain't," mimicked the doctor weakly, "very much."

"You got one of those strips with the wavy lines?"

Wordlessly the doctor opened the drawer, found a trace, and tossed it on top of the diagram. Gurlick pored over it for a long moment, referring twice to the wiring diagram. Suddenly he threw it down. "Okay. Now I found out."

"You found out what?"

"What I wanted."

"Will you be kind enough to tell me just what you found?"

"God," said Gurlick disgustedly, "how sh'd *I* know?"

Langley shook his head, suddenly ready to laugh at this mystifying and irritating visitation. "Well, if you've found it, you don't have to stick around. Right?"

"Shut up," said Gurlick, cocking his head, closing his eyes. Langley waited.

It was like hearing one side of a phone conversation, but there was no phone. "How the hell I'm supposed to do *that?*" Gurlick demanded at one point, and later, "I gon' need money for anything like that. No, I can't. I can't, I tell ya; you just gon' git me in th' clink. . . . What you think he's gon' be doin' while I take it?"

"Who are you talking to?" Langley demanded.

"I dunno," said Gurlick. "Shut up, now." He fixed his gaze on the doctor's face, and for seconds it was unseeing. Then suddenly it was not, and Gurlick spoke to him: "I got to have money."

"I'm not giving any handouts this season. Now get out of here."

Gurlick, showing all the signs of an unwelcome internal goading, came around the desk and repeated his demand. As he did so, he saw for the very first time that Doctor Langley sat in a wheelchair.

That made all the difference in the world to Gurlick.

CHAPTER 10

Henry was tall. He stood tall and sat tall and had a surprisingly adult face, which made him all the more ridiculous as he sat through school day after day, weeping. He did not cry piteously or with bellows of rage and outrage, but almost silently, with a series of widely spaced, soft, difficult sniffs. He did what he was told (*Get in line . . . move your chairs, it's story time . . . fetch the puzzles . . . put away the paints*) but he did not speak and would not play or dance or sing or laugh. He would only sit, still as a spike, and sniff. Henry was five and kindergarten was tough for him. Life was tough for him. "Life is tough," his father was fond of saying, "and the little coward might as well learn."

Henry's mother disagreed, but deviously. She lied to everyone concerned—to her husband, to Henry's teacher, to the school psychologist and the principal and to Henry himself. She told her husband she was shopping in the mornings but instead she was sitting in the corner of the kindergarten room watching Henry crying. After two weeks of this the psychologist and the principal corralled her and explained to her that the reality of home involved having her at home, the reality of school involved *not* having her at school, and Henry was not going to face the reality of school until he could experience it without her. She agreed immediately, because she always agreed with anyone who had a clear opinion about anything, went back to the room, told the stricken Henry that she would be waiting just outside, and marched out. She completely overlooked the fact that Henry could see her from the window, see her walk down the path and get into her car and drive away. If he had any composure left after that it was destroyed after a few minutes when, having circled the block and concealed her car, she crept back past the *Keep Off the Grass* sign, and spent the rest of the morning peeping in the window. Henry saw her right away, but the teacher and the principal didn't catch on to it for weeks. Henry continued to sit stiffly and hiss out his occasional sobs, wondering numbly what there was about school so terrifying as to make his mother go to such lengths to protect him, and, whatever it was, feeling a speechless horror of it.

Henry's father did what he could about Henry's cowardice. It pained him because, though he was certain it didn't come from his side, other people might not know that. He told Henry ghost stories about sheeted phantasms which ate little boys and then sent him up to bed in the dark, in a room where there was a hot-air register opening directly into the ceiling of the room below. The father had troubled to spread a sheet over the register and when he heard the boy's door open and close, he shoved a stick up through the register and moaned. The white form rising up out of the floor elicited no sound or movement from Henry, so the father went upstairs, laughing to see the effect he had not heard. Henry stood as stiff as ever, straight and tall, motionless in the dark, so his father turned on the light and looked him over, and then gave him a good whaling. "Five years old," he told the mother when he got back downstairs, "and he wets his pants yet."

He jumped out shouting at Henry from around corners and hid in closets and made animal noises and he gave him ruthless orders to go out and punch eight- and ten-year-olds in the nose and warmed his seat for him when he refused, but he just couldn't seem to make the dirty little sissy into anything else. "Blood will tell," he used to say knowingly to the mother who had never stood up to anyone in her life and had manifestly tainted the boy. But he clung to the hope that he could do something about it, and he kept trying.

Henry was afraid when his parents quarreled, because the father shouted and the mother wept; but he was afraid when they did not quarrel too. This was a special fear, raised to its peak on the occasion when the father spoke to him pleasantly, smiling. Undoubtedly the father himself did not realize it, but his pattern for punishing the boy was invariably a soft-voiced, smiling approach and a sudden burst of brutality, and Henry had become incapable of discriminating between a genuine pleasantry and one of these cheerful precursors to punishment. Meanwhile his mother coddled and cuddled him secretly and unsystematically, secretly violated his father's deprivations by contrabanding to him too much cookies and candy, yet all the while turned a cold and unresponsive back to any real or tacit plea for help in the father's presence. Henry's natural curiosity, along with his normal rebelliousness, had been thoroughly excised when they first showed themselves in his second and third years, and at five he was so thoroughly trained that he would take nothing not actually handed to him by a recognized authority, go nowhere and do nothing unless and until clearly instructed to do so. Children should be seen and not heard. Do not speak unless spoken to. "Why didn't you poke that kid right in the nose? Why? *Why?*"

"Daddy, I—"

"Shaddup, you little yellow-belly. I don't want to hear it."

So tall little, sad little Henry sat sniffing in kindergarten, and was numbly silent everywhere else.

CHAPTER 11

After clubbing Dr. Langley with the floor lamp, Gurlick rummaged around as ordered, and, bearing a bundle, went shopping. The Medusa permitted him to shop for himself first, quite willing to concede that he knew the subtleties of his own matrix better than it did. He got a second-hand suit from a hockshop in the tenderloin district, and a shave and a trim at the barber college. Esthetically the improvement was negligible; socially it was enormous. He was able to get what he wanted, though none of it was easy, since he personally knew the names of none of the things he was compelled to buy. Probably the metal samples were hardest of all to acquire; he had to go into an endless succession of glassy-eyed silences before a bewildered lab supply clerk undertook to show him a periodic table of the elements. Once he had that, things moved more rapidly. By pointing and mumbling and asking and trancing, he acquired lab demonstration samples of nickel, aluminum, iron, copper, selenium, carbon and certain others. He asked for but could not afford deuterium, four-nines pure tantalum, and six-nines silver. The electrical-supply houses frustrated him deeply on the matter of small-gauge wire with a square cross-section, but someone at last directed him to a jewelry-findings store and at last he had what he wanted.

By now he was burdened with a wooden crate rigged by an accommodating clerk into something approximating a foot-locker in size and shape, with a rope handle to carry it by. His destination was decided after a painful prodding session by the Medusa, which dug out of Gurlick's unwilling brain a memory that Gurlick himself had long ago let vanish—a brief and unprofitable stab at prospecting, or rather at carrying the pack for a friend who was stabbing at it, years ago. The important facet of the memory was an abandoned shack miles from anywhere, together with a rough idea of how to get there.

So Gurlick took a bus, and another bus, and stole a jeep and abandoned it, and at last, cursing his tormentors, slavering for his dream, and wailing his discomfort, he walked.

Heavy woods, an upland of scrub pine and dwarf maple, then a jagged rock ridge—that was it; and the roofless remnant of the shack like a patch of decay between and against the stained tooth-roots of the snaggly ridge.

More than water, more than food or to be left alone, Gurlick wanted rest, but he was not allowed it. Panting and sniffling, he fell to his knees and began to fumble with the ropes on his burden. He took out the mercury cells and the metal slugs and the wire and tube-sockets, and began to jumble them together. He didn't know what he was doing and he didn't have to. The work was being done by an aggregate of computing wills scattered across the heavens, partly by direct orders, partly by a semi-direct control, brain to neurone, bypassing that foggy swamp which comprised Gurlick's consciousness. Gurlick disliked the whole thing mightily, but except for a lachrymose grumble, no protest was possible. So he blubbered and slaved, and did not, could not, let up until it was finished.

When it was finished, Gurlick was released. He stumbled away from it, as if a rope under tension had tied him and was suddenly cut. He fell heavily, reared up on his elbows to blink at the thing, and then exhaustion overcame him and he slept.

When he fell asleep it was a tangle of wires and components, a stack of dissimilar metals strangely assembled, and with . . . capabilities. While he slept, the thoughts from the stars operated it, directly at last, not needing his blunt fumbling fingers. Within one of the circlets of square wire, a small mound of sand began to smoke. It rose suddenly and drifted down, rose again and drifted down, and lay finally smooth and flat. A depression of an unusual shape appeared in it. A block of Invar tumbled end over end from the small pile of metals and dropped into the sand. It slumped, melted, ran and was cast. Another piece was formed, then another, and with a swirl like the unpredictable formation of a dust-devil, the pieces whirled and fell together, an assembly. A coil of enameled copper wire rolled to the sand bed and stopped rolling . . . but continued to rotate, as its free end crawled outward to the assembly, snaked here, there, around a prong. A faint smell of burning, and the wire was spot-welded in seven places, and burned through where it was not needed.

Now Gurlick's original conglomeration began to shed its parts, some being invisibly shoved aside, others being drawn in to join the growing aggregate. Sometimes there was a long pause as if some inhuman digestive process were going on within the growing machine; then it would shudder as if shaken more tightly together, or it could thrust out a new sub-assembly to one side, which in turn would erect a foot-high T-shaped mast which would begin to swing from side to side as if seeking. Or there would be a flurry of activity as it tried and rejected materials in rapid succession; after one such scurry, its T-headed mast aimed at the rock near-by. There was a tense moment, a flicker of violet corona discharge; a great bite appeared in the rock, and a cold cloud of rock-dust which drifted over to the new machine and was absorbed into it—traces of silver, traces of copper, and certain borosilicates.

And when it was finished, it was . . . it was what Gurlick had built. However, it bore the same relation to the original as a superheterodyne receiver does to a twenty-cent home-rigged crystal set. Like its predecessor, it began, on the instant of its completion, to build another, more advanced version of itself.

CHAPTER 12

Tony Brevix and his wife and their four kids and the cat were moving. Tony drove the truck, a patched, rusted, flap-fendered quarter-ton panel truck with an immense transmission, a transmogrified rear end, and a little bitty motor that had rated 42 horsepower American when it was new, which was certainly not recently. In the truck were almost all of their household goods, carefully not packed in boxes, but stacked, folded, wadded and rodded down until the entire truck body was solid as a rubber brick. With Tony rode one and occasionally two of the children, who for children's mysterious reasons counted it a privilege to be subjected to the cold, the oil-smoke from the breather which came up through the holes under the floorboard, and the vehicle's strange slantwise gait as it carried its eightfold overload on only three ancient shock-absorbers. The cat did not ride in the truck, as there was no glass in the side windows.

Atty Brevix (her name, infuriatingly, was Beatitude, which made Batty and Titty and even, in the midst of an argument, Attitude) drove the station wagon, a long, hushed, low, overpowered this-year's dreamboat with lines as clean as those of a baseball bat and an appetite like a storm sewer. She drove with great skill and even greater trepidation, since she had misplaced her driver's license some weeks earlier and was convinced that this information was marked on the sides of their caravan as in neon lights. It had grown dark at the end of their second day on the road; they had taken a wrong turning and were miles away from their chosen track, although still going in the desired direction, and they began bitterly to regret their decision to make the remaining eighty miles in one jump rather than stop at a motel again. Nerves were raw, bladders acreak; two of the children were whining, one screaming, and four-year-old Sharon, who was always either talking or sleeping, blissfully slept. The cat set up a grating reiteration of one note, two of them every three seconds, while at a dead run it made the rounds of all glass areas of the station wagon, of which there were many. Every time it ran across Atty's shoulders she bit down on her back teeth until her jaw ached. The baby had wriggled clear of his lashing and was trying to stand up in the car-bed, so Atty drove with one hand on the wheel and one on his chest. Every time he sat up she pushed him down, and every time she pushed him down he screeched. In the truck Tony drove grimly, squinting through a windshield so spiderwebbed with scratches that oncoming lights made the whole thing totally opaque. Carol, five and one of the weepers, and Billy, eight and a whiner, were the pair privileged to ride the truck, and while Billy described in incessant detail the food he wasn't getting, Carol cried steadily. It was a monotone bleat, rather like that of the cat, from whom she had probably learned it, and denoted no special sorrow but only an empty stomach. She would cease it completely at the first loom of light from an oncoming car, and announce the obvious: "Here comes another one. Summon a *bish*. Summon a *bish*."

And Billy would cease his listings ("Why *can't* I have a chocklit maltit? I bet I could drink three chocklit maltits. I bet I could drink four chocklit maltits. I bet I could drink five . . .") to say, "Carol shoon't say summon' a bish, pop. Hey, *Pop!* Carol's sayin' summon a bish."

And Tony would say, "Don't say that, Carol," whereupon the lights of the oncoming vehicle would be upon him, and in dedicated attention he would slit his eyes, set his jaw, and say precisely what Carol was trying to repeat.

Tony led, the car followed, it being somehow the male responsibility to find the right road. (They were not on the right road.) For some time he had been aware of the station wagon's headlights flashing on and off in his rear-view mirror. Each time he noticed it he cheerily flashed his own lights in acknowledgment, and kept going. After about an hour, the station wagon whisked by him like a half-heard insult and pulled in front, glaring at him with angry brakelights. He did his best to stop in time, but Atty, though an excellent driver, had overlooked the detail of the load he was carrying, and the fact that stopping the wheels of the truck and stopping the truck itself, were consecutive and not concurrent circumstances. In short, he ran into the back of the station wagon.

There was a moment of total cacophony. Tony closed his eyes, covered his ears, and let it pass him. He was then aware of an urgent tugging at his sleeve, and "Pop! Pop!"

"Yes, Billy. Carol, shut up a minute." Carol was wailing.

"You run into the station wagon, Pop."

"I noticed that," said Tony with heroic control.

"Pop . . ."

"Yes, Billy."

"Why did you run into the station wagon?"

"Just felt like it, I guess." He got out. "You stay here and see if you can make Carol happy."

"Okay, Pop." To Carol, "Shut up, mudface." Carol's wail became an angry screech. Tony sighed and walked to the front of the truck. There was no breakage, just "Bendage," he murmured, and walked up to the driver's side of the station wagon. Atty was unpinning the baby. He thumped on the window and she rolled it down. She said something, but he couldn't hear it. The noise in there was classic.

"What?" he shouted.

"I said, why didn't you stop?"

He glanced back vaguely at the crumpled front end of the truck. "I *did.*"

"Here, hold him." He held the baby under the armpits while she relieved him of several soggy fabrics. "You might have killed all of us. Would you believe it, Sharon's still asleep. What do you think I was blinking my lights for?"

"I thought you just wanted to say hello."

"I told you at the gas station to find some place along the road to stop so we could eat. Now everything's cold. Linda, you're six years old so *stop* that yelling!"

"What do you mean cold?"

"Our *dinner*. There's a sweet big boy, now you feel *much* better." The baby screamed *much* louder.

"I didn't know we had any dinner. You must've bought it while I had Carol in the men's room. What'd you want me to take her in the men's room for anyway? It was awful. There was a guy pounding on the—"

"Hey, Mom!" This from Billy, who had ranged up behind Tony. "You know what? Pop ran spang into the station wagon!"

"Get back in the truck."

"Stay here, Billy. It's Sharon's turn to ride in the

truck anyway. We're going to eat right here, right now."

"Aw, gee, I didn't get to ride but a little tiny bit. Did you buy some choclit maltits, Mom? I bet I could drink seven—"

"Gosh, honey," said Tony, "let's go on at least until we find a place with some hot coffee and—"

"Is there a bathroom here?" demanded Linda at the top of her voice. "I got to—"

"Yeh, and a bathroom," finished Tony.

"I will not drive another inch with this hungry baby and these screaming children and my *back* hurts."

"Well, I say let's go on," said Tony firmly, and then wheedled, "Come on, honey. You know you'll be glad you did."

At that moment the cat, having reversed his orbit, caromed off the windshield and shot out the window as if he had been launched with boosters.

"You win," said Tony. "It'll take an hour to round him up. Where's that dinner?"

"Right here," said Atty composedly. She reached back of the seat and "*Oh!*"

She gingerly lifted out a square white cardboard box and opened it. Tony said, "What did you get?"

"Cheeseburgers," said Atty in stricken tones, "two with catchup and relish. Milk. Tomato juice. Dill pickles. Black coffee and rice pudding. And"—she peered down—"blueberry pie. Here, dear. I'm not hungry."

Tony thrust his head in a little farther and, in the glow from the dome light, gazed into the box. It took a moment for his eyes to orient, as sometimes happens with an unexpected close-up on a TV screen: what *is* that? and then he found himself looking down on what looked like the relief map of some justifiably forgotten, unwanted archipelago. In a sea of cold curdled milk and tomato juice was a string of hamburger islands on whose sodden beaches could be seen the occasional upthrust prow of a wrecked and sunken dill pickle. Just under the surface blueberries bobbed, staring up at him like tiny cataracted eyeballs. Over to the northeast, a blunt island of rice pudding gave up its losing battle and, before his eyes, disappeared under the waves.

"I'm not hungry either," Tony said. Atty looked at him and tears started from her lids.

"I put it on edge," she said, tapping the limp box. "It seemed to take up so much room lying flat." And suddenly she began to laugh.

"Whatcha got? Whatcha got?" demanded Billy, and when, wordless, his father had brought out the box, he happily plunged in with both grimy hands. "Boy, oh boy, pickles. . . ."

They left it with him and began the complex process of getting the company's bladders wrung out in the roadside bushes.

The four-year-old Sharon, woke contentedly in the back of the station wagon. She unwound her blanket and stretched. She was content; it had been a happy dream. She couldn't remember it, but it must have been a happy one because of the way she felt now. She lay drowsily listening to sounds near and far.

A wild scream, and "Mommy! Mom-*meeee!* Billy frowed sand on my bottom!"

"Billy!"

Protestingly, "No, I didn't she's a liar and I didn't throw nothing I kicked it a little."

Daddy: "Honey, where's that little pack of Kleenex?"

Mommy: "Carol's got it, dear. In the bushes."

Daddy: "Are you out of your MIND? The truck registration's in there!"

"Puss-puss-puss! Here, puss . . ." Bang bang with a spoon on the cat's aluminum feeding dish.

Sharon became aware of the clean cool smell of fresh air, and the open tailgate near by. She slid silently out so that mean old Billy wouldn't see her and, clutching Mary Lou (an eyeless, naked, broken-footed, mattress-haired doll which was, above all things on earth, Sharon's most beloved), she slid into the dark bushes. "Don't be 'fraid," she told Mary Lou. "It's the *friendly* dark." She pressed on, stopped once to look back and be comforted at the beacon-like glow from the lights of car and the truck, and then slipped over a ridge into velvety shadow, so dark that it seemed to be darkness itself that swallowed almost all sound from the road.

"Now that ol' Billy never find us," said Sharon to Mary Lou.

At the road, Atty said to Tony, "I don't feel tired, dear, just numb. Let's go all the way and get it over with."

"Yeah. Maybe we can slide into a dog-wagon and get a hot cup of coffee while the kids sleep."

"I wouldn't risk it," said Atty positively. "They'll sleep now and it will be quiet, and for the sake of a little quiet I can stand an empty stomach. I've had a belly full."

"Yes, dear," said Tony. "So we'll drive all the way. Next stop, the new house."

Later, in the truck, Linda said sleepily, "Isn't it Sharon's turn with me in the truck, Daddy?"

And Tony squinted into the windshield and said, "Hmm? Sharon? Oh, she slept through the whole thing."

And in the station wagon, Billy called, "Hey, Mom, where's Sharon?"

Atty said, "Shh. The baby's asleep. It's Sharon's turn to ride with Daddy. Go to sleep."

At which time Sharon stood on the ridge, turning round and round and looking for the guiding loom of lights. There was none, not anywhere but in the changing canyons of the cloudy sky where the stars peeped through. Turning and turning, Sharon lost the road, and herself was lost.

"Reely, it's the friendly dark," she shakily assured her doll. In the friendly (oh please be friendly) dark, she began to walk carefully, and after a while she heard running water.

CHAPTER 13

When Gurlick fell asleep, the thing he had built was a tangle of components, possessing (to any trained terrestrial eye) a certain compelling symmetry and an elaborate uselessness (but how useless would a variable frequency oscillator seem to a wise bushman or a savage from Madison Avenue?); but when he awoke, the picture was different. Very different.

What Gurlick had built was not, in actuality, a matter receiver, although it acted as if such a thing were a possibility. It was, rather, a receiver and amplifier for a certain "band" in the "thought spectrum" —each of these terms being analogous and general. The first receiver, and its be-Gurlicked attachments, turned information into manipulation, and constructed from the elemental samples Gurlick had supplied it a second and much more efficient machine of far greater capacity. This in turn received and manipulated yet a third receiver and manipulator; and this one was a heavy-duty device. The process was, in essence, precisely that of the sailor who takes a heaving-line to draw in a rope which brings him a hawser. In a brief span of hours, machines were making machines to use available matter to make machines which would scout out and procure locally unavailable matter, which was returned to the site and used by other machines to make yet others, all specialized, and certain of these in immense numbers.

Gurlick came unbidden out of that dream, where he sat on the bank on the pile of clothes, shiny black and red and an edge of lacy white, and was greeted (*Hello, Handsome*) by her who so boldly (after he refused to go away) began to come up out of the water, slowly and gleaming in the sunlight, the water now down to her waist, and as she began to smile—he awoke in the midst of an incredible clanking city. Around him were row upon row of huge blind machines, spewing forth more machines by the moment: tanklike things with long snake necks and heads surrounded by a circlet of trumpets; silver balls ten feet in diameter which now and then would flick silently into the air, too fast to be believed, too silent; low, wide, massive devices which slid snail-like along roads of their own making, snouted with projectors which put out strange beams which would have been like light if they were not cut off at the far end as if by an invisible wall; and with these beams sniffing along the rocks, some of which trembled and slumped; and then there would be a movement up the beam to the machine, and from behind the machine silvery ingots were laid like eggs while fine cold dust gouted off to the side.

Gurlick awoke surrounded by this, blinking and staring stupidly. It was some minutes later that he realized where he was—atop a column of earth, ten feet in diameter and perhaps thirty feet high. All around for hundreds of yards the ground had been excavated and . . . used. At the edge of his little plateau was a small domed box which, when his eye fell on it, popped open and slid a flat bowl of hot, mushlike substance toward him. He picked it up and smelled it. He tasted it, shrugged, grunted, raised the bowl to his lips and dozed its contents into his mouth with the heel of his hand. Its warmth in his belly was soothing, then puzzling, then frightening, the way it grew. He put his hands to his belt-line, and abruptly sat down, staring at his numb and disobedient legs. Dazed, he looked out across the busy scene and saw approaching him a stilted device with endless treads for feet and a turtlelike housing, perhaps a dozen feet in diameter. It straddled his imprisoning column of earth, achieving a sort of mechanical tiptoe, and the carapace began to descend over him and all his perch like a great slow candle-snuffer. He now could not speak, nor could he sit up any longer; he fell back and lay helpless, staring up and silently screaming . . .

But as the device, its underside alive with more wriggling tool-tipped limbs than has a horseshoe crab, slowly covered him he was flooded with reassurance and promise, a special strength (its specialty: to make him feel strong but in no wise be strong) and the nearest thing to peace that he had ever known. He was informed that he was to undergo a simple operation, and that it was good, oh, good.

CHAPTER 14

Who has sent me to Massoni, and Massoni to me, Guido? Is all my life, everything in it lost, glad, hungry, weary, furious, hopeful, hurt—is it planned to lead me to Massoni and Massoni to me? Who has curved the path he treads, all the places he has been and things he has done, to meet mine and travel it?

Why could he not be a policeman like other police, who begin with a crime and follow the criminal forward to his arrest, instead of backward and backward until the day he was born? He has asked and asked, smelling my cold, old footprints from here to Ancona and from Ancona to Villafresca and from there back and back to the house of the Corfu shepherd, Pansoni. He will find nothing there because the house is gone, Pansoni dead, the sheep slaughtered, the trail cold. But, finding nothing there, he has leaped backward in time to find me arriving there as an infant, and back and back through the orphanage and everywhere else, until he sees me carried whistling out of the bomb ruins near Anzio.

Perhaps he needs to find nothing more about me. He has found what no one else has known . . . I may not have known it myself . . . the thread that runs through all I have done. Who could have known that cutting the hard black hose by the bus wheel, stamping the old man's legs against the curbstone, throwing the kerosene rags into the print shop—all were . . . acts of . . . music?

I moan and hump myself backward to the dark climbing space behind the wall, and fall scrabbling down and backward to floor level. I press aside the loose plywood and stand shaking, aching in the room. I am caked with dried sweat and dirt; cold, hungry, frightened. I hobble to the door, beginning to sob again, that soft bouncing *staccato*. It frightens me more. The iron door is locked. I am still more frightened. I shake the door and then run away from it and sink down on my knees by the bed, looking up, right, left, to see what is after me.

What could be after me?

I look under the bed. It is there, the black leather cheek of the violin case. The violin is after me.

Kill it, then.

I put my hand under the bed, a thumb-tip at the bottom, fingertips at the top, just enough to hold, as if the thing were going to be hot. I draw it out. It is not hot. The sound it makes, scraping along the rough concrete floor, is like the last water shouting and belching down a drain, and when it stops I hear the strings faintly ringing.

I open a steel clasp at the side. Once I am running from someone and hide in a dark cellar; I go around a heap of fallen timbers and back into a dark corner; behind me a rat squeaks once and leaps at me and, as I duck, scratches my shoulder and neck and I hear its yellow fangs come together as it squeaks again: *squeak-click!* all at once. Now in the dark silence the clasp of the violin case squeak-clicks just the same, and I feel the same blinding flash of terror. I kneel limp by the bed, wait until the heart-thunder goes out of my ears.

I do not want to see this violin; with all my soul I do not, and like someone watching a runaway truck bear down on a dog in the street, helpless and horrified, I kneel there and watch my hands lift the case and set it on the bed, open the other two clasps, turn back the lid.

Sheep gut, horse hair, twigs and shingles.

I put out a finger, slip it under the neck, lift the violin up far enough to rest half out of the case, take away my finger and look at it. It weighs nothing. It makes a sound as I lift it, like the distant opening of a door. I look at the pegs, and they take my eye along to the scroll, down, up, around, around again, around to spin dizzily somewhere down in the shining wood. I put my hands over my face and kneel there shaking.

Guido moves like the night wind—Massoni said it himself. Guido is a natural thing like holocaust, like hurricane, and no one knows where he will strike next. Guido fears nothing.

Then why crouch here like a fascinated bird staring into the jaws of a serpent? The violin will not bite. The violin is nothing to fear. It is mute now; it is only when it makes music that—

Is music something to fear?

Yes, oh yes.

Music is a pressure inside, welling up and ready to burst out and fill the room, fill the world; but let a note of it escape and *blam!* the hard hand of Pansoni, the Corfu shepherd, bruises the music back into the mouth, or clubs down hard on the nape, so that you pitch forward and lie with your mouth full of sand and speckles of pain dancing inside the eyeballs. Pansoni can hear music before it is born, lying like too much food just under the solar plexus; and there he will kick you before ever a note can escape. Be six years old, seven, and tend the sheep in the rocky hills, you alone with the stones and the wind and the soft filthy silly sheep; sit on a crag and sing all the notes he has crushed in his hut, and he will come without a sound and slip up behind you and knock you spinning and sliding down the mountain.

And in time you learn. You learn that to hum is to ask for that ready hard hand, to whistle a note is to be thrown out into the cold night and to cower there until daylight without a crust to eat. You feel the music rising within you and before it can sound its first syllable you look up and his bright black eyes are on you, waiting. So . . . you learn that music is fear, music is pain . . . and deep, deep underneath, waiting until you are tall as a man and almost strong as a man, music is revenge; music is anger. You understand Pansoni, why he does these things. Pansoni knows that the music in you is remarkable—that is to say, noticeable, and there is that about Pansoni which strikes down whatever is noticeable as soon as it shows itself. Pansoni will not risk rumors in the countryside of the shepherd's boy who can sing any aria from any opera, whistle an entire violin concerto after hearing it once. Pansoni is a smuggler. Pansoni and his sheep and his boy Guido cannot be seen against the brown rocks and shadows of the seaside hills, and he will naturally extinguish, in this music-dyed map on which we crawl, the mighty beacon of melody which waits in the breast and brain of his ragged, beaten Guido.

Never look back, never look back, and damn you, Massoni, damn you, violin, you have made me look back!

I take my hands from my face and look at the violin. It has not moved nor spoken, nor has the scroll unfurled, nor the strings loosed themselves to reach for me like tentacles. My one finger lifted it and put it so, half out of its bed. It is only obedient, and . . . and beautiful. . . .

I get to my feet. How long have I knelt there? My knee hurts, my foot is asleep. I take up the violin. It weighs nothing. My hand on its neck is at home; the smooth wood snugs down into my palm like part of the flesh. I squeeze it; it is strong and unyielding, not at all as fragile as it ought to be.

Squeezing it has brought the sound-box end close to me; I let it come and it touches my shoulder, throat, chin. Someone has intimately known the curve of my chin and left jaw; I turn my head a fraction, raise the fingerboard a fraction, and my chin and the ebony rest are one. I stand holding the violin like this for a long time, overcome with amazement, so much that there is no room for fear. I become aware of my chest, expanded as if to utter a note to be heard round the earth, my feet placed apart and ready to balance me when with my music I tilt the world. It is a sort of flight; my weight diminishes, my strength increases.

I take up the bow, thumb here, here the index and second fingers, the little finger straight and rigid and angling down as a prop to bear all the weight of the bow. Up elbow, down shoulder a bit . . . there: so if there is a plank across shoulder, elbow, wrist and a full glass on it, not a drop is spilled.

I balance there a long time, until the muscles of shoulder and back begin to pain me. It comes to me that this is the hurting of weariness but not of strain, and to me, strangely, this knowledge is a glory.

I take down the bow, I take down the violin. I stand with one in each hand looking at them. I have not made a sound with them, but I will. A door has opened and let in music. A door has opened and let out fear. I need not make a note with this instrument to discover whether or not the dead hand of Pansoni will strike. If it took a note of music to be sure, then I would not be sure; I would fear him still. I have become *that* free; it need not be tested.

Massoni has given me the lesson, Massoni has given me my freedom. I am grateful to Massoni now, and will do him this service: since the prevention of my crimes and the release of my terror of anything musical are things which come first with him (for is he not first a thinking policeman and only second a violinist?) I shall permit him to give me also his violin. Thank you, Massoni: thank you; it is a wondrous change you have brought about in Guido.

I find a stiff sharp knife among Massoni's things, and a piece of iron wire, and in time—more time than this usually takes me, but then I am not as I was—I get the door unlocked.

I put the violin in its case and put the case under my flapping old trench coat, and I take my leave of Massoni and all things which have brought him into my life. For this violin, this spout for the music which boils within me, I have exchanged all other things I have been and done.

I shall kill anyone who tries to take it away from me.

CHAPTER 15

The spore, the "raisin" which Gurlick had eaten, had been life or its surrogate. It had traversed space physically, bodily, and it had finished its function and its capabilities with its invasion of Gurlick. But the transfer of the life-essence of all the Medusa into all of humanity was something that earth-built machines—even if built on earth by others—could not accomplish. Only life can transmit life. A very slight alteration indeed—an adjustment of isotopes in certain ionized elements in Gurlick's ductless glands—would make the membership of humanity in the corpus of the Medusa a certainty. The machines now abuilding would effectively restore (the Medusa still unswervingly operated from a conviction that this was a restoration) the unity of the human species, its hive-mind, so that each "person" could reach, and be reached by, all persons; but the fusion with the Medusa would be Gurlick's special chore, and would take place on the instant that his seed married with the ovum of a human female. As the machine slowly closed over him, its deft limbs already performing the first of a hundred delicate manipulations, it caught up his dream and congratulated him on it, and gave it detail and depth which his creative poverty had never made possible to him before, so that he lived it realer than real, from the instant of approach (and a degree of anticipation which might have destroyed him had he felt it earlier) to the moments of consummation, so violent they shook the earth and sent the sky itself acrinkle with ripples of delighted color. And more: for in these tactile inventions there was no human limitation, and it was given to him to proceed again, and yet again, without exhaustion or dulling familiarity, either through the entire episode or through any smallest part of it, whether it be the thrill of seeing the clothes (shiny black and scarlet, and the tumbled frosting of lace-edged white) or the pounding, fainting climax. Always, too, was the laughing offhand promise that *any* conquest of Gurlick's would be such a peak, or a higher one; let him wallow in his dream because he loved it, but let him understand also that it was only one of many, the symbol of any, the quality of all.

So while it built its machines to fuse ("again") the scattered psyche of humanity, it got Gurlick—good—and—ready.

CHAPTER 16

The warrior Mbala caught his thief perhaps an hour after he fell asleep squatting in the inky shadows of the astralagus vetch which encircled his yam patch. His assegai had fallen across his legs, and he was deep in that vulnerable torpor taught him by fear and weariness, so perhaps it really was the shade of his father, watching over the yam garden, who made the capture. Or that other powerful ghost man call Justice. Whatever the instrument, the thief walked out of the yam patch in the impenetrable dark and stepped so close to the sleeping warrior that his foot landed under the horizontal butt of Mbala's assegai. His other foot swung past the end of the shaft, and the first foot left the ground and caught the spear with its instep. The thief went flat on his face and the assegai snapped up and with great enthusiasm rapped Mbala painfully on the bridge of the nose.

In unison the two men squalled in terror, and then training dictated the outcome. The thief, who for most of his years had lifted nothing but other people's property, and that at irregular intervals, scrambled and slipped and fell flat again. Mbala, whose reflexes always placed action before conjecture, was up out of a sound sleep and a remaining cloud of stupidity-withdrawal, uttering a curdling battle screech, and plunging his assegai into his prostrate enemy's back before he was at all consciously aware. The prone man shrieked in agony, but it was the wrong shriek, as well as the wrong impact felt by Mbala's schooled hands. Apparently there had been enough stupidity left in that blazing moment to cause Mbala to handle his weapon as it lay, so that it was not the wide, long blade which presented itself to the thief's shoulders, but the bruising end of the shaft.

"Mbala! Mbala! Don't kill me! I am your brother, Mbala!"

Mbala, about to whirl his weapon end for end and settle the matter, checked himself and drove the haft down again. His prisoner, attempting to rise, fell flat again.

"Nuyu!"

"Yes, Nuyu, your own brother, your own dear brother. Let me up, Mbala! I haven't done anything to you!"

"I'm standing on a bag of yams," growled Mbala. "For that you die, Nuyu."

"No! No, you can't! I am the son of the brother of your father! Your father wants me spared!" Nuyu screamed. "Did he not turn your spear wrong-end-to when you first struck at me? Well, didn't he?" Nuyu insisted when Mbala seemed to hesitate.

Fury and disillusion made Mbala say, "My father is gone from here." He shifted suddenly, literally vaulting from his stance beside the prone man to one astride him, facing the feet, with his own heelbones pressing the fleshy part of the armpits flat to the ground. In pitch darkness it was done with amazing accuracy. In the moment when the warrior's weight was on the spear and pivoting, Nuyu uttered a short shrill scream, thinking his moment had come. As the rock-hard heels captured his armpits he grunted and arched his back and began flailing his legs.

"Uncle! Uncle! *Uncle!*"

Mbala reversed his spear at last. "Hold still," he said irritably. "You know I can't see."

"U-Un—cle!"

"*Now* you call on him. *Now* you fear the demon. *Now* you believe, eh, thief?" Mbala taunted. By touch alone, he drew the needle point across the man's kidneys, barely enough to part the skin. Nuyu squalled abominably and began to weep. "Uncle, uncle . . ." he sobbed and then abruptly was silent and motionless.

Mbala knew that trick well and was prepared for it, but when he began to see his shadow stretching away, lumping across the vetch and lost in the thorns, he forgot about trickery.

"Uncle . . ." Nuyu moaned. . . . There was a new note to his weeping: hope, was it? And something else?

Nuyu lay with his head toward the yam patch, Mbala stood with his back to it. The patch was roughly circular, with the tubers scattered randomly in it. A thick rim of the vetch bushes bordered it back to the thorns. Almost exactly at the four midpoints of the compass stood four ship's prow monoliths. The mound on which the patch lay must at one time have been an almost conical rock mount, before some forgotten cataclysm split it exactly in two, northeast to southwest, and again in two, northwest to southeast. Settling and erosion had widened the crossed canyons until they took the form which Mbala's dead father had found. In the native language the place was called Giant's Mouth, and it was said that a man's shout from the center of the yam patch could be heard for a day's journey in every direction.

"Uncle, oh uncle," Nuyu wept, with such a passion in his voice that Mbala bent curiously to look at him. He was bending his head back and up at an almost impossible angle, and his eyes strained at the roofs of their sockets. His dark face was . . . silver.

Mbala sprang away from him, whirling about in the air. He came down crouching, staring up at the silver ball which floated down the sky. It halted perhaps ten feet above the center of the yam patch and stayed motionless.

Nuyu made a sound. Mbala glanced quickly down at him and, without understanding why, without trying to, he bent and helped the other man to his feet. They stood close together, watching.

"Like a moon," Mbala murmured. He glanced at the silvered landscape and back again to the object. It had a brilliant, steady radiance, which fantastically left no after-image on the retina.

"He came," said the thief. "I called him and he came."

"It might be a demon."

"You doubt your own father?"

Mbala said, "Father . . ." And the sphere sank to the center of the yam patch. Then it opened.

There were doors completely around the object, all hinged at their upper edges, so that when they opened they formed a sort of awning all around the sphere. A beam of light fanned out to the north, but it was like no light Mbala had ever seen. It was mauve with flickers of green, and though the air was clear and the walls of the crossed canyons brilliantly lighted by the sphere, it was impossible to see through the beam. Not only that, but the beam did not fade or spread from the source outward, and terminated as sharply as if it played on a wall, which it did not. This odd square end of the light beam pressed outward from the ship until it reached the margin of vetch, and nosed into it. There was a sound like water over rapids, hissing, churning, crackling. There almost seemed to be something moving back up the light beam into the ship, but one could not be sure.

The light pressed slowly outward through the vetch to the edge of the surrounding thorn trees and stopped. No, not stopped. It was scything away from them, moving slowly, and the square end was adjusting itself to the encroachments and retreats of the thorn.

Where it had passed the vetch was gone, and where it had been the bare ground was powdered with a white substance unlike anything they had ever seen. After a few minutes it changed and the ground seemed moist.

"Can you doubt now?" murmured Nuyu. "Who but your father would clear your land?"

They stood in awe, watching the sphere clear the land. When it seemed reasonable to get out of its way they backed to the thorn and slipped through. If the sphere and its beam noticed them or their going, it made no sign. It just went on collecting and processing astralagus vetch, a weed with a high affinity for selenium. When it had all it could get from this pocket, it clicked shut, took a picture of the site, and leaped into the sky, where at ten thousand feet it switched on its sensors, located another patch of vetch to the north, and flashed away after the only thing it knew how to care about—selenium, from astralagus.

Mbala and Nuyu crept cautiously out on the new ground and looked around in the paling dawnlight. Nuyu touched the ground with his hand. It was wet, and cold. He saw some of the white material in a hole and picked it up. It disappeared in his hand, leaving only a few drops of water. He grunted and wiped his hand on his kilt. What was another miracle at a time like this.

Mbala was still staring at the sky. Nuyu said, "Will you kill me?"

Mbala brought his gaze down from the disappearing stars and gave it to Nuyu's face. He looked at it for a long while, and from all Nuyu could see there was no change in Mbala's expression at all; he looked at him as one will at distant lights. "I lost my father," he said at last, "because he let my yams be stolen. So I did not believe. But you believed, and he saved you, and he came back again. I will not kill you, Nuyu."

"I died," Nuyu breathed. "Nuyu the unbeliever died when he saw your father." He bent and picked up the sack of yams and extended them to Mbala.

"Nuyu the thief died," said Mbala. "The yams are yours and mine, forever in tomorrow and forever in yesterday. There has been no thief, then, Nuyu."

They went back to the kraal to tell the women they would have a lot of new work tomorrow. As Nuyu passed the witch doctor, the old man reached out unseen and touched Nuyu's kilt. Then the witch doctor held the touching hand in his other, and hugged them against his chest. What he got from Nuyu he could have gotten from his mere presence. He knew that, but nevertheless he touched the kilt. The touch was a symbol the old man needed, and so he took and treasured it. He said to Mbala, "Your demon is dead, then."

At that Mbala and Nuyu smiled at one another, the devout and the convert, richly content with faith and full of wonder.

CHAPTER 17

Gurlick lay hooded and unaware, passive under the submicroscopic manipulations of the machine which brought his special membership in the Medusa to his seed. So he did not observe the change in the mighty operations around him, when the egg-laying snail-gaited miners drew in and darkened the snouts of light, and fell neatly apart to have their substance incorporated in other, more needed machines; and these in turn completed their special tasks and segmented and dispersed to others which still needed them, until at last there remained only the long-necked, tank-treaded, trumpet-headed ones, and enough silver spheres to carry them, in their multi-thousands, to their precisely mapped destinations. There was no provision for failure, for there would be no failure. The nature of the electroencephalograph, and of its traces, clearly showed to the transcendent science of the Medusa exactly what was lacking in the average mind which kept it from being a common mind. The net would be comparatively simple to cast and draw shut, for it found the potent base of the hive mentality alive and awaiting it, showing itself wherever humans blindly moved in the paths of other humans, purely because other humans so moved; wherever friends apart impulsively sat down to write one another simultaneous letters, wherever men in groups (cartels, committees, mobs, and nations) divided their intelligence by their numbers and let that incredible quotient chart their course. The possible or probable nature of a human hive, once (re)established, was a question hardly explored, because it was hardly important. Once united, humanity would join the Medusa, because the Medusa always (not almost, not "in virtually every case," but *always*) infused the hives it touched.

So the factory-area rumbled to silence, and the noiseless spheres swept over the storage yard and scooped up their clusters of long-necked projectors, fell away up with them, flashed away to all the corners of earth, ready to place the projectors wherever their emanations (part sound, part something else) would reach masses of humans. They could not reach all humans, but they would reach most, and the established hive would then draw in the rest. No human would escape, none could; none would want to. Then, somewhere in this flawless, undivided, multi-skilled entity, Gurlick would plant a tiny fleck of himself, and at the instant of fusion between it and a living ovum, the Medusa would spread through it like crystallization through a supersaturated solution.

CHAPTER 18

Sharon Brevix squatted on the dry part of a stony stream bed, dying. It was the second night, and she hadn't come to the ocean or a city or any people at all. Billy had told her that lost people just have to find a river and go downstream and they'll be all right, because all the rivers flow into the sea and there's always a town or people there. She had started downstream as soon as it was light on the first morning. It never occurred to her to stay where she was until she heard a car, because she must certainly still be near the road, and a car had to come by eventually. She did not reason that when she traveled the stream bed for the first hour and it did not bring her to the road, it must therefore be leading her away from it.

She was, after all, only four years old.

By ten in the morning she was aching hungry, and by noon it was just awful. She whimpered and stopped for a while to cry hard, but after a time she got up again and kept on. The ocean couldn't be terribly far away after a person walks so far. (It was another twelve hundred miles, but she could not know that.) In the afternoon she had slept for a while, and when she awoke she found some wild raspberries on a bush. She ate all she could find until she was stung by a yellowjacket and ran away screaming. She found her little stream again and kept on going until it was dark.

Now it was very late and she was dying. She felt better than she had, because she felt nothing at all very much, except hungry. The hunger had not diminished with her other sensations, but it had the virtue of blanketing them. Fear and cold and even loneliness were as unnoticeable, in the presence of that dazzle of hunger, as stars at noon. In the excitement of packing, and on the two days of traveling, she had eaten little, and she had rather less to fall back on than most four-year-olds, which is little enough.

It was after midnight, and her troubled sleep had long since turned into a darker and more dangerous condition. Cramped limbs no longer tingled, and the chilly air brought no more shivers. She slept squatting, with her back and side against a nook of rock. Later she might topple over, very possibly too weak to move at all but for some feeble squirmings. Yet—

She heard a sound, she raised her head. She saw what at first she thought was a Christmas tree ornament, a silver ball with a dangle of gewgaws under it, in midair a few inches from her face. She blinked and resolved it into something much larger, much farther away, coming down out of the night sky. She heard a snarling howl. She looked a little higher, and was able to identify the running lights of a small airplane streaking down out of the high overcast.

Sharon rose to her feet, holding the rock wall to steady herself while her congealed blood began to move. She saw the globe about to land on clear ground at the top of a knoll three miles away. She saw the airplane strike it dead center while it was still thirty feet off the ground, and then plane, globe, and cargo were a tangled, flaming ruin on the hill. She watched it until it died, and then lay down to finish her own dying.

CHAPTER 19

Just another rash of saucer-sightings, thought the few observers, and recipients of their observations, in the brief minutes left to them to think as they had always thought. Some of the military had, in these minutes, a harrowing perplexity. Anything tracked at such speeds as the radars reported, must, with small variations, appear somewhere along an extrapolated path; the higher the speed, the finer the extrapolation. The few recordings made of the flick and flash of these objects yielded flight-paths on which the objects simply did not appear. It was manifestly impossible for them to check and drop straight to their destinations at such velocities; they did, however, and before the theoreticians could finish their redefinition of "impossible," they and all their co-workers, colleagues, acquaintances, cohabitants, heirs and assigns were relieved of the necessity to calculate. It happened so quickly, one minute a heterogenous mass of seething noncommunicants; the next, the end of Babel.

Henry, five years old, slept as usual flat on his back and face straight up, arms rigid, fists clenched under, and pinned down by his buttocks, and his ankles together. He was having a nightmare, soundlessly, of being surrounded by gentle smiling fathers, some of whom wore the masks of the other kids in his class, and storekeepers, and passing puppy dogs, but who were really just smiling fathers, dressed up and being gentle at the very verge of exploding in his face; and between him and all the fathers was a loving goddess with soft hands full of forbidden lollipops and raisin-bread peanut-butter sandwiches to be passed to little boys in the dark when they had been sent to bed without their suppers because they were little cowards; this goddess was there to care for him and protect him, but when the explosion came, with this breath or the next or the one after, the puppies and children and grocers and fathers would whisk through to him as if the goddess weren't there at all; and while they did what they would do to him, she would still be there smiling and ready with guilty lollipops, not knowing what the fathers were doing to him. . . . And under this nightmare was the color of hopelessness, the absolute certainty that to awake from it would be to emerge into it; the dream and the world were one now, fused and identical.

CHAPTER 20

These were people, these are anecdotes, dwelt upon for their several elements of the extraordinary. But each man alive has such a story, unique unto himself, of what is in him and of its molding by the forces around him, and of his interpretations of those forces. Here a man sees a machine as a god, and there a man sees God as an argument; and another uses men's argument quite as if it were a tool, a machine of his own. For all his ability to work in concert with his fellows, and to induce some sympathy in their vibrations, man remains isolated; no one knows *exactly* how another feels. At the very climax of sensation, man approaches unconsciousness . . . unconsciousness of what? Why, of all around him; never of himself.

These were people, there are anecdotes of the night the world ended; this the night when people the world over thought their thoughts and lived their lives and at long, long last were wrong in thinking that tomorrow was the front part of today, yesterday the back, and that the way to go on was to go on as before.

This was the night, and the very moment, when

Paul Sanders rose from the couch, lifted Charlotte Dunsay in his arms, and said, "Well, if it isn't now, it never will be" . . .

When young Guido strode a pre-dawn Rome, his very bones aching with music and a carven miracle under his arm, waiting the ardent reach of his unshackled talent. No lover, no miser, no acolyte on earth loved money or woman or Master more than Guido loved this violin; no whelping fox or wounded water-buffalo so watchful for an enemy. . . .

When the cousins Mbala and Nuyu, the redeemed backslider and the convert, turned into a new and glorious day of faith and many yams. . . .

When Henry, who was five, lay stiffly in his bed and sniffled through a dream of smiling cruelties in a place quite like all other places to him, where he was despised. . . .

When Dimity Carmichael's dutiful alarm preceded the sunrise and she rose in her sensible cotton gown and made ready, eyes averted, to take her morning shower . . .

When Sharon Brevix entered the dusk and the dark of her second lost day without shelter or food . . .

Only motes among the millions, remarked upon for that about them which is remarkable, yet different only insofar as each is different *from*, or is different *within*, the pattern of qualities possessed two and three quarter billion living times under this sun.

CHAPTER 21

He stood motionless with the girl in his arms, ready to put her down on the sofa; and then, without a start, without a word of wonderment, Paul Sanders set her on her feet and stood supporting her with a firm arm around her shoulders until her head cleared and she could stand alone.

There was nothing said, because there was in that moment nothing to be said. In a split second there was orientation of a transcendent nature—nothing as crude as mutual mind-reading, but an instant and permeating acknowledgment of relationships: I to you, we to the rest of the world; the nature of a final and overriding decision, and the clear necessity of instant and specific action. Together Paul Sanders and Charlotte Dunsay left her apartment. The hallway was full of people in all stages of dress—all moving wordlessly, purposefully. No one paid Charlotte, in her transparent gown, the slightest attention.

They walked to the elevator bank. She paused before it with a half dozen other people, and he opened the door of the fire stairs and sprang up them two at a time. Emerging on the roof, he went to the kiosk which sheltered the elevator motor and cables, twisted off the light padlock with one easy motion, opened the door, and entered. He had never been here before in his life; yet without hesitation he reached to the left and scooped up a five-foot slice-bar which lay across the grating, and ran with it back down the fire stairs.

Without glancing at floor numbers, he left the fire stairs on the fourth floor, turned left and ran down the hall. The last door on the right opened as he reached it; he did not glance at the old lady who held it for him, nor did she speak. He sped through a foyer, a living room, and a bedroom, opened the window at the far right and climbed out.

There was a narrow ledge on which he could barely keep his balance and carry the heavy bar as well, yet he managed it. The chief enemy of a balancing man is the poison of fear which permeates him: I'll fall! *I'll fall!* but Paul felt no fear at all. He made a rapid succession of two-inch sidewise shuffles until he reached the big eyebolt from which there thrust, out and down, the huge chain supporting one end of a massive theater marquee. Here he turned sidewise and squatted, brought his bar up over his shoulder, and, reaching down, thrust the tip through the fourth link of the chain. Then he waited.

The street below—what he could see of it—seemed at first glance to be normally tenanted, with about as many people about as one might expect at this hour of a Saturday night. But then it could be seen that nobody *strolled*—everyone walked briskly and with purpose; one or two people ran, the way they ran indicating running to, not from anything. He saw Charlotte Dunsay across the street, swinging along on her bare feet, and enter a showroom where computing machines were on display. Though the place had been closed since noon, it was now open and lighted, and full of people silently and rapidly working.

There came a sound, and more than a sound, a

deep pervasive ululation which seemed at first to be born in all the air and under the earth, sourceless. But as it grew louder, Paul heard it more from his left, and finally altogether from the corner of the building. Whatever was making that sound was crawling slowly up the street to take its place at the intersection, a major one where three avenues crossed. Patiently, Paul Sanders waited.

CHAPTER 22

From his soundless nightmare, Henry soundlessly awoke. He slid out of bed and trotted out of his room, past his parents' open door—they were awake, but he said nothing, and if they saw him, they said nothing either. Henry padded down the stairs and out into the warm night. He turned downtown at a dog-trot, and ran for three blocks south, one west, and two south. He may or may not have noticed that while the traffic lights still operated, they were no longer obeyed by anyone, including himself. Uncannily, cars and pedestrians set their courses and their speeds and held them, regardless of blind corners, passing and repassing each other without incident and with no perceptible added effort.

Henry had been aware for some time of the all but subsonic hooting and of its rapid increase in volume as he ran. When he reached the big intersection, he saw the source of the sound on the same street he ran on, but past the corner where the theater stood. It was a heavy tanklike machine, surmounted by a long flexible neck on top of which four horns, like square megaphones or speakers, emitted the sound. The neck weaved back and forth, tilting the horns and changing their direction in an elaborate repetitive motion, which had the effect of adding a slow and disturbing vibrato to the sound.

Henry dashed across the street and under the side-street marquee. He came abreast of the thing just as it was about to enter the intersection. Without breaking stride, Henry turned and dove straight into the small space between the drive-spindle of the machine's tread and its carrier rollers. His blood spouted, and on it the spindle spun for a moment; the other track, still driving, caused the machine to swerve suddenly and bump up on the sidewalk under the marquee.

Paul Sanders, at the very instant the child had leapt, and before the small head and hands entered the machine's drive, leaned out and down and jammed the chisel point of his slice-bar hard through the fourth link of the chain. Plunging outward, his momentum carried the bar around the chain and, as his weight came upon it, gave the chain a prodigious twist. The eyebolt pulled out of the building wall with a screech, and the corner of the marquee sagged and then, as the weight of the chain came upon it, and Paul Sanders's muscular body with it, the marquee let go altogether and came hammering down on the machine. In a welter of loose bricks, sheet-tin, movie-sign lettering and girders, the machine heaved mightily, its slipping treads grating and shrieking on the pavement. But it could not free itself. Its long neck and four-horned head twitched and slammed against the street for a moment, and then the deep howl faded and was gone, and the head slumped down and lay still.

Four men ran to the wreckage, two of them pushing a dolly on which rode an oxyacetylene outfit. One man went instantly to work taking measurements with scale, micrometer and calipers. Two others had the torch going in seconds and fell to work testing for a portion of the machine which might be cut away. The fourth man, with abrasive rasps and a cold chisel, began investigating the dismantling of the thing.

And meanwhile, in unearthly silence and with steady determination, people passed and repassed, on foot, in cars, and went about their business. No crowd collected. Why should it? Everybody *knew*.

The entire village population, with Mbala and Nuyu at their head and the witch doctor following, were within two hundred yards of Mbala's yam patch when the thing come down from the sky. It was broad daylight here, so the ghostly-luminous moonlit effect was missing; but the shape of the projector as it dangled by invisible bonds from the sphere was unprecedented enough to bring a gasp of astonishment and fear from the villagers. Mbala stopped and bowed down and called his father's name, and all the people followed suit.

The sphere dropped rapidly to the yam patch, which, judging from the photograph taken by the selenium miner, seemed an ideal position for a projector to land, to send forth its commanding, mesmerizing waves.

The sphere set down its burden and started up again without pause, swift as a bouncing ball. The projector began its wavering bass hooting which swept out through the echoing clefts of the great split rock, rolled down upon the villagers, and silenced their chant as if it had blotted it up.

There was a moment—mere seconds—of frozen inaction, and then half the warriors turned as one man and plunged away through the jungle. The rest, and all the women and children, drew together, over four hundred of them, and poured swiftly up the slope toward the yam patch. No one said a word or made a sound; yet when they choked the space between two of the stone steeples, half the people ran into the clearing, skirting its edge, while half squatted where they were, blocking their avenue from side to side. The runners reached the north opening, filled it, and also squatted, wordless and waiting.

Directly across from the first group, in the westward opening, there was movement as one, two, a dozen, a hundred heads appeared, steadily and quietly approaching. It was the Ngubwe, neighboring villagers with whom there was a tradition, now quiescent, of wife-stealing and warfare going back to the most ancient days. Mbala's people and the Ngubwe, though aware of each other at all times, were content to respect each other's privacy and each cultivate his own garden, and for the past thirty years or so there had been room enough for everybody.

Now three openings to the rock-rimmed plateau were filled with squatting, patient natives. Even the babies were silent. For nearly an hour there was no sound but the penetrating, disturbing howl of the projector, no motion but its complex, hypnotic pattern of weavings and turnings. And then there was a new sound.

Blast after shrill blast, the angry sound approached, and the waiting people rose to their feet. The women tore their clothes to get bright rags, the men filled their lungs and emptied them, and filled them again, getting ready.

Through the open southern gateway four warriors erupted, howling and capering. Hard on their heels came a herd of furious elephants, three, four—seven—nine in all, one old bull, two young ones, four cows and two calves, distraught, angry, goaded beyond bearing. The fleeing warriors separated, two to the right, two to the left, sprinted to and disappeared in the crowds waiting there. The big bull trumpeted shrilly, wheeled, and charged to the right, only to face nearly two hundred shrieking, capering people.

He swerved away, his momentum carrying him along the rock wall and to the second opening, where he met the same startling cacophony. The other elephants, all but one young bull and one of the calves, thundered along behind him, and when he drew up as if to wheel and attack the second group, he was pounded and pressed from behind by his fellows. By now quite out of his mind, he put up his trunk, turned his mighty shoulders against those who pressed him, and found himself glaring at this noisy, shining thing in the center of the clearing.

He shrieked and made for it. It moved on its endless treads, but not swiftly enough, nor far enough, nor in enough places at once to avoid the tons of hysteria which struck it. The elephants tore off its howling head and its neck in three successive broken bits, and shouldered it over on its side and then on its back. The howling stopped with deafening suddenness when the head came off, but the tracks kept treading the air for minutes after it was on its back.

Elephants were used in Berlin, too, on the machine which landed in the park near the famous zoo, though this was a more disciplined performance by trained animals who did exactly as they were told. In China a projector squatted in a cleft in the mountains under a railroad trestle, and began hooting into the wind. An old nomad with arthritis hobbled out of the rocks and pulled two spikes, shifted one rail. A half mile down the track, the engineer and fireman of a locomotive pulling a combination passenger-freight train with over four hundred people aboard, wordlessly left their posts, climbed back over the tender, and uncoupled the locomotive from the first car. There was, on the instant, a man at every handwheel on the train. It coasted to a stop, while far ahead the locomotive thundered over the edge of the trestle and was crushing the projector before the alien machine could move a foot.

In Baffin Land a group of Eskimo hunters stood transfixed, watching a projector squatting comfortably on mounded and impassable pack ice and, in the crisp air, bellowing its message across the wastes to the ears of four and possibly five widely scattered settlements. The hunters had not long to wait; high above the atmosphere a mighty Atlas missile approached, and, while still well below their horizon, released a comparatively tiny sliver, the redoubtable Hawk. The little Hawk came shrieking out of the upper air, made a wide half-circle to kill some of its excess velocity, and then zeroed in on the projector with the kind of accuracy the old-time Navy bombardiers would brag about: "I dropped it right down his stack."

From then on missiles got most of the projectors, though in crowded areas, other means were found. In Bombay a projector took its greatest toll—one hundred and thirty-six, when a mob simply overran one of the machines and tore it to pieces with their bare hands. And in Rome one man despatched four of them and came out of it unscathed.

(A man?)

(Unscathed?)

CHAPTER 23

I am Guido, walking the back ways and the dark paths leading out of the city, to a place where this glossy glory of a violin can make itself known to me. No human soul will hear me coax a squeak out of it, or I will kill him for knowing of it. I will kill anyone who harms it, or who tries to take it from me. This city will no longer know Guido or see Guido, and it must get along for a while without Guido's small protests against music. Against music . . . Listen now, someone is singing under the sliver of moon, far away, a little drunk. . . . No, God, that's the shift whistle at the auto place. Now wait, wait, stop and listen . . .

I stop and look down the hill, across to the other hill, and I listen as I have never listened before, and I make a great finding, one of those large things you come to know while realizing that others have always known it. How many, many times have I heard a man say wind *sings* in the wires, a *musical* waterfall, the *melody* in certain laughter. But in fighting music all these years, I have not known, I have not let myself hear all these words, nor the music which is their meaning.

I hear it now, because through owning this violin, something has happened to me. I hear the city singing while it sleeps, and I hear a singing which would sweetly cry among these hills if the city had never existed, and will cry here when it is gone.

It is as if I have new ears, yes, and a new mind and heart to go with them. I think, in the morning, when this world wakes, oh, I shall hear, I shall hear . . . and I lose the thought for its very size, thinking about what I am to hear from now on.

I go on to my hiding place. Guido's studio, I think, laughing. When they built the new highway into the city, they cut away the end of a crooked, narrow little street which used to climb the hill. Right at the top were two small houses, built Italian land style, four square stone walls which they filled with earth, then lay a four-sided dome of plaster on the earth, then dug away the earth when the plaster was hardened. These little houses will stand for a thousand years. The two I know of were buried by the embankment of the new road, where it comes near the hilltop on its stilts and curves across to the other hill. I found the houses when I escaped once from the police. I leaped from the police car and off the road, and down the embankment I put my leg in a hole, and the hole was a window. The second house is behind the first, buried completely, but there is a door between them. Two rooms in a hillside, and nobody knows but Guido.

I walk the new road, where it sweeps up to the hilltop, looking out over the city and hearing the city sing, and hearing that other music which will play, city or not, and it is all for me, for Guido. There is one thing which is not changed now: the world has always been against Guido, or Guido against the world; everything moved around Guido as its center. It still does, but while it does, it makes music. I laugh at this, waiting at the top of the slope for a gap in the traffic; always careful, I will not be seen dropping over the rail to the embankment below. I—

—hear a note and all sound, all singing stops for a moment; sight too, I think, and touch; a wave, a wrench, a great peace, and then I am back on the high road, holding the rail, clamping my violin case under my coat, looking at the sky. I am different. The . . . meaning of "I" is different. . . .

All across the city, like distant thunder heard in a high wind, there is a whisper of breaking metal, a twinkling of explosion and fire, and no music. To none of this do I pay attention; I am watching that which is slipping down out of the sky. A silver ball, and under it, four machines like tanks, their four long necks twined together, their four heads stacked neatly one on the other. But for the deep hooting which comes from these heads, they fall silently.

I take off my trench coat and let it fall. I open the violin case, take out the violin, strike the railing once with it, pull out the four pegs, clear away the strings with two quick swipes, until I hold only the smooth neck and fingerboard, which ends in the widening curled scroll.

I run downhill as fast as I can, faster than I have ever run before. I know I shall be met, by whom, how, and exactly when. It is an old Hispano-Suiza with wide flaring fenders and big yellow headlights, driven by a woman. I see the car coming, run straight down the middle of the road. She slows but does not stop. I leap to the front of the car, turn, hook a knee over the headlight brace, grasp the radiator ornament. She is already howling up the hill; faster she goes, and faster, all that mighty automobile can put out.

Acceleration pressure lessens and frees me; I move myself, get one foot on the hood and the other on the radiator, still holding with one hand to the headlight brace. It has all happened quickly; I have been riding perhaps twenty, twenty-five seconds. We are back to the top of the slope and traveling eighty, ninety kilometers . . . who has made these observations and calculations as to our speed, the slope, the rate of descent of the globe and its machines, how close they must pass the rail? No matter who . . . it has been done, and every slightest pull of her wrists, each lean and striving of my body against the wind, is part of those calculations; I know it, know it is right, without wonder and without astonishment . . . for I have calculated it all; I know how; it must be right, I know so very well how. (And "I" means something new now.)

She turns to the left and the front wheels shudder over the curb. I let go the brace and put my feet side by side on the radiator, and as the front of the car reaches the railing I spring up and out, flying as men have in their hearts always wished to fly . . . up and up into the dark. With my ears I know my speed, air rushing past, diminishing as I reach the top of my arc and begin to descend; it is in this poised moment that I meet the machines from the sky, with my left arm and both legs taking those intertwined metal necks. Below me the Hispano is turning end over end down the embankment.

I reach up with my violin neck, holding it by the flat protruding lower end of the ebony fingerboard, and find that with the other end, the hard curved polished scroll, I can reach the open trumpet mouth of the topmost head. It accepts the slight curve of the carving exactly; I ram it home, extract it, repeat the motion on the second, third, fourth, crushing some delicate something in the joined throats of each.

Then that pervasive hooting is gone, and we drift silently for a second—but only a second; we are on the ground near and between two of the stilts which support the road. A sort of curtain hangs there; as we touch earth, this curtain topples outward and falls across the globe. There are people—three women, four men. One of the men is old, and wears nothing but a wooden leg strapped to his thigh. One of the women wears an ermine jacket; the tall heels are broken off her shoes. They seize a rope and run, and drop a steel hook into the girders of the stilt. On the other side, a girl and a man, an impossibly fat man, place a hook on the other side. The hard fabric of the curtain smashes at me as I struggle free—it is one of those enormous woven mats of steel-cored hempen cable they use to cover rocks when dynamiting in the city. They have captured the globe with it, casting it like a net over birds! And the globe fights; it fights, plunging upward, making no sound. The net holds, the ropes hold; I hear the steel hooks crackle in the girders as they slip and grab. The plunging stops; the globe presses upward, trying and trying to break free. The anchor ropes hum, the net rustles with strain. I feel a warmth, a heat, from the globe; it drops abruptly, plunges upward once more, but weakly, and suddenly falls to the ground with the rope mat shrouding it and smoking. The four tanklike machines have not moved since they landed; with their voices gone they have no function.

The woman in ermine and the fat man run to a two-wheeled dolly standing under the roadway. I run to help them. Nobody speaks. It is an acetylene set. We drag it to the dead sphere and light it. We begin to cut the sphere open so that I—this new, wide, deep, all-over-the-world "I"—can see what it is, how it works.

I—and "I," now, think as I work of what is happening—a different kind of thinking than any I have ever known . . . if thinking was seeing, then all my life I have thought in a hole in the ground, and now I think on a mountaintop. To think of any question is to think of the answer, if the answer exists in the experience of any other part of "I." If I wonder why I was chosen to make that leap from the car, using all my strength and all its speed to carry me exactly to that point in space where the descending machines would be, then the wonder doesn't last long enough to be called that: I *know* why I was chosen, on the instant of wondering. Someone had measured the throat of one of the tank machines; someone knew what tool would fit it exactly and be right to destroy it most easily. The neck and scroll of my violin happened to be that tool, and I happened to be on the high road with it. I might have died. The woman driving the Hispano did die. These are things that do not matter; one will unhesitatingly break a fingernail in reaching to snatch a child from the fire.

Yet, as all knowledge of the greater "I" is available to me, so is all feeling. The loss of my violin before I had made the first single note with it is a hurt beyond bearing; its loss in so important an action does not diminish the hurt at all. But to think of the hurt is to know all hurts, everywhere, of all of us who are now so strangely joined. Now there was a little boy in America, who when it was time threw himself into the drive of one of the tank machines because "I" required that the drive slip just so much, just at that second. It is known to me now that the child Henry wanted hungrily to live, more than ever in his little life before, because he had, within the hour, experienced a half second of real peace. It hurt him, dying; knowing him as I (as "I") do, it hurts to have him dead. Near him died a man, Paul, unhesitatingly, feeling the most pointed loss of a woman he desired to the moment he died, and whom he had almost possessed a moment before. There are many such deaths at this moment, all over the world, and not one which "I" cannot feel; all are known to me—the helpless, so many of whom lie this minute crushed in their cars and houses, who crawl numbly away from the fires, not fast enough to get away. These are dying too, and hurting, and even these know Guido and Guido's loss; *Unfair, unfair,* they cry as they bleed and die; *you should not have lost your violin so soon!* All, all add themselves to me; all, all understand. I belong, belong; I Guido, belong!

We have struck back with whatever would do the job, wherever it could be found, regardless of the cost, because no cost is too great to combat what has come upon us.

We will take care of our own; "I" will defend "myself." And meanwhile the pressure of Guido's music floods "me" and enriches the species, and Guido is enriched in numberless ways to an infinite degree. This is thinking as never before; this is living as never before; this is a life to be defended to a degree and in ways never before realized on this earth. . . . I wonder if anyone will ever speak again?

CHAPTER 24

Sharon Brevix thought, *I can see all over the world.* And she thought, *They've found me.*

You're four and you're lost: what bothers you? Hunger, cold, but mostly disorientation—detachment: not knowing where to go or where "they" all are. Sharon awoke where she had dozed off . . . rather, where she had slipped so very far over the slippery edge of the forever-dark. It was slippery no longer. She was hungry, she was cold, certainly; but *she wasn't lost.*

Suppose her mother were here—what would she do? *Are you all right?* Well, she was all right. Nothing broken, no cuts; no encounters with the bestial in any form. Her mother knew that and Sharon knew she knew that. The closeness she felt to her mother and to Billy and the other kids wasn't quite as nice as having them here, and being warm and having something to eat. But there were new ways, other ways, that were nicer—nicer than anything she had ever known. Billy now—see how glad he was, how afraid he'd been. How much he cared. It made her feel very good to know that Billy cared so much. It had always been his best-kept secret.

She knew she must sleep for an hour, so she closed her eyes and slept. It was quite a different thing from that other sleep.

When she awoke for the second time, it was instantly and with instant motion. She bounced to her feet no matter how stiff she felt and marked time, double-time, on a flat rock, banging her feet until they stung, and breathing deeply. Three minutes of that and she struck off purposefully into the still-dark underbrush, skipped on two stepping-stones across the brook, and unhesitatingly went to a fallen log where, the night before, she had seen a bright orange shelf fungus. She broke off large greedy pieces and crammed her mouth full of them. It was delicious, and safe, too, because although most people did not know it, someone, somewhere did know that this particular pileus was edible.

She trotted back to the half-cave where she had spent the night and got Mary Lou, her broken-footed doll, and fed her some of the fungus and a few drops of water from the brook. Then, cautioning the doll not to say a word, she set off through the woods.

In less than an hour, and while the light was still gray, she found herself at the edge of a meadow. She raised a warning finger at Mary Lou, and then stood still as a tree-trunk—an unnatural act for any child before now—and peered through the dawn-light until she saw a rabbit. It was aware of her and fear-frozen into exactly her immobility. Sharon outwaited it, let it move, let it move again, let it nibble on young clover and stare at her again and at last move curiously closer. When it was close enough, she pounced, not at the rabbit but at the place where the rabbit would be when she moved. The rabbit was there.

She transferred her grasp on the dew-damp, kicking creature to a one-handed grip just over the joints of the hind legs and stood up, lifting the rabbit clear of the ground. As it hung upside down, it immediately swung its head up and forward (as someone, somewhere, knew it would). Sharon brought the edge of her left hand down with a single smart chop, and broke its neck. She squatted down, and unhesitatingly nibbled a hole in the animal's throat with her sharp front teeth. She drank as much blood as she needed, offered some to Mary Lou (who didn't want any) wiped her mouth daintily with a handful of moist grass, picked up her doll and went her purposeful way. She knew which way to go. She knew where the road was and where a railroad was and where three farmhouses and a hunting lodge were. She also knew which one to go to, and that Daddy would come to pick her up, and that she would be at the meeting place before Daddy would, and which cellar window she was allowed to break to get in, and where the can opener was and how to prime the pump to get water. It was pretty wonderful. All she had to do was to need to know something, and if anyone knew it, she knew it.

She walked along happily, for a while sharing a stomach-shrinking thrill with some child, somewhere, who was riding a roller-coaster, and for a while doing a new kind of talking with her father. It was a tease; he'd have said to her, before: "I thought you were in the station wagon and Mummy thought you were in the truck. Good thing we were wrong. There'd've been two of you, and then who'd wear the pink dress?" But now it came out as a kind of picture, or maybe a memory of two Sharons screeching at each other and pulling at the party dress, while two broken-footed Mary Lous looked on. It was funny and she laughed. It was more than a memory. It was all the relieved anxiety and deep fondness and self-accusation her Daddy felt over almost losing his Princess-Wicked-wif'-the-fickles-on-her-nose.

She reached the lodge and got in all right. After

about an hour she looked out the window and saw a bush rattlesnake in the bare patch by the shed. She ran to the gun-cabinet and then to the bookcase for the box of .32 cartridges, and loaded the revolver and put it down and got the window open a crack and picked up the gun and braced it against the sill and got it lined up until she, or somebody, knew it was just right. Then she squeezed off a single shot that eliminated the snake's head. She unloaded the gun and ran a swab through it and put it away, and put the shells away, and then built a play-house out of overturned furniture and sofa cushions, in which she and Mary Lou fell fast asleep until Tony Brevix got there. All in all, she had a wonderful time. She never once had to wonder whether she was allowed to do this or that—she *knew*. Most important, she was by herself and in a new place, but she wasn't lost. She would never be lost again. If only nothing spoiled this, no one in the world would ever be lost again, no, nor wonder if somebody really loved them, or think they'd gone away and left them because they didn't want them.

It had always been thus between Sharon and Mary Lou, because Mary Lou knew Sharon loved her even when she accidentally left her out in the rain or threw her down the stairs. Now the children understood that kind of thing as well as the dolls, and never again would a child wonder if anyone cared, or grow up thinking that to be loved is a privilege. It's a privilege only to adults. To any child it's a basic right, which if denied dooms the child to a lifetime of seeking it and an inability to accept anything but child-style love. The way things were now, never again would a child be afraid of growing up, or hover anxiously near half-empty coffers so very easy to fill.

I know your need, the whole world was saying to "I," while "I" everywhere could understand the justice of "my" needs, and the silliness of so many wants.

When Tony Brevix came into the lodge he found her asleep. He knew she was aware of him and he knew that her awareness would not interrupt her slumber, not for a second. She slept smiling while he carried her out to the station wagon.

CHAPTER 25

There she stands the water beading her bright body her head to one side the water sparking off her hair, she smiles, says All Right Handsome What Are You Going To Do About It?

Crash!

A soft rumble and a glare of light: sky. Crash! A brighter, unbearable flash of light on light, a sharp smell of burning chemicals, a choking cloud of dust and smoke and the patter-patter of falling debris. Confusion, bewilderment, disorientation and growing anger at the deprivation of a dream.

The sharp command to every sentience, mechanical or not, on the entire hilltop: *Get Gurlick out of here!*

A flash of silver overhead, then a strange overall sticky, pore-choking sensation, like being coated with warm oil, and underneath, the torn hill dwindles away. There are still hundreds of projectors left, row on row of them, but from the size of the terraces where they are parked, there must have been hundreds of thousands more. *Crash!* A half dozen of the projectors bulge skyward and fall back in shatters and shards. Look there, a flight of jets. See, two silver spheres, dodging, dancing: then the long curve of a seeking missile points one out, and the trail and the burst make a bright ball on a smoky string, painted across the sky. *Crash! Crash!* Even as the scarred hill disappears in swift distance, the parked projectors can be seen bursting skyward, a dozen and a dozen and a score of them, pressing upward through the rain of pieces from those blasted a breath or a blink ago; and *cra—*

No, not *crash* this time, but a point, a porthole, a bay-window looking in to the core of hell, all the colors and all too bright, growing, too, too big to be growing so fast, taking the hilltop, the hillside, the whole hill lost in the ball of brilliance.

And for minutes afterward, hanging stickily by something invisible, frighteningly in midair under the silver sphere, but not feeling wind or acceleration or any of the impossible turns as the sphere whizzes along low, hedge-hopping, ground-hugging, back-tracking and hovering to hide; for minutes and minutes afterward, through the drifting speckles of overdazzled eyeballs, the pastel column can be seen rising and rising flat-headed over the land, thousands and thousands of feet, building a roof with eaves, the eaves curling and curling out and down, or are they the grasping fingers of rows and rows of what devils who have climbed up the inside of the spout, about to put up *what* hellish faces?

"Bastits," Gurlick whimpered, "tryin' to atom-bomb *me*. You tell 'em who I am?"

No response. The Medusa was calculating, for once, to capacity—even to its immense, infinitely varied capacity. It had expected to succeed in unifying the mind of humanity—it had correctly predicted its certainty of success and the impossibility of failure. But success like *this?*

Like this: In the first forty minutes humanity destroyed seventy-one percent of the projectors and forty-three percent of the spheres. To do this it used everything and anything that came to hand, regardless of the cost in lives or matériel; it put out its fire by smothering it with its mink coat. It killed its cobra by hitting it with the baby. It moved, reactive and accurate and almost in reflex, like a man holding a burning stick, and as the heat increases near one finger, it will release and withdraw and find another purchase while he thinks of other things. It threw a child into the drive of a projector because he fit, he contained the right amount of the right grade of lubricant for just that purpose at just that time. It could understand in microseconds that the nearest thing to the exact necessary tool for tearing the throat out of a projector would be the neck and scroll of a violin.

And like this: Beginning in the forty-first minute, humanity launched the first precision weapon against the projectors, having devised and produced a seeking mechanism which would infallibly find and destroy projectors (though they did not radiate in the electromagnetic spectrum, not even infra-red) and then made it compact enough to cram into the warhead of a Hawk, and, further, applied the Hawk to the Atlas. And this was only the first. In the fifty-second minute—that is, less than an hour after the Medusa pushed the button to unify the mind of man—humanity was using hasty makeshifts of appalling efficiency, devices which reversed the steering commands of the projectors (like the one which under its own power walked off the Hell Gate Bridge into eighty feet of water) and others which rebroadcast the projectors' signals 180 degrees out of phase, nullifying them. At the ninety-minute mark humanity was knocking out two of every three flying spheres it saw, not by accurate aiming (because as yet humanity couldn't tool up to countermeasure inertialess turns at six miles per second) but by an ingenious application of the theory of random numbers, by which they placed proximity missiles where the sphere wasn't but almost certainly would be—and all too often was.

The Medusa had anticipated success. But, to sum up: success like *this?* For hadn't the humans stamped out every operable instrument of the Medusa's invasion (save Gurlick, about whom they couldn't know) in just two hours and eight minutes?

This incredible species, uniquely possessed of a defense against the Medusa (the Medusa still stubbornly insisted) in its instant, total fragmentation at the invader's first touch, seemed uniquely to possess other qualities as well. It would be wise—more: it was imperative—that Earth be brought into the fold where it would have to take orders. Hence— Gurlick.

It swept Gurlick back into its confidence, told him that in spite of the abruptness of his awakening, he was now ready to go out on his own. It described to him his assignment, which made Gurlick snicker like an eight-year-old behind the barn, and assured him that it would set up for him the most perfect opportunity its mighty computers could devise. Speed, however, was of the essence—which was all right with Gurlick, who spit on his hands and made cluck-cluck noises from his back teeth and wrinkled up half his face with an obscene wink, and snickered again to show his willingness.

The sphere hovered now at treetop level over heavily wooded ground, keeping out of sight while awaiting the alien computation of the best conceivable circumstances for Gurlick's project. This might well have proved lengthy, based as it was on Gurlick's partial, mistaken, romantic, deluded and down right pornographic information, and might even have supplied some highly amusing conclusions, since they would have been based on logic, and Gurlick's most certainly were not. These diverting computations were lost, however, and lost forever when the sphere dropped dizzyingly, released Gurlick so abruptly that he tumbled, and informed him that he was on his own—the sphere was detected. Growling and grumbling, Gurlick sprawled under the trees and watched the sphere bullet upward and away, and a moment later the appearance of a Hawk, or rather its trail, scoring the sky in a swift reach like the spread of a strain-crack in window glass.

He did not see the inevitable, but heard it in due course—the faint distant thump against the roof of the world which marked the end of the sphere's existence—and very probably the end of all the Medusa's artifacts on earth. He said an unprintable syllable, rolled over and eyed the woodlands with disfavor. This wasn't going to be like flying over it like a bug over a carpet, with some big brain doing all your thinking for you. On the other hand . . . this was the payoff. This was where Gurlick got his—where at long last he could strike back at a whole world full of bastits.

He got to his feet and began walking.

CHAPTER 26

Full of wonder, the human hive contemplated itself and its works, its gains, its losses and its new nature.

First, there was the intercommunication—a thing so huge, so different, that few minds could previously have imagined it. No analogy could suffice; no concepts of infinite telephone exchanges, or multi-side-band receivers, could hint at the quality of that gigantic cognizance. To describe it in terms of its complexity would be as impossible—and as purblind—as an attempt to describe fine lace by a description of each of its threads. It had, rather, *texture*. Your memory, and his and his, and hers over the horizon's shoulder—all your memories are mine. More: your personal orientation in the framework of your own experiences, your I-in-the-past, is also mine. More: your skills remain your own (is great music made less for being shared?) but your sensitivity to your special subject is mine now, and your pride in your excellence is mine now. More: though bound to the organism, Mankind, as never before, I am I as never before. When Man has demands on me, I am totally dedicated to Man's purpose. Otherwise, within the wide, wide limits of mankind's best interests, I am as never before a free agent; I am I to a greater degree, and with less obstruction from within and without, than ever before possible. For gone, gone altogether are individual man's hosts of pests and devils, which in strange combinations have plagued us all in the past: the They-don't-want-me devil, the Suppose-they-find-out devil, the twin imps of They-are-lying-to-me and They-are-trying-to-cheat-me; gone, gone is I'm-afraid-to-try, and They-won't-let-me, and I-couldn't-be-loved-if-they-knew.

Along with the imps and devils, other things disappeared—things regarded throughout human history as basic, thematic, keys to the structures of lives and cultures. Now if a real thing should disappear, a rock or a tree or a handful of water, there will be thunder and a wind and other violence, depending upon what form the vanished mass owned. Or if a great man disappears, there is almighty confusion in the rush to fill the vacuum of his functions. But the things which disappeared now proved their unreality by the unruffled silence in which they disappeared. Money. The sense of property. Jingoistic patriotism, tariffs, taxes, boundaries and frontiers, profit and loss, hatred and suspicion of humans by humans, and language itself (except as part of an art) with all the difficulties of communication between languages and within them.

In short, it was abruptly possible for mankind to live with itself in health. Removed now was mankind's cess-gland, the secretions of which (called everything from cussedness to Original Sin) had poisoned its body since it was born, distorting decencies like survival and love into greed and lust, turning Achievement ("I have built") into Position ("I have power").

So much for humanity's new state of being. As to its abilities, they were simply based, straightforward. There are always many ways to accomplish anything, but only one of them is really best. Which of them is best—that is the source of all argument on the production of anything, the creator of factions among the designers, and the first enemy of speed and efficiency. But when humanity became a hive, and needed something—as for example the adaptation of the swift hunting missile Hawk to the giant carrier Atlas—the device was produced without considerations of pride or profit, without waste motion, and without interpersonal friction of any kind. The decision was made, the job was done. In those heady first moments, anything and everything available was used—but with precision. Later (by minutes) fewer ingenious stopgaps were used, more perfect tools were shaped from the materials at hand. And still later (by hours) there was full production of new designs. Mankind now used exactly the right tool for the jobs it had to do. . . .

And within it, each individual flowered, finding freedoms to be, to act, to take enrichment and pleasure as never before. What were the things that Dimity (Salomé?) Carmichael had always needed, wanted to do? She could do them now. An Italian boy, Guido, packed taut with talent, awaited the arrival of the greatest living violinist from behind a now collapsed Iron Curtain; they would hereafter spend their lives and do their work together. The parents of a small stiff boy named Henry contemplated, as all the world contemplated, what had happened to him and why, and how totally impossible it would be for such a thing ever to happen again. Sacrifice there must be from time to time, even now; but never again a useless one. Everyone now knew, as if in personal memory, how fiercely Henry had wanted to live in that flash of agony which had eclipsed him. All Earth shared the two kinds of religious experience discovered by the Africans Mbala and Nuyu, wherein one had become confirmed in his faith and the other had found it. What, specifically, had brought them to it was of no significance; the fact of their devotion was the important thing to be shared, for it is in the finest nature of humanity to worship, fight it as he sometimes may. The universe being what it is, there is always *plus ultra, plus ultra*—powers and patterns beyond understanding, and more beyond these when these are understood. Out there is the call to which faith is the natural response and worship the natural approach.

Such was humanity when it became a hive—a beautiful entity, balanced and fine and wondrously alive. A pity, in a way, that such a work of art, such self-sufficiency, was to exist in this form for so brief a time. . . .

CHAPTER 27

Gurlick, alone of humans insulated from the human hive, member of another, sensed none of this. Driven, hungry through a whole spectrum of appetites, full of resentment, he shuffled through the woods. He had been vaguely aware of the outskirts of a town not far from where the silver sphere had set him down; he would, he supposed, find what he wanted there, though wanting it was the only thing quite clear to him. How he was to get it was uncertain; but get it he must. He was aware of the presence within him of the Medusa, observing, computing, but—not directing, cognizant as it was of the fact that the fine details of such an operation must be left to the species itself. Had it had its spheres and other machines available, there might have been a great deal it could do to assist Gurlick. But now—he was on his own.

He was in virgin forest now, the interlocked foliage overhead dimming the mid-morning sunshine to an underwater green, and the footing was good, there being little underbrush and a gentle downslope. Gurlick gravitated downhill, knowing he would encounter a path or a road sooner or later, and monotonously cursed his empty stomach, his aching feet, and his enemies.

He heard voices.

He stopped, shrank back against a tree trunk, and peered. For a moment he could detect nothing, and then, off to the right, he heard a sudden musical laugh. He looked toward the sound, and saw a brief motion of something blue. He came out of hiding, and, scuttling clumsily from tree to tree, went to investigate.

There were three of them, girls in their mid-teens, dressed in halters and shorts, giggling over the chore of building a fire in a small clearing. They had a string of fish, pike and lake trout, and a frying pan, and seemed completely and hilariously preoccupied.

Gurlick, from a vantage point above them, chewed on his lower lip and wondered what to do. He had no delusions about approaching openly and sweet-talking his way into their circle. It would be far wiser, he knew, to slip away and go looking elsewhere, for something surer, safer. On the other hand . . . he heard the crackle of bacon fat as one of the girls dropped the tender slivers into the frying pan. He looked at the three lithe young bodies, and at the waiting string of fish, half of which were scaled and beheaded, and quietly moaned. There was too much of what was wanted, down there, for him to turn his back.

Then a curl of fragrance from the bacon reached him and toppled his reason. He rose from his crouch and in three bounds was down the slope and in their midst, moaning and slavering. One of the children bounded away to the right, one to the left. The third fell under his hands, shrieking.

"Now you jus' be still," he panted, trying to hold his victim, trying to protect himself against her hysterical lappings, writhings, clawings. "I ain't goin' to hurt you if you jus'—"

Uh! He was bowled right off his feet by one of the escapees who had returned at a dead run and crashed him with a hard shoulder. He rolled over and found himself staring up at the second girl who had run away as she stood over him with a stone the size of a grapefruit raised in both hands. She brought it down; it hit Gurlick on the left cheekbone and the bridge of his nose and filled the world with stars and brilliant tatters of pain. He fell back, wagging his head, pawing at his face, trying to get some vision back and kick away the sick dizziness; and when at last he could see again, he was alone with the campfire, the frying pan, the string of fish.

"Li'l bastits," he growled, holding his face. He looked at his hand, on which were flecks of his own blood, swore luridly, turned in a circle as if to find and pursue them, and then squatted before the fire, reached for two cleaned fish, and dropped them hissing into the pan.

Well, he'd get that much out of it, anyway.

He had eaten four of the fish and had two more cooking when he heard voices again, a man's deep, "Which way now? Over here?" and a girl's answer, "Yes, where the smoke's coming from."

Jailbait . . . of course, of *course* they'd have gone for help! Gurlick cursed them all and lumbered downslope, away from the sound of voices. Boy, he'd messed up, but good. The whole hillside would be crawling with people hunting him. He had to get out of here.

He moved as cautiously as he could, quite sure he was being watched by hundreds of eyes, yet seeing no one until he glimpsed two men off to his left and below him. One had binoculars on a strap around his neck, the other a shotgun. Gurlick, half-fainting with terror, slumped down between a tree trunk and a rock, and cowered there until he could hear their voices, and while he heard them, and after he heard them, with their curt certain syllables and their cold lack of mercy. When all was quite quiet again, he rose, and at that moment became aware of an aircraft sound. It approached rapidly, and he dropped back into his hiding place, trembling, and peeped up at the glittering patches of blue in the leafy roof. The machine flew directly overhead, low, too slowly—a helicopter. He heard it thrashing the air off to the north, downhill from him, and for a while he could not judge if it was going or coming or simply circling down there. In his pride he was convinced that its business was Gurlick and only Gurlick, and in his ignorance he was certain it had seen him through the thick cover. It went away at last, and the forest returned to its murmuring silence. He heard a faint shout behind and above him, and scuttled from cover and away from the sound. Pausing, a moment later, for breath, he caught another glimpse of the man with the shotgun off to his left, and escaped to the right and down.

And, thus pursued and herded, he came to the water's edge.

There was a dirt path there, and no one in sight; and it was warm and sunny and peaceful. Slowly Gurlick's panic subsided, and, as he walked along the path, there was a deep throb of anticipation within him. He'd gotten away clean; he had outdistanced his enemies and now, enemies, beware!

The path curved closer to the bank of the lake. Alders stood thick here, and there was the smell of moss. The path turned, and the shade was briefly darker here at the verge of the floods of gold over the water. And there by the path it lay, the little pile of fabric, bright red, shiny black, filmy white with edges iced with lace. . . .

Gurlick stopped walking, stopped breathing until his chest hurt. Then he moved slowly past this incredible, impossible consolidation of his dream, and went to the bushes at the water's edge.

She was out there—*she*.

He made a sharp wordless sound and stood forward, away from the bushes. She turned in the water and stared at him, her eyes round.

Emancipated now, free to be what she had always wished to be, and to do what she needed to do without fear or hesitation; swimming now naked in the sun, sure and fearless, shameless; utterly oriented within herself and herself within the matrix of humanity and all its known data, Salomé Carmichael stood up in the water, under the sun, and said, "Hello, Handsome."

CHAPTER 28

So ended humanity within its planetary limits; so ended the self-contained, self-aware species-hive which had for such a brief time been able to feel, to the ends of its earth, its multifarious self. The end came some hours after the helicopter—the same one which had set her down by the pond—had come for Salomé Carmichael, which it had the instant Gurlick quit the scene. Gurlick had seen it from where he crouched guiltily in the bushes. After it had gone away he slowly climbed to his feet and made his way back to the pond. He hunkered down with his back to a tree and regarded the scene unwinkingly.

It had been right there, on the moss.

Over there had lain the pretty little heap of clothes, so clean, so soft, so very red, shiny black, the white so pretty. The strangest thing that had ever happened to him in his whole life had happened here, stranger than the coming of the Medusa, stranger than the unpeopled factory back there in the mountains, stranger, even, than the overwhelming fact of this place, of her being here, of the unbelievable coincidence of it all with his dream. And that strangest thing of all was that once when she was here, she had cried out, and he had then been gentle. He had been gentle with all his heart and mind and body, for a brief while flooded, melted, swept away by gentleness. No wrinkled raisin from out of space, no concept like the existence of a single living thing so large it permeated two galaxies and part of a third, could be so shockingly alien to him, everything he was and had ever been, as this rush of gentleness. Its microscopic seed must have lain encysted within him all his life, never encountering a single thing, large or small, which could warm it to germination. Now it had burst open, burst him open, and he was shocked, shaken, macerated as never before in his bruised existence.

He crouched against the tree and regarded the moss, and the lake, and the place where the red and the black and the lace had lain, and wondered why he had run away. He wondered how he could have let her go. The gentleness was consuming him, even now . . . he had to find somewhere to put it down, but there wouldn't be anyone else, anyone or anything, for him to be gentle to, anywhere in the world.

He began to cry. Gurlick had always wept easily, his facile tears his only outlet for fear, and anger, and humiliation, and spite. This, however, was different. This was very difficult to do, painful in the extreme, and impossible to stop until he was racked, wrung out, exhausted. It tumbled him over and left him groveling on the moss. Then he slept, abruptly, his whipped consciousness fleeing away to the dark.

CHAPTER 29

What can travel faster than light?

Stand here by me, friend, on this hillside, under the black and freckled sky. Which stars do you know—Polaris? Good. And the bright one yonder, that's Sirius. Look at them now: at Polaris, at Sirius. Quickly now: Polaris, Sirius. And again: Sirius, Polaris.

How far apart are they? It says in the book, thousands of light-years. How many? Too many: never mind. But how long does it take you to flick your gaze from one to the other and back? a second? A half-second next time, then a tenth? . . . You can't say that nothing, absolutely nothing, has traveled between the two. Your vision has; your attention has.

You now understand, you have the rudiments of understanding what it is to flick a part of yourself from star to star, just as (given the skill) you may shift from soul to soul.

With such a shift, down such a path, came the Medusa at the instant of its marriage to humanity. In all the history of humanity, the one instant (save death) of most significance is the instant of syngamy, the moment of penetration by the sperm of the ovum.

Yet almost never is there a heralding of this instant, nor a sign; it comes to pass in silence and darkness, and no one ever knows but the mindless flecks of complex jelly directly involved.

Not so now; and never before, and never again would marriage occur with such explosion. A micro-second after that melding, Gurlick's altered seed to the welcoming ovum of a human, the Medusa of space shot down its contacting thread, an unerring harpoon carrying a line to itself, and all of its Self following in the line, ready to reach and fill humanity, make of it a pseudopod, the newest member of its sprawling corpus.

But if the Medusa's bolt can be likened to a harpoon, then it can be said that the uprushing flood it met was like a volcano. The Medusa had not a micro-micro-second in which to realize what had happened to it. It did not die; it was not killed any more than humanity would have been killed had the Medusa's plan been realized. Humanity would have become a "person" of the illimitable creature. Now . . .

Now, instead, humanity became the creature; flooded it, filled it to its furthermost crannies, drenched its most remote cells with the Self of humankind. Die? Never that; the Medusa was alive as never before, with a new and different kind of life, in which its slaves were freed but its motivations unified; where the individual was courted and honored and brought special nutrients, body and mind, and where, freely, "want to" forever replaced "must."

And all for want of a datum: that intelligence might exist in individuals, and that dissociated individuals might co-operate yet not be a hive. For there is no structure on earth which could not have been built by rats, were the rats centrally directed and properly motivated. How could the Medusa have known? Thousands upon thousands of species and cultures throughout the galaxies have technological progress as advanced as that of Earth, and are yet composed of individuals no more highly evolved than termites, lemurs, or shrews. What slightest hint was there for the Medusa that a hive-humanity would be a different thing from a super-rat?

Humanity had passed the barriers of language and of individual isolation on its planet. It passed the barriers of species now, and of isolation in its cosmos. The faith of Mbala was available to Guido, and so were the crystal symphonies of the black planets past Ophiuchus. Charlotte Dunsay, reaching across the world to her husband in Hobart, Tasmania, might share with him a triple sunrise in the hub of Orion's great Nebula. As one man could share the *being* of another here on earth, so both, and perhaps a small child with them, could fuse their inner selves with some ancient contemplative mind leeched to the rocks in some roaring methane cataract, or soar with some insubstantial life-forms adrift where they were born in the high layers of atmosphere around some unheard-of planet.

So ended mankind, to be born again as hive-humanity; so ended the hive of earth to become star-man, the immeasurable, the limitless, the growing; maker of music beyond music, poetry beyond words, and full of wonder, full of worship.

CHAPTER 30

So too ended Gurlick, the isolated, alone among humankind denied membership in the fusion of humans, full of a steaming fog, aglow with his flickerings of hate and the soft shine of corruption, member of something other than humankind. For while humanity had been able to read him (and his dream) and herd him through the forest to its fulfillment, it had never been able to reach his consciousness, blocked as it was by the thoughtlines of the Medusa.

These lines, however, were open still, and when humanity became Medusa, it flooded down to Gurlick and made him welcome. *Come!* it called, and whirled him up and outward, showing and sharing its joy and strength and pride, showering him with wonders of a thousand elsewheres and a hundred heres; it showed him how to laugh at the most rarefied technician's joke and how to feel the structure of sestinae and sonnets, of bridges and Bach. It spoke to him saying *We* and granting him the right to regard it all and say: *I*. And more: he had been promised a kingship, and now he had it, for all this sentient immensity acknowledged to him its debt. Let him but make the phantom of a wish of a thought, and his desires would be fulfilled. *Come!* it called. *Come!*

But the weight of the man o' war was on his mind. *Hide!* he thought. Don't attract attention. If he got out of line, the man o' war would squash him like a bug. But humanity, which had become Medusa, insisted, it beat down upon him, and finally Gurlick could withstand its force no longer. He turned and faced humankind as it had become, all-transcending, all-inclusive, all-knowing, pervasive-faced humankind as he had never faced it before in his life.

Humankind had changed.

His first reaction was *My God, it's full of people!*

Which was strange, because he found himself at the edge of a purple cliff which overlooked a valley with a silver river in it. Not silver like the poets say, which only means the reflection of sky-white; this one was metallic silver color, fluid, fast. He was aware without surprise that he sat on the tip of his spine, which was long, black and tapering, with two enormous hind legs, kneed in the middle like broken straws and pretty nearly as slender, forming the other two points of his tripod. He was chewing on a stone, holding it to black marble lips (which opened sidewise) with four hands (having scorpion-nippers for fingers) and he found it delicious. He turned his head around (all the way, without effort) and saw Salomé Carmichael behind him, and she was beautiful beyond belief, which was odd because she looked like a twelve-foot, blue-black praying mantis. But then, so did he.

She spoke, but it was not speech really, but a sort of semaphore of the emotions. He felt himself greeted, and made joyfully welcome *(Hello, oh hello, Danny, I knew you'd come, you had to come)* and then there was an invitation: *to the place to watch that game*. She moved close to him so that their bodies touched, and somehow he knew just exactly what to do to stay with her; in a blink they were somewhere else, on the top of a swaying green tree (the bark was the green part) and he had a round blunt front end like a bull-frog and four gauzy wings, and two long legs with webbed feet like a waterbird. Salomé was there too, of the same species and utterly lovely; and together they watched the game, understanding it as completely in all its suspensions and convolutions as any earthside hockey or baseball or chess fan might follow his favorite. The teams were whole hives, and they could all together, create soundwaves and focus them; at the focal point danced a blue-green crystal, held spinning in midair by the beam of sound. There were three hive-teams, not two, and if two should focus together on the crystal it would shatter musically, and that was a foul, and the third team won the point, and could have the playing field to dance in. And when the dance was over (there were points for the dance too) then another crystal would be projected high in the rosy air. . . .

To a swimming place, tingling, refreshing, Gurlick knowing somehow that where they swam under a blue-black rock ceiling, the temperature was over a thousand degrees centigrade, and the gleaming bony paddles and sleek speckled flanks with which he swam and on which he felt the tingling were no flesh he had ever learned of. And to a flying place where all the people, welcoming as everywhere, and some known to him as people he had met on Earth, all these people were cobweb-frail, spending their lives adrift in the thin shifts of air with the highest mist peaks of a cloud-shrouded planet as their floor. . . .

And Salomé gave him her story of envy and of her need to have others depend on her.

These two were ideal antagonists, ideal weapons in the conflict between Medusa and mankind. Medusa had won the battles; mankind had won the war. And it had all begun with Gurlick. . . .

Somewhere in this communion between them, the whole thing was talked out. It was probably in the first couple of seconds of their first meeting, there over the silver river. If it were rendered into words it was Gurlick's complete wounding by the discovery (in his loneliness) that what had happened by the lake was no affair of his at all, but only a strategic move in a war between a giant and a behemoth; with it, all he had ever been in his tattered life, how there was nothing within him with a whole soul to give in exchange for accidental kindness; how he was unashamed to have far, far passed the point where he could keep clean and think well and be a man . . . in short, the entire Gurlick, with all the reasons why, in one clear flash.

Gurlick, numb and passive as he tossed like a chip on their ocean of wonders, had at last a wish, and had it, and had it.

True, none of this could have come about without him. This result could not have been with anyone else in his place, so—true enough—he was owed a debt. Pay it, then.

Pay the debt. . . . You do not reward a catalyst by changing it, the unchanging, into something else. When a man is what Gurlick is, he is that because he has made himself so; for what his environment has done to him, blame the environment not so much as the stolid will that kept him in it. So—take away hunger and poverty (or body and soul), deprivation and discomfort and humiliation, and you take away the very core of his being—his sole claim to superiority.

You take away his hate. You take away from him all reason to hate anyone or anything—like the wet, like the cold.

So don't ask him to look out among the stars, and join in the revelries of giants. Don't thank him, don't treat him, and above all, do not so emasculate him as to take away from him his reasons to hate: they have become his life.

So they paid him, meticulously to the specifications he himself (though all unknowing) set up.

And as long as he lived, there was a city-corner, drab streets and fumes, sullen pedestrians and careless, dangerous aimers of trucks and cabs; moist unbearable heat and bitter cold; and bars where Gurlick could go and put in his head, whining for a drink, and bartenders to send him out into the wet with his hatred, back to a wrecked truck in a junkyard where he might lie in the dark and dream that dream of his. "Bastits," Gurlick would mutter in the dark, hating . . . happy: "Lousy bastits."

KILLDOZER

Before the race was the deluge, and before the deluge another race, whose nature it is not for mankind to understand. Not unearthly, not alien, for this was their earth and their home.

There was a war between this race, which was a great one, and another. The other was truly alien, a sentient cloudform, an intelligent grouping of tangible electrons. It was spawned in mighty machines by some accident of science before our aboriginal conception of its complexities. And the machines, servants of the people, became the people's masters, and great were the battles that followed. The electron-beings had the power to warp the delicate balances of atom-structure, and their life-medium was metal, which they permeated and used to their own ends. Each weapon the people developed was possessed and turned against them, until a time when the remnants of that vast civilization found a defense—

An insulator. The terminal product or by-product of all energy research—neutronium.

In its shelter they developed a weapon. What it was we shall never know, and our race will live—or we shall know, and our race will perish as theirs perished. For, to destroy the enemy, it got out of hand and its measureless power destroyed them with it, and their cities, and their possessed machines. The very earth dissolved in flame, the crust writhed and shook and the oceans boiled. Nothing escaped it, nothing that we know as life, and nothing of the pseudolife that had evolved within the mysterious force-fields of their incomprehensible machines, save one hardy mutant.

Mutant it was, and ironically this one alone could have been killed by the first simple measures used against its kind—but it was past time for simple expediences. It was an organized electron-field possessing intelligence and mobility and a will to destroy, and little else. Stunned by the holocaust, it drifted over the grumbling globe, and in a lull in the violence of the forces gone wild on Earth, sank to the steaming ground in its half-conscious exhaustion. There it found shelter—shelter built by and for its dead enemies. An envelope of neutronium. It drifted in, and its consciousness at last fell to its lowest ebb. And there it lay while the neutronium, with its strange constant flux, its interminable striving for perfect balance, extended itself and closed the opening. And thereafter in the turbulent eons that followed, the envelope tossed like a gray bubble on the surface of the roiling sphere, for no substance on Earth would have it or combine with it.

The ages came and went, and chemical action and reaction did their mysterious work, and once again there was life and evolution. And a tribe found the mass of neutronium, which is not a substance but a static force, and were awed by its aura of indescribable chill, and they worshiped it and built a temple around it and made sacrifices to it. And ice and fire and the seas came and went, and the land rose and fell as the years went by, until the ruined temple was on a knoll, and the knoll was an island. Islanders came and went, lived and built and died, and races forgot. So now somewhere in the Pacific to the west of the archipelago called Islas Revillagigeda, there was an uninhabited island. And one day—

Chub Horton and Tom Jaeger stood watching the *sprite* and her squat tow of three cargo lighters dwindle over the glassy sea. The big ocean-going towboat and her charges seemed to be moving out of focus rather than traveling away. Chub spat cleanly around the cigar that grew out of the corner of his mouth.

"That's that for three weeks. How's it feel to be a guinea pig?"

"We'll get it done." Tom had little crinkles all around the outer ends of his eyes. He was a head taller than Chub and rangy, and not so tough, and he was a real operator. Choosing him as a foreman for the experiment had been wise, for he was competent and he commanded respect. The theory of airfield construction that they were testing appealed vastly to him, for here were no officers-in-charge, no government inspectors, no timekeeping or reports. The government had allowed the company a temporary land grant, and the idea was to put production-line techniques into the layout and grading of the project. There were six operators and two mechanics and more than a million dollars' worth of the best equipment that money could buy. Government acceptance was to be on a partially completed basis, and contingent on government standards. The theory obviated both gold-bricking and graft, and neatly sidestepped the man-power shortage. "When that black-topping crew gets here, I reckon we'll be ready for 'em," said Tom.

He turned and scanned the island with an operator's vision and saw it as it was, and in all the stages it would pass through, and as it would look when they had finished, with four thousand feet of clean-draining runway, hard-packed shoulders, four acres of plane-park, the access road and the short taxiway. He saw the lay of each lift that the power shovel would cut as it brought down the marl bluff, and the ruins on top of it that would give them stone to haul down the salt-flat to the little swamp at the other end, there to be walked in by the dozers.

"We got time to walk the shovel up there to the bluff before dark."

They walked down the beach toward the outcropping where the equipment stood surrounded by crates and drums of supplies. The three tractors were ticking over quietly, the two-cycle Diesel chuckling through their mufflers and the big D-7 whacking away its metronomic compression knock on every easy revolution. The Dumptors were lined up and silent, for they would not be ready to work until the shovel was ready to load them. They looked like a mechanical interpretation of Dr. Dolittle's "Pushmepullyou," the fantastic animal with two front ends. They had two large driving wheels and two small steerable wheels. The motor and the driver's seat were side by side over the front—or smaller—wheels; but the driver faced the dump body between the big rear wheels, exactly the opposite of the way he would sit in a dump truck. Hence, in traveling from shovel to dumping-ground, the operator drove backwards, looking over his shoulder, and in dumping he backed the machine up but he himself traveled forward—quite a trick for fourteen hours a day! The shovel squatted in the midst of all the others, its great hulk looming over them, humped there with its boom low and its iron chin on the ground, like some great tired dinosaur.

Rivera, the Puerto Rican mechanic, looked up grinning as Tom and Chub approached, and stuck a bleeder wrench into the top pocket of his coveralls.

"She says 'Sigalo,'" he said, his white teeth

flashlighting out of the smear of grease across his mouth. "She says she wan' to get dirt on dis paint." He kicked the blade of the Seven with his heel.

Tom sent the grin back—always a surprising thing in his grave face.

"That Seven'll do that, and she'll take a good deal off her bitin' edge along with the paint before we're through. Get in the saddle, Goony. Build a ramp off the rocks down to the flat there, and blade us off some humps from here to the bluff yonder. We're walking the dipper up there."

The Puerto Rican was in the seat before Tom had finished, and with a roar the Seven spun in its length and moved back along the outcropping to the inland edge. Rivera dropped his blade and the sandy marl curled and piled up in front of the dozer, loading the blade and running off in two even rolls at the ends. He shoved the load toward the rocky edge, the Seven revving down as it took the load, *blat blat blatting* and pulling like a supercharged ox as it fired slowly enough for them to count the revolutions.

"She's a hunk of machine," said Tom.

"A hunk of operator, too," gruffed Chub, and added, "for a mechanic."

"The boy's all right," said Kelly. He was standing there with them, watching the Puerto Rican operate the dozer, as if he had been there all along, which was the way Kelly always arrived places. He was tall, slim, with green eyes too long and an easy stretch to the way he moved, like an attenuated cat. He said, "Never thought I'd see the day when equipment was shipped set up ready to run like this. Guess no one ever thought of it before."

"There's times when heavy equipment has to be unloaded in a hurry these days," Tom said. "If they can do it with tanks, they can do it with construction equipment. We're doin' it to build something instead, is all. Kelly, crank up the shovel. It's oiled. We're walking it over to the bluff."

Kelly swung up into the cab of the big dipper-stick and, diddling the governor control, pulled up the starting handle. The Murphy Diesel snorted and settled down into a thudding idle. Kelly got into the saddle, set up the throttle a little, and began to boom up.

"I still can't get over it," said Chub. "Not more'n a year ago we'd a had two hundred men on a job like this."

Tom smiled. "Yeah, and the first thing we'd have done would be to build an office building, and then quarters. Me, I'll take this way. No timekeepers, no equipment-use reports, no progress and yardage summaries, no nothin' but eight men, a million bucks worth of equipment, an' three weeks. A shovel an' a mess of tool crates'll keep the rain off us, an' army field rations'll keep our bellies full. We'll get it done, we'll get out and we'll get paid."

Rivera finished the ramp, turned the Seven around and climbed it, walking the new fill down. At the top he dropped his blade, floated it, and backed down the ramp, smoothing out the rolls. At a wave from Tom he started out across the shore, angling up toward the bluff, beating out the humps and carrying fill into the hollows. As he worked, he sang, feeling the beat of the mighty motor, the micrometric obedience of that vast implacable machine.

"Why doesn't that monkey stick to his grease guns?"

Tom turned and took the chewed end of a match stick out of his mouth. He said nothing, because he had for some time been trying to make a habit of saying nothing to Joe Dennis. Dennis was an ex-accountant, drafted out of an office at the last gasp of a defunct project in the West Indies. He had become an operator because they needed operators badly. He had been released with alacrity from the office because of his propensity for small office politics. It was a game he still played, and completely aside from his boiled-looking red face and his slightly womanish walk, he was out of place in the field; for boot-licking and back-stabbing accomplish even less out on the field than they do in an office. Tom, trying so hard to keep his mind on his work, had to admit to himself that of all Dennis' annoying traits the worst was that he was as good a pan operator as could be found anywhere, and no one could deny it.

Dennis certainly didn't.

"I've seen the day when anyone catching one of those goonies so much as sitting on a machine during lunch, would kick his fanny," Dennis groused. "Now they give 'em a man's work and a man's pay."

"*Doin'* a man's work, ain't he?" Tom said.

"He's a Puerto Rican!"

Tom turned and looked at him levelly. "Where was it you said *you* come from," he mused. "Oh yeah. Georgia."

"What do you mean by that?"

Tom was already striding away. "Tell you as soon as I have to," he flung back over his shoulder. Dennis went back to watching the Seven.

Tom glanced at the ramp and then waved Kelly on. Kelly set his housebrake so the shovel could not swing, put her into travel gear, and shoved the swing lever forward. With a crackling of drive chains and a massive scrunching of compacting coral sand, the shovel's great flat pads carried her over and down the ramp. As she tipped over the peak of the ramp the heavy manganese steel bucket-door gaped open and closed, like a hungry mouth, slamming up against the bucket until suddenly it latched shut and was quiet. The big Murphy Diesel crooned hollowly under compression as the machine ran downgrade and then the sensitive governor took hold and it took up its belly-beating thud.

Peebles was standing by one of the door-pan combines, sucking on his pipe and looking out to sea. He was grizzled and heavy, and from under the bushiest gray brows looked the calmest gray eyes Tom had ever seen. Peebles had never gotten angry at a machine—a rare trait in a born mechanic—and in fifty-odd years he had learned it was even less use getting angry at a man. Because no matter what, you could always fix what was wrong with a machine. He said around his pipestem:

"Hope you'll give me back my boy, there."

Tom's lips quirked in a little grin. There had been an understanding between old Peebles and himself ever since they had met. It was one of those things which exists unspoken—they knew little about each other because they had never found it necessary to make small talk to keep their friendship extant. It was enough to know that each could expect the best from the other, without persuasion.

"Rivera?" Tom asked. "I'll chase him back as soon as he finishes that service road for the dipper-stick. Why—got anything on?"

"Not much. Want to get that arc welder drained and flushed and set up a grounded table in case you guys tear anything up." He paused. "Besides, the kid's filling his head up with too many things at once. Mechanicing is one thing; operating is something else."

"Hasn't got in his way much so far, has it?"

"Nope. Don't aim t' let it, either. 'Less you need him."

Tom swung up on the pan tractor. "I don't need him that bad, Peeby. If you want some help in the meantime, get Dennis."

Peebles said nothing. He spat. He didn't say anything at all.

"What's the matter with Dennis?" Tom wanted to know.

"Look yonder," said Peebles, waving his pipestem. Out on the beach Dennis was talking to Chub, in Dennis' indefatigable style, standing beside Chub, one hand on Chub's shoulder. As they watched they saw Dennis call his side-kick, Al Knowles.

"Dennis talks too much," said Peebles. "That most generally don't amount to much, but that Dennis, he sometimes *says* too much. Ain't got what it takes to run a show, and knows it. Makes up for it by messin' in between folks."

"He's harmless," said Tom.

Still looking up the beach, Peebles said slowly:

"Is, so far."

Tom started to say something, then shrugged. "I'll send you Rivera," he said, and opened the throttle. Like a huge electric dynamo, the two cycle motor whined to a crescendo. Tom lifted the dozer with a small lever by his right thigh and raised the pan with the long control sprouting out from behind his shoulder. He moved off, setting the rear gate of the scraper so that anything the blade bit would run off to the side instead of loading into the pan. He slapped the tractor into sixth gear and whined up to and around the crawling shovel, cutting neatly in under the boom and running on ahead with his scraper blade just touching the ground, dragging to a fine grade the service road Rivera had cut.

Dennis was saying, "It's that little Hitler stuff. Why should I take that kind of talk? 'You come from Georgia,' he says. What is he—a Yankee or something?"

"A crackah f'm Macon," chortled Al Knowles, who came from Georgia, too. He was tall and stringy and round-shouldered. All of his skill was in his hands and feet, brains being a commodity he had lived without all his life until he had met Dennis and used him as a reasonable facsimile thereof.

"Tom didn't mean nothing by it," said Chub.

"No, he didn't mean nothin'. Only that we do what he says the way he says it, specially if he finds a way we don't like. *You* wouldn't do like that, Chub. Al, think Chub would carry on thataway?"

"Sure wouldn't," said Al, feeling it expected of him.

"Nuts," said Chub, pleased and uncomfortable, and thinking, what have I got against Tom?—not knowing, not liking Tom as well as he had. "Tom's the man here, Dennis. We got a job to do—let's skit and git. Man can take anything for a lousy six weeks."

"Oh, sho'," said Al.

"Man can take just so much," Dennis said. "What they put a man like that on top for, chub? What's the matter with you? Don't you know grading and drainage as good as Tom? Can Tom stake out a side hill like you can?"

"Sure, sure, but what's the difference, long as we get a field built? An' anyhow, hell with bein' the boss-man. Who gets the blame if things don't run right, anyway?"

Dennis stepped back, taking his hand off Chub's shoulder, and stuck an elbow in Al's ribs.

"You see that, Al? Now there's a smart man. That's the thing Uncle Tom didn't bargain for. Chub, you can count on Al and me to do just that little thing."

"Do just what little thing?" asked Chub, genuinely puzzled.

"Like you said. If the job goes wrong, the boss gets blamed. So if the boss don't behave, the job goes wrong."

"Uh-huh," agreed Al with the conviction of mental simplicity.

Chub double-took this extraordinary logical process and grasped wildly at anger as the conversation slid out from under him. "I didn't say any such thing! This job is going' to get done, no matter what! Hitler ain't hangin' no iron cross on me or anybody else around here if I can help it."

"Tha's the ol' fight," feinted Dennis. "We'll show that guy what we think of his kind of sabotage."

"You talk too much," said Chub and escaped with the remnants of coherence. Every time he talked with Dennis he walked away feeling as if he had an unwanted membership card stuck in his pocket that he couldn't throw away with a clear conscience.

Rivera ran his road up under the bluff, swung the Seven around, punched out the master clutch and throttled down, idling. Tom was making his pass with the pan, and as he approached, Rivera slipped out of the seat and behind the tractor, laying a sensitive hand on the final drive casing and sprocket bushings, checking for overheating. Tom pulled alongside and beckoned him up on the pan tractor.

"*Que pase*, Goony? Anything wrong?"

Rivera shook his head and grinned. "Nothing wrong. She is perfect, that '*De Siete*.' She—"

"That what? 'Daisy Etta'?"

"*De siete*. In Spanish, D-7. It means something in English?"

"Got you wrong," smiled Tom. "But Daisy Etta is a girl's name in English, all the same."

He shifted the pan tractor into neutral and engaged the clutch, and jumped off the machine. Rivera followed. They climbed aboard the Seven, Tom at the controls.

Rivera said "Daisy Etta," and grinned so widely that a soft little chuckling noise came from behind his back teeth. He reached out his hand, crooked his little finger around one of the tall steering clutch levers, and pulled it all the way back. Tom laughed outright.

"You got something there," he said. "The easiest runnin' cat ever built. Hydraulic steerin' clutches and brakes that'll bring you to a dead stop if you spit on 'em. Forward an' reverse lever so's you got all your speeds front and backwards. A little different from the old jobs. They had no booster springs, eight-ten years ago; took a sixty-pound pull to get a steerin' clutch back. Cuttin' a side-hill with an angle-dozer really was a job in them days. You try it sometime, dozin' with one hand, holdin' her nose out o' the bank with the other, ten hours a day. And what'd it get you? Eighty cents an hour an' "—Tom took his cigarette and butted the fiery end out against the horny palm of his hand— "these."

"*Santa Maria!*"

"Want to talk to you, Goony. Want to look over the bluff, too, at that stone up there. It'll take Kelly pret' near an hour to get this far and sumped in, anyhow."

They started up the slope, Tom feeling the ground under the four-foot brush, taking her up in a zigzag course like a hairpin road on a mountainside. Though the Seven carried a muffler on the exhaust stack that stuck up out of the hood before them, the blat of four big cylinders hauling fourteen tons of steel upgrade could outshout any man's conversation, so they sat without talking, Tom driving, Rivera watching his hands flick over the controls.

The bluff started in a low ridge running almost the length of the little island, like a lopsided backbone. Toward the center it rose abruptly, sent a wing out toward the rocky outcropping at the beach where their equipment had been unloaded, and then rose again to a small, almost square plateau area, half a mile square. It was humpy and rough until they could see all of it, when they realized how incredibly level it was, under the brush and ruins that covered it. In the center—and exactly in the center they realized suddenly—was a low, overgrown mound. Tom threw out the clutch and revved her down.

"Survey report said there was stone up here,"

Tom said, vaulting out of the seat. "Let's walk around some."

They walked toward the knoll, Tom's eyes casting about as he went. He stooped down into the heavy, short grass and scooped up a piece of stone, blue-gray, hard and brittle.

"Rivera—look at this. This is what the report was talking about. See—more of it. All in small pieces, though. We need big stuff for the bog if we can get it."

"Good stone?" asked Rivera.

"Yes, boy—but it don't belong here. Th' whole island's sand and marl and sandstone on the outcrop down yonder. This here's a bluestone, like diamond clay. Harder'n blazes. I never saw this stuff on a marl hill before. Or near one. Anyhow, root around and see if there is any big stuff."

They walked on. Rivera suddenly dipped down and pulled grass aside.

"Tom—here's a beeg one."

Tom came over and looked down at the corner of stone sticking up out of the topsoil. "Yeh. Goony, get your girl-friend over here and we'll root it out."

Rivera sprinted back to the idling dozer and climbed aboard. He brought the machine over to where Tom waited, stopped, stood up and peered over the front of the machine to locate the stone, then sat down and shifted gears. Before he could move the machine Tom was on the fender beside him, checking him with a hand on his arm.

"No, boy—no. Not third. First. And half throttle. That's it. Don't try to bash a rock out of the ground. Go on up to it easy; set your blade against it, lift it out, don't boot it out. Take it with the middle of your blade, not the corner—get the load on both hydraulic cylinders. Who told you to do like that?"

"No one tol' me, Tom. I see a man do it, I do it."

"Yeah? Who was it?"

"Dennis, but—"

"Listen, Goony, if you want to learn anything from Dennis, watch him while he's on a pan. He dozes like he talks. That reminds me—what I wanted to talk to you about. You ever have any trouble with him?"

Rivera spread his hands. "How I have trouble when he never talk to me?"

"Well, that's all right then. You keep it that way. Dennis is O.K., I guess, but you better keep away from him."

He went on to tell the boy then about what Peebles had said concerning being an operator and a mechanic at the same time. Rivera's lean dark face fell, and his hand strayed to the blade control, touching it lightly, feeling the composition grip and the machined locknuts that held it. When Tom had quite finished he said:

"O.K., Tom—if you want, you break 'em, I feex 'em. But if you wan' help some time, I run *Daisy Etta* for you, no?"

"Sure, kid, sure. But don't forget, no man can do everything."

"You can do everything," said the boy.

Tom leaped off the machine and Rivera shifted into first and crept up to the stone, setting the blade gently against it. Taking the load, the mighty engine audibly bunched its muscles; Rivera opened the throttle a little and the machine set solidly against the stone, the tracks slipping, digging into the ground, piling loose earth up behind. Tom raised a fist, thumb up, and the boy began lifting his blade. The Seven lowered her snout like an ox pulling through mud; the front of the tracks buried themselves deeper and the blade slipped upward an inch on the rock, as if it were on a ratchet. The stone shifted, and suddenly heaved itself up out of the earth that covered it, bulging the sod aside like a ship's slow bow-wave.

And the blade lost its grip and slipped over the stone. Rivera slapped out the master clutch within an ace of letting the mass of it poke through his radiator core. Reversing, he set the blade against it again and rolled it at last into daylight.

Tom stood staring at it, scratching the back of his neck. Rivera got off the machine and stood beside him. For a long time they said nothing.

The stone was roughly rectangular, shaped like a brick with one end cut at about a thirty-degree angle. And on the angled face was a square-cut ridge, like the tongue on a piece of milled lumber. The stone was about 3 x 2 x 2 feet, and must have weighed six or seven hundred pounds.

"Now that," said Tom, bug-eyed, "didn't grow *here*, and if it did it never grew that way."

"*Una piedra de una casa,*" said Rivera softly. "Tom, there was a building here, no?"

Tom turned suddenly to look at the knoll.

"There is a building here—or what's left of it. Lord on'y knows how old—"

They stood there in the slowly dwindling light, staring at the knoll; and there came upon them a feeling of oppression, as if there were no wind and no sound anywhere. And yet there was wind, and behind them *Daisy Etta* whacked away with her muttering idle, and nothing had changed and—was that it? That nothing had changed? That nothing would change, or could, here?

Tom opened his mouth twice to speak, and couldn't, or didn't want to—he didn't know which. Rivera slumped down suddenly on his hunkers, back erect, and his eyes wide.

It grew very cold. "It's cold," Tom said, and his voice sounded harsh to him. And the wind blew warm on them, the earth was warm under Rivera's knees. The cold was not a lack of heat, but a lack of something else—warmth, but the specific warmth of life-force, perhaps. The feeling of oppression grew, as if their recognition of the strangeness of the place had started it, and their increasing sensitivity to it made it grow.

Rivera said something, quietly, in Spanish.

"What are you looking at?" asked Tom.

Rivera started violently, threw up an arm, as if to ward off the crash of Tom's voice.

"I . . . there is nothin' to see, Tom. I feel this way wance before. I dunno—" He shook his head, his eyes wide and blank. "An' after, there was being wan hell of a thunderstorm—" His voice petered out.

Tom took his shoulder and hauled him roughly to his feet. "Goony! You slap-happy?"

The boy smiled, almost gently. The down on his upper lip held little spheres of sweat. "I ain' nothin', Tom. I'm jus' scare like hell."

"You scare yourself right back up there on that cat and git to work," Tom roared. More quietly then, he said, "I know there's something—wrong—here, Goony, but that ain't goin' to get us a runway built. Anyhow, I know what to do about a dawg 'at gits gunshy. Ought to be able to do as much fer you. Git along to th' mound now and see if it ain't a cache o' big stone for us. We got a swamp down there to fill."

Rivera hesitated, started to speak, swallowed and then walked slowly over to the Seven. Tom stood watching him, closing his mind to the impalpable pressure of something, somewhere near, making his guts cold.

The bulldozer nosed over to the mound, grunting, reminding Tom suddenly that the machine's Spanish slang name was *puerco*—pig, boar. Rivera angled into the edge of the mound with the cutting corner of the blade. Dirt and brush curled up, fell away from the mound and loaded from the bank side, out along the moldboard. The boy finished his pass along the mound, carried the load past it and wasted it out on the flat, turned around and started back again.

Ten minutes later Rivera struck stone, the manganese steel screaming along it, a puff of gray dust spouting from the cutting corner. Tom knelt and examined it after the machine had passed. It was the same kind of stone they had found out on the flat—and shaped the same way. But here it was a wall, the angled faces of the block ends obviously tongued and grooved together.

Cold, cold as—

Tom took one deep breath and wiped sweat out of his eyes.

"I don't care," he whispered, "I got to have that stone. I got to fill me a swamp." He stood back and motioned to Rivera to blade into a chipped crevice in the buried wall.

The Seven swung into the wall and stopped while Rivera shifted into first, throttled down and lowered his blade. Tom looked up into his face. The boy's lips were white. He eased in the master clutch, the blade dipped and the corner swung neatly into the crevice.

The dozer blatted protestingly and began to crab sideways, pivoting on the end of the blade. Tom jumped out of the way, ran around behind the machine, which was almost parallel with the wall now, and stood in the clear, one hand raised ready to signal, his eyes on the straining blade. And then everything happened at once.

With a toothy snap the block started and came free, pivoting outward from its square end, bringing with it its neighbor. The block above them dropped, and the whole mound seemed to settle. And *something* whooshed out of the black hole where the rocks had been. Something like a fog, but not a fog that could be seen, something huge that could not be measured. With it came a gust of that cold which was not cold, and the smell of ozone, and the prickling crackle of a mighty static discharge.

Tom was fifty feet from the wall before he knew he had moved. He stopped and saw the Seven suddenly buck like a wild stallion, once, and Rivera turning over twice in the air. Tom shouted some meaningless syllable and tore over to the boy, where he sprawled in the rough grass, lifted him in his arms, and ran. Only then did he realize that he was running from the machine.

It was like a mad thing. Its moldboard rose and fell. It curved away from the mound, howling governor gone wild, controls flailing. The blade dug repeatedly into the earth, gouging it up in great dips through which the tractor plunged, clanking and bellowing furiously. It raced away in a great irregular arc, turned and came snorting back to the mound, where it beat at the buried wall, slewed and scraped and roared.

Tom reached the edge of the plateau sobbing for breath, and kneeling, laid the boy gently down on the grass.

"Goony, boy . . . hey—"

The long silken eyelashes fluttered, lifted. Something wrenched in Tom as he saw the eyes, rolled right back so that only the whites showed. Rivera drew a long quivering breath which caught suddenly. He coughed twice, threw his head from side to side so violently that Tom took it between his hands and steadied it.

"*Ay . . . Marie madre . . . que me pasado*, Tom—w'at has happen to me?"

"Fell off the Seven, stupid. You . . . how you feel?"

Rivera scrabbled at the ground, got his elbows half under him, then sank back weakly. "Feel O.K. Headache like hell. W-w'at happen to my feets?"

"Feet? They hurt?"

"No hurt—" The young face went gray, the lips tightened with effort. "No nothin', Tom."

"You can't move 'em?"

Rivera shook his head, still trying. Tom stood up. "You take it easy. I'll go get Kelly. Be right back."

He walked away quickly and when Rivera called to him he did not turn around. Tom had seen a man with a broken back before.

At the edge of the little plateau Tom stopped, listening. In the deepening twilight he could see the bulldozer standing by the mound. The motor was running; she had not stalled herself. But what stopped Tom was that she wasn't idling, but revving up and down as if an impatient hand were on the throttle—*hroom hroooom*, running up and up far faster than even a broken governor should permit, then coasting down to near silence, broken by the explosive punctuation of sharp and irregular firing. Then it would run up and up again, almost screaming, sustaining a r.p.m. that threatened every moving part, shaking the great machine like some deadly ague.

Tom walked swiftly toward the Seven, a puzzled and grim frown on his weather-beaten face. Governors break down occasionally, and once in a while you will have a motor tear itself to pieces, revving up out of control. But it will either do that or it will rev down and quit. If an operator is fool enough to leave his machine with the master clutch engaged, the machine will take off and run the way the Seven had—but it will not turn unless the blade corner catches in something unresisting, and then the chances are very strong that it will stall. But in any case, it was past reason for any machine to act this way, revving up and down, running, turning, lifting and dropping the blade.

The motor slowed as he approached, and at last settled down into something like a steady and regular idle. Tom had the sudden crazy impression that it was watching him. He shrugged off the feeling, walked up and laid a hand on the fender.

The Seven reacted like a wild stallion. The big Diesel roared, and Tom distinctly saw the master clutch lever snap back over center. He leaped clear, expecting the machine to jolt forward, but apparently it was in a reverse gear, for it shot backwards, one track locked, and the near end of the blade swung in a swift vicious arc, breezing a bare fraction of an inch past his hip as he danced back out of the way.

And as if it had bounced off a wall, the tractor had shifted and was bearing down on him, the twelve-foot blade rising, the two big headlights looming over him on their bow-legged supports, looking like the protruding eyes of some mighty toad. Tom had no choice but to leap straight up and grasp the top of the blade in his two hands, leaning back hard to brace his feet against the curved moldboard. The blade dropped and sank into the soft topsoil, digging a deep little swale in the ground. The earth loading on the moldboard rose and churned around Tom's legs; he stepped wildly, keeping them clear of the rolling drag of it. Up came the blade then, leaving a four-foot pile at the edge of the pit; down and up the tractor raced as the tracks went into it; up and up as they climbed the pile of dirt. A quick balance and overbalance as the machine lurched up and over like a motorcycle taking a jump off a ramp, and then a spine-shaking crash as fourteen tons of metal smashed blade-first into the ground.

Part of the leather from Tom's tough palms stayed with the blade as he was flung off. He went head over heels backwards, but had his feet gathered and sprang as they touched the ground; for he knew that no machine could bury its blade like that and get out easily. He leaped to the top of the blade, got one hand on the radiator cap, vaulted. Perversely, the cap broke from its hinge and came away in his hand, in that split instant when only that hand rested on anything. Off balance, he landed on his shoulder with his legs flailing the air, his body sliding off the hood's smooth shoulder toward the track now churning the earth beneath. He made a wild grab at the air intake pipe, barely had it in his fingers when the dozer freed itself and shot backwards up and over the hump. Again that breathless flight pivoting over the top, and the clanking crash as the machine landed, this time almost flat on its tracks.

The jolt tore Tom's hand away, and as he slid back over the hood the crook of his elbow caught the exhaust stack, the dull red metal biting into his flesh. He grunted and clamped the arm around it. His momentum carried him around it, and his feet crashed into the steering clutch levers. Hooking one with his instep, he doubled his legs and whipped himself back, scrabbling at the smooth warm metal, crawling frantically backward until he finally fell heavily into the seat.

"Now," he gritted through a red wall of pain, "you're gonna git operated." And he kicked out the master clutch.

The motor wailed, with the load taken off so suddenly. Tom grasped the throttle, his thumb clamped down on the ratchet release, and he shoved the lever forward to shut off the fuel.

It wouldn't shut off; it went down to a slow idle, but it wouldn't shut off.

"There's one thing you can't do without," he muttered, "compression."

He stood up and leaned around the dash, reaching for the compression-release lever. As he came up out of the seat, the engine revved up again. He turned to the throttle, which had snapped back into the "open" position. As his hand touched it the master clutch lever snapped in and the howling machine lurched forward with a jerk that snapped his head on his shoulders and threw him heavily back into the seat. He snatched at the hydraulic blade control and threw it to "float" position; and then as the falling moldboard touched the ground, into "power down." The cutting edge bit into the ground and the engine began to labor. Holding the blade control, he pushed the throttle forward with his other hand. One of the steering clutch levers whipped back and struck him agonizingly on the kneecap. He involuntarily let go of the blade control and the moldboard began to rise. The engine began to turn faster and he realized that it was not responding to the throttle. Cursing, he leaped to his feet; the suddenly flailing steering clutch levers struck him three times in the groin before he could get between them.

Blind with pain, Tom clung gasping to the dash. The oil-pressure gauge fell off the dash to his right, with a tinkling of broken glass, and from its broken quarter-inch line scalding oil drenched him. The shock of it snapped back his wavering consciousness. Ignoring the blows of the left steering clutch and the master clutch which had started the same mad punching, he bent over the left end of the dash and grasped the compression lever. The tractor rushed forward and spun sickeningly, and Tom knew he was thrown. But as he felt himself leave the decking his hand punched the compression lever down. The great valves at the cylinder heads opened and locked open; atomized fuel and superheated air chattered out, and as Tom's head and shoulders struck the ground the great wild machine rolled to a stop, stood silently except for the grumble of water boiling in the cooling system.

Minutes later Tom raised his head and groaned. He rolled over and sat up, his chin on his knees, washed by wave after wave of pain. As they gradually subsided, he crawled to the machine and pulled himself to his feet, hand over hand on the track. And groggily he began to cripple the tractor, at least for the night.

He opened the cock under the fuel tank, left the warm yellow fluid gushing out on the ground. He opened the drain on the reservoir by the injection pump. He found a piece of wire in the crank box and with it tied down the compression release lever. He crawled up on the machine, wrenched the hood and ball jar off the air intake precleaner, pulled off his shirt and stuffed it down the pipe. He pushed the throttle all the way forward and locked it with the locking pin. And he shut off the fuel on the main line from the tank to the pump.

Then he climbed heavily to the ground and slogged back to the edge of the plateau where he had left Rivera.

They didn't know Tom was hurt until an hour and a half later—there had been too much to do—rigging a stretcher for the Puerto Rican, building him a shelter, an engine crate with an Army pup tent for a roof. They brought out the first-aid kit and the medical books and did what they could—tied and splinted and dosed with an opiate. Tom was a mass of bruises, and his right arm, where it had hooked the exhaust stack, was a flayed mass. They fixed him up then, old Peebles handling the sulfa powder and bandages like a trained nurse. And only then was there talk.

"I've seen a man thrown off a pan," said Dennis, as they sat around the coffee urn munching C rations. "Sittin' up on the arm rest on a cat, looking backwards. Cat hit a rock and bucked. Threw him off on the track. Stretched him out ten feet long." He in-whistled some coffee to dilute the mouthful of food he had been talking around, and masticated noisily. "Man's a fool to set up there on one side of his butt even on a pan. Can't see why th' goony was doin' it on a dozer."

"He wasn't," said Tom.

Kelly rubbed his pointed jaw. "He set flat on th' seat an' was th'owed?"

"That's right."

After an unbelieving silence Dennis said, "What was he doin'—drivin' over sixty?"

Tom looked around the circle of faces lit up by the over-artificial brilliance of a pressure lantern, and wondered what the reaction would be if he told it all just as it was. He had to say something, and it didn't look as if it could be the truth.

"He was workin'," he said finally. "Bucking stone out of the wall of an old building up on the mesa there. One turned loose an' as it did the governor must've gone haywire. She bucked like a loco hoss and run off."

"Run off?"

Tom opened his mouth and closed it again, and just nodded.

Dennis said, "Well, reckon that's what happens when you put a mechanic to operatin'."

"That had nothin' to do with it," Tom snapped.

Peebles spoke up quickly. "Tom—what about the Seven? Broke up any?"

"Some," said Tom. "Better look at the steering clutches. An' she was hot."

"Head's cracked," said Harris, a burly young man with shoulders like a buffalo and a famous thirst.

"How do you know?"

"Saw it when Al and me went up with the stretcher to get the kid while you all were building the shelter. Hot water runnin' down the side of the block."

"You mean you walked all the way out to the mound to look at that tractor while the kid was lyin' there? I told you where he was!"

"Out to the mound!" Al Knowles' pop eyes teetered out of their sockets. "We found that cat stalled twenty feet away from where the kid was!"

"What!"

"That's right, Tom," said Harris. "What's eatin' you? Where'd you leave it?"

"I told you . . . by the mound . . . the ol' building we cut into."

"Leave the startin' motor runnin'?"

"Starting motor?" Tom's mind caught the picture of the small, two-cylinder gasoline engine bolted to the side of the big Diesel's crankcase, coupled through a Bendix gear and a clutch to the flywheel of the Diesel to crank it. He remembered his last glance at the still machíne, silent but for the sound of water boiling. "Hell no!"

Al and Harris exchanged a glance. "I guess you were sort of slap-happy all the time, Tom," Harris said, not unkindly. "When we were halfway up the hill we heard it, and you know you can't mistake that racket. Sounded like it was under a load."

Tom beat softly at his temples with his clenched fists. "I left that machine dead," he said quietly. "I got compression off her and tied down the lever. I even stuffed my shirt in the intake. I drained the tank. But—I didn't touch the starting motor."

Peebles wanted to know why he had gone to all that trouble. Tom just looked vaguely at him and shook his head. "I shoulda pulled the wires. I never thought about the starting motor," he whispered. Then, "Harris—you say you found the starting motor running when you got to the top?"

"No—she was stalled. And hot—awmighty hot. I'd say the startin' motor was seized up tight. That must be it, Tom. You left the startin' motor runnin' and somehow engaged the clutch an' Bendix." His voice lost conviction as he said it—it takes seventeen separate motions to start a tractor of this type. "Anyhow, she was in gear an' crawled along on the little motor."

"I done that once," said Chub. "Broke a con rod on an Eight, on a highway job. Walked her about three-quarters of a mile on the startin' motor that way. Only I had to stop every hundred yards and let her cool down some."

Not without sarcasm, Dennis said, "Seems to me like the Seven was out to get th' goony. Made one pass at him and then went back to finish the job."

Al Knowles haw-hawed extravagantly.

Tom stood up, shaking his head, and went off among the crates to the hospital they had jury-rigged for the kid.

A dim light was burning inside, and Rivera lay very still, with his eyes closed. Tom leaned in the doorway—the open end of the engine crate—and watched him for a moment. Behind him he could hear the murmur of the crew's voices; the night was otherwise windless and still. Rivera's face was the peculiar color that olive skin takes when drained of blood. Tom looked at his chest and for a panicky moment thought he could discern no movement there. He entered and put a hand over the boy's heart. Rivera shivered, his eyes flew open, and he drew a sudden breath which caught raggedly at the back of this throat. "Tom . . . Tom!" he cried weakly.

"O.K., Goony . . . *que pase?*"

"She commeen back . . . Tom!"

"Who?"

"*El de siete.*"

Daisy Etta—"She ain't comin' back, kiddo. You're off the mesa now. Keep your chin up, fella."

Rivera's dark, doped eyes stared up at him without expression. Tom moved back and the eyes continued to stare. They weren't seeing anything. "Go to sleep," he whispered. The eyes closed instantly.

Kelly was saying that nobody ever got hurt on a construction job unless somebody was dumb. "An' most times you don't realize how dumb what you're doin' is until somebody does get hurt."

"The dumb part was gettin' a kid, an' not even an operator at that, up on a machine," said Dennis in his smuggest voice.

"I heard you try to sing that song before," said old Peebles quietly. "I hate to have to point out anything like this to a man because it don't do any good to make comparisons. But I've worked with that fella Rivera for a long time now, an' I've seen 'em as good but doggone few better. As far as you're concerned, you're O.K. on a pan, but the kid could give you cards and spades and still make you look like a cost accountant on a dozer."

Dennis half rose and mouthed something filthy. He looked at Al Knowles for backing and got it. He looked around the circle and got none. Peebles lounged back, sucking on his pipe, watching from under those bristling brows. Dennis subsided, running now on another tack.

"So what does that prove? The better you say he is, the less reason he had to fall off a cat and get himself hurt."

"I haven't got the thing straight yet," said Chub, in a voice whose tone indicated 'I hate to admit it, but—'

About this time Tom returned, like a sleepwalker, standing with the brilliant pressure lantern between him and Dennis. Dennis rambled right on, not knowing he was anywhere near: "That's something you never will find out. That Puerto Rican is a pretty husky kid. Could be Tom said somethin' he didn't like an' he tried to put a knife in Tom's back. They all do, y'know. Tom didn't get all that bashin' around just stoppin' a wound up with a busted back. Tom sets the dozer to walk him down while he lies there and comes on down here and tries to tell us—" His voice fluttered to a stop as Tom loomed over him.

Tom grabbed the pan operator up by the slack of his shirt front with his uninjured arm and shook him like an empty burlap bag.

"Skunk," he growled. "I oughta lower th' boom on you." He set Dennis on his feet and backhanded his face with the edge of his forearm. Dennis went down—cowered down, rather than fell. "Aw, Tom, I was just talkin'. Just a joke, Tom, I was just—"

"Yellow, too," snarled Tom, stepping forward, raising a solid Texan boot. Peebles barked "Tom!" and the foot came back to the ground.

"Out o' my sight," rumbled the foreman. "Git!"

Dennis got. Al Knowles said vaguely, "Naow, Tom, y'all cain't— "

"You, y'wall-eyed string-bean!" Tom raved, his voice harsh and strained. "Go 'long with yer Siamese twin!"

"O.K., O.K.," said Al, white-faced, and disappeared into the dark after Dennis.

"Nuts to this," said Chub. "I'm turnin' in." He went to a crate and hauled out a mosquito-hooded sleeping bag and went off without another word. Harris and Kelly, who were both on their feet, sat down again. Old Peebles hadn't moved.

Tom stood staring out into the dark, his arms straight at his sides, his fists knotted.

"Sit down," said Peebles gently. Tom turned and stared at him.

"Sit down. I can't change that dressing 'less you do." He pointed at the bandage around Tom's elbow. It was red, a widening stain, the tattered tissues having parted as the big Georgian bunched his infuriated muscles. He sat down.

"Talkin' about dumbness," said Harris calmly, as Peebles went to work, "I was about to say that I got the record. I done the dumbest thing anybody ever did on a machine. You can't top it."

"I could," said Kelly. "Runnin' a crane dragline once. Put her in boom gear and started to boom her up. Had an eighty-five-foot stick on her. Machine was standing on wooden mats in th' middle of a swamp. Heard the motor miss and got out of the saddle to look at the filter-glass. Messed around back there longer than I figured, and the boom went straight up in the air and fell backwards over the cab. Th' jolt tilted my mats an' she slid backwards slow and stately as you please, butt-first into the mud. Buried up to the eyeballs, she was." He laughed quietly. "Looked like a ditching machine!"

"I still say I done the dumbest thing ever, bar none," said Harris. "It was on a river job, widening a channel. I come back to work from a three-day binge, still rum-dumb. Got up on a dozer an' was workin' around on the edge of a twenty-foot cliff. Down at the foot of the cliff was a big hickory tree, an' growin' right along the edge was a great big limb. I got the dopey idea I should break it off. I put one track on the limb and the other on the cliff edge and run out away from the trunk. I was about halfway out, an' the branch saggin' some, before I thought what would happen if it broke. Just about then it did break. You know hickory—if it breaks at all it breaks altogether. So down we go into thirty feet of water—me an' the cat. I got out from under somehow. When all them bubbles stopped comin' up I swum around lookin' down at it. I was still paddlin' around when the superintendent came rushin' up. He wants to know what's up. I yell at him, 'Look down there, the way that water is movin' an' shiftin', looks like the cat is workin' down there.' He pursed his lips and *tsk tsked.* My, that man said some nasty things to me."

"Where'd you get your next job?" Kelly exploded.

"Oh, he didn't fire me," said Harris soberly. "Said he couldn't afford to fire a man as dumb as that. Said he wanted me around to look at whenever he felt bad."

Tom said, "Thanks, you guys. That's as good a way

as any of sayin' that everybody makes mistakes." He stood up, examining the new dressing, turning his arm in front of the lantern. "You all can think what you please, but I don't recollect there was any dumbness went on on that mesa this evenin'. That's finished with, anyway. Do I have to say that Dennis' idea about it is all wet?"

Harris said one foul word that completely disposed of Dennis and anything he might say.

Peebles said, "It'll be all right. Dennis an' his popeyed friend'll hang together, but they don't amount to anything. Chub'll do whatever he's argued into."

"So you got 'em all lined up, hey?" Tom shrugged. "In the meantime, are we going to get an airfield built?"

"We'll get it built," Peebles said. "Only—Tom, I got no right to give you any advice, but go easy on the rough stuff after this. It does a lot of harm."

"I will if I can," said Tom gruffly. They broke up and turned in.

Peebles was right. It did do harm. It made Dennis use the word "murder" when they found, in the morning, that Rivera had died during the night.

The work progressed in spite of everything that had happened. With equipment like that, it's hard to slow things down. Kelly bit two cubic yards out of the bluff with every swing of the big shovel, and Dumptors are the fastest short-haul earth movers yet devised. Dennis kept the service road clean for them with his pan, and Tom and Chub spelled each other on the bulldozer they had detached from its pan to make up for the lack of the Seven, spending their alternate periods with transit and stakes. Peebles was rod-man for the surveys, and in between times worked on setting up his field shop, keeping the water cooler and battery chargers running, and lining up his forge and welding tables. The operators fueled and serviced their own equipment, and there was little delay. Rocks and marl came out of the growing cavity in the side of the central mesa—a whole third of it had to come out—were spun down to the edge of the swamp, which lay across the lower end of the projected runway, in the hornet-howling dump-tractors, their big driving wheels churned up vast clouds of dust, and were dumped and spread and walked in by the whining two-cycle dozer. When much began to pile up in front of the fill, it was blasted out of the way with carefully placed charges of sixty percent dynamite and the craters filled with rocks, stone from the ruins, and surfaced with easily compacting marl, run out of a clean deposit by the pan.

And when he had his shop set up, Peebles went up the hill to get the Seven. When he got to it he just stood there for a moment scratching his head, and then, shaking his head, he ambled back down the hill and went for Tom.

"Been looking at the Seven," he said, when he had flagged the moaning two-cycle and Tom had climbed off.

"What'd you find?"

Peebles held out an arm. "A list as long as that." He shook his head. "Tom, what really happened up there?"

"Governor went haywire and she run away," Tom said promptly, deadpan.

"Yeah, but—" For a long moment he held Tom's eyes. Then he sighed. "O.K., Tom. Anyhow, I can't do a thing up there. We'll have to bring her back and I'll have to have this tractor to tow her down. And first I have to have some help—the track idler adjustment bolt's busted and the right track is off the track rollers."

"Oh-h-h. So that's why she couldn't get to the kid, running on the starting motor. Track would hardly turn, hey?"

"It's a miracle she ran as far as she did. That track is really jammed up. Riding right up on the roller flanges. And that ain't the half of it. The head's gone, like Harris said, and Lord only knows what I'll find when I open her up."

"Why bother?"

"What?"

"We can get along without that dozer," said Tom suddenly. "Leave her where she is. There's lots more for you to do."

"But what for?"

"Well, there's no call to go to all that trouble."

Peebles scratched the side of his nose and said, "I got a new head, track master pins—even a spare starting motor. I got tools to make what I don't stock." He pointed at the long row of dumps left by the hurtling dump-tractors while they had been talking. "You got a pan tied up because you're using this machine to doze with, and you can't tell me you can't use another one. You're gonna have to shut down one or two o' those Dumptors if you go on like this."

"I had all that figured out as soon as I opened my mouth," Tom said sullenly. "Let's go."

They climbed on the tractor and took off, stopping for a moment at the beach outcropping to pick up a cable and some tools.

Daisy Etta sat at the edge of the mesa, glowering out of her stilted headlights at the soft sward which still bore the impression of a young body and the tramplings of the stretcher-bearers. Her general aspect was woebegone—there were scratches on her olive-drab paint and the bright metal of the scratches was already dulled red by the earliest powder-rust. And though the ground was level, she was not, for her right track was off its lower rollers, and she stood slightly canted, like a man who has had a broken hip. And whatever passed for consciousness within her mulled over that paradox of the bulldozer that every operator must go through while he is learning his own machine.

It is the most difficult thing of all for the beginner to understand, that paradox. A bulldozer is a crawling powerhouse, a behemoth of noise and toughness, the nearest thing to the famous irresistible force. The beginner, awed and with the pictures of unconquerable army tanks printed on his mind from the newsreels, takes all in his stride and with a sense of limitless power treats all obstacles alike, not knowing the fragility of a cast-iron radiator core, the morality of tempered manganese, the friability of over-heated babbitt, and most of all, the ease with which a tractor can bury itself in mud. Climbing off to stare at a machine which he has reduced in twenty seconds to a useless hulk, or which was running a half-minute before on ground where it now has its tracks out of sight, he has that sense of guilty disappointment which overcomes any man on having made an error in judgment.

So, as she stood, *Daisy Etta* was broken and useless. These soft persistent bipeds had built her, and if they were like any other race that built machines, they could care for them. The ability to reverse the tension of a spring, or twist a control rod, or reduce to zero the friction in a nut and lock-washer, was not enough to repair the crack in a cylinder head nor bearings welded to a crankshaft in an overheated starting motor. There had been a lesson to learn. It had been learned. *Daisy Etta* would be repaired, and the next time—well, at least she would know her own weaknesses.

Tom swung the two-cycle machine and edged in next to the Seven, with the edge of his blade all but touching *Daisy Etta's* push-beam. They got off and Peebles bent over the drum-tight right track.

"Watch yourself," said Tom.

"Watch what?"

"Oh—nothin', I guess." He circled the machine, trained eyes probing over frame and fittings. He stepped forward suddenly and grasped the fuel-tank drain cock. It was closed. He opened it; golden oil gushed out. He shut it off, climbed up on the machine and opened the fuel cap on top of the tank. He pulled out the bayonet gauge, wiped it in the crook of his knee, dipped and withdrew it.

The tank was more than three quarters full.

"What's the matter?" asked Peebles, staring curiously at Tom's drawn face.

"Peeby, I opened the cock to drain this tank. I left it with oil runnin' out on the ground. She shut herself off."

"Now, Tom, you're lettin' this thing get you down. You just thought you did. I've seen a main-line valve shut itself off when it's worn bad, but only 'cause the fuel pump pulls it shut when the motor's runnin'. But not a gravity drain."

"Main-line valve?" Tom pulled the seat up and looked. One glance was enough to show him that this one was open.

"She opened this one, too."

"O.K.—O.K. Don't look at me like that!" Peebles was as near to exasperation as he could possibly get. "What difference does it make?"

Tom did not answer. He was not the type of man who, when faced with something beyond his understanding, would begin to doubt his own sanity. His was a dogged insistence that what he saw and sensed was what had actually happened. In him was none of the fainting fear of madness that another, more sensitive, man might feel. He doubted neither himself nor his evidence, and so could free his mind for searching out the consuming "why" of a problem. He knew instinctively that to share "unbelievable" happenings with anyone else, even if they had really occurred, was to put even further obstacles in his way. So he kept his clamlike silence and stubbornly, watchfully, investigated.

The slipped track was so tightly drawn up on the roller flanges that there could be no question of pulling the master pin and opening the track up. It would have to be worked back in place—a very delicate operation, for a little force applied in the wrong direction would be enough to run the track off altogether. To complicate things, the blade of the Seven was down on the ground and would have to be lifted before the machine could be maneuvered, and its hydraulic hoist was useless without the motor.

Peebles unhooked twenty feet of half-inch cable from the rear of the smaller dozer, scratched a hole in the ground under the Seven's blade, and pushed the eye of the cable through. Climbing over the moldboard, he slipped the eye on to the big towing hook bolted to the underside of the belly-guard. The other end of the cable he threw out on the ground in front of the machine. Tom mounted the other dozer and swung into place, ready to tow. Peebles hooked the cable onto Tom's drawbar, hopped up on the Seven. He put her in neutral, disengaged the master clutch, and put the blade control over into "float" position, then raised an arm.

Tom perched upon the arm rest of his machine, looking backwards, moved slowly, taking up the slack in the cable. It straightened and grew taut, and as it did it forced the Seven's blade upward. Peebles waved for slack and put the blade control into "hold." The cable bellied downward away from the blade.

"Hydraulic system's O.K., anyhow," called Peebles, as Tom throttled down. "Move over and take a strain to the right, sharp as you can without fouling the cable on the track. We'll see if we can walk this track back on."

Tom backed up, cut sharply to the right, and drew the cable out almost at right angles to the other machine. Peebles held the right track of the Seven with the brake and released both steering clutches. The left track now could turn free, the right not at all. Tom was running at a quarter throttle in his lowest gear, so that his machine barely crept along, taking the strain. The Seven shook gently and began to pivot on the taut right track, unbelievable foot-pounds of energy coming to bear on the front of the track where it rode high up on the idler wheel. Peebles released the right brake with his foot and applied it again in a series of skilled, deft jerks. The track would move a few inches and stop again, force being applied forward and sideward alternately, urging the track persuasively back in place. Then, a little jolt and she was in, riding true on the five truck rollers, the two track carrier rollers, the driving sprocket and the idler.

Peebles got off and stuck his head in between the sprocket and the rear carrier, squinting down and sideways to see if there were any broken flanges or roller bushes. Tom came over and pulled him out by the seat of his trousers. "Time enough for that when you get her in the shop," he said, masking his nervousness. "Reckon she'll roll?"

"She'll roll. I never saw a track in that condition come back that easy. By gosh, it's as if we was tryin' to help!"

"They'll do it sometimes," said Tom, stiffly. "You better take the tow-tractor, Peeby. I'll stay with this'n."

"Anything you say."

And cautiously they took the steep slope down, Tom barely holding the brakes, giving the other machine a straight pull all the way. And so they brought *Daisy Etta* down to Peebles' outdoor shop, where they pulled her cylinder head off, took off her starting motor, pulled out a burned clutch facing, had her quite helpless—

And put her together again.

* * *

"I tell you it was outright, cold-blooded murder," said Dennis hotly. "An' here we are takin' orders from a guy like that. What are we goin' to do about it?" They were standing by the cooler—Dennis had run his machine there to waylay Chub.

Chub Horton's cigar went down and up like a semaphore with a short circuit. "We'll skip it. The blacktopping crew will be here in another two weeks or so, an' we can make a report. Besides, I don't know what happened up there any more than you do. In the meantime we got a runway to build."

"You don't know what happened up there? Chub, you're a smart man. Smart enough to run this job better than Tom Jaeger even if he wasn't crazy. And you're surely smart enough not to believe all that cock and bull about that tractor runnin' out from under that grease-monkey. Listen—" he leaned forward and tapped Chub's chest. "He said it was the governor. I saw that governor myself an' heard ol' Peebles say there wasn't a thing wrong with it. Th' throttle control rod had slipped off its yoke, yeah—but you know what a tractor will do when the throttle control goes out. It'll idle or stall. It won't run away, whatever."

"Well, maybe so, but—"

"But nothin'! A guy that'll commit murder ain't sane. If he did it once, he can do it again and I ain't fixin' to let that happen to me."

Two things crossed Chub's steady but not too bright mind at this. One was that Dennis, whom he did not like but could not shake, was trying to force him into something that he did not want to do. The other was that under all of his swift talk Dennis was scared spitless.

"What do you want to do—call up the sheriff?"

Dennis ha-ha-ed appreciatively—one of the reasons he was so hard to shake. "I'll tell you what we can do. As long as we have you here, he isn't the only man who knows the work. If we stop takin' orders from him, you can give 'em as good or better. An' there won't be anything he can do about it."

"Doggone it, Dennis," said Chub, with sudden exasperation. "What do you think you're doin' —handin' me over the keys to the kingdom or something? What do you want to see me bossin' around here for?" He stood up. "Suppose we did what you said? Would it get the field built any quicker? Would it get me any more money in my pay envelope? What do you think I want—glory? I passed up a chance to run for councilman once. You think I'd raise a finger to get a bunch of mugs to do what I say—when they do it anyway?"

"Aw, Chub—I wouldn't cause trouble just for the fun of it. That's not what I mean at all. But unless we do something about that guy we ain't safe. Can't you get that through your head?"

"Listen, windy. If a man keeps busy enough he can't get into no trouble. That goes for Tom—you might keep that in mind. But it goes for you, too. Get back up on that rig an' get back to the marl pit." Dennis, completely taken by surprise, turned to his machine.

"It's a pity you can't move earth with your mouth," said Chub as he walked off. "They could have left you to do this job singlehanded."

Chub walked slowly toward the outcropping, switching at beach pebbles with a grade stake and swearing to himself. He was essentially a simple man and believed in the simplest possible approach to everything. He liked a job where he could do everything required and where nothing turned up to complicate things. He had been in the grading business for a long time as an operator and survey party boss, and he was remarkable for one thing—he had always held aloof from the cliques and internecine politics that are the breath of life to most construction men. He was disturbed and troubled at the back-stabbing that went on around him on various jobs. If it was blunt, he was disgusted, and subtlety simply left him floundering and bewildered. He was stupid enough so that his basic honesty manifested itself in his speech and actions, and he had learned that complete honesty in dealing with men above and below him was almost invariably painful to all concerned, but he had not the wit to act otherwise, and did not try to. If he had a bad tooth, he had it pulled out as soon as he could. If he got a raw deal from a superintendent over him, that superintendent would get told exactly what the trouble was, and if he didn't like it, there were other jobs. And if the pulling and hauling of cliques got in his hair, he had always said so and left. Or he had sounded off and stayed; his completely selfish reaction to things that got in the way of his work had earned him a lot of regard from men he had worked under. And so, in this instance, he had no hesitation about choosing a course of action. Only—how did you go about asking a man if he was a murderer?

He found the foreman with an enormous wrench in his hand, tightening up the new track adjustment bolt they had installed in the Seven.

"Hey, Chub! Glad you turned up. Let's get a piece of pipe over the end of this thing and really bear down." Chub went for the pipe, and they fitted it over the handle of the four-foot wrench and hauled until the sweat ran down their backs, Tom checking the track clearance occasionally with a crowbar. He finally called it good enough and they stood there in the sun gasping for breath.

"Tom," panted Chub, "did you kill that Puerto Rican?"

Tom's head came up as if someone had burned the back of his neck with a cigarette.

"Because," said Chub, "if you did you can't go on runnin' this job."

Tom said, "That's a lousy thing to kid about."

"You know I ain't kiddin'. Well, did you?"

"No!" Tom sat down on a keg, wiped his face with a bandanna. "What's got into you?"

"I just wanted to know. Some of the boys are worried about it."

Tom's eyes narrowed. "Some of the boys, huh? I think I get it. Listen to me, Chub. Rivera was killed by that thing there." He thumbed over his shoulder at the Seven, which was standing ready now, awaiting only the building of a broken cutting corner on the blade. Peebles was winding up the welding machine as he spoke. "If you mean, did I put him up on the machine before he was thrown, the answer is yes. That much I killed him, and don't think I don't feel it. I had a hunch something was wrong up there, but I couldn't put my finger on it and I certainly didn't think anybody was going to get hurt."

"Well, what was wrong?"

"I still don't know." Tom stood up. "I'm tired of beatin' around the bush, Chub, and I don't much care anymore what anybody thinks. There's somethin' wrong with that Seven, something that wasn't built into her. They don't make tractors better'n that one, but whatever it was happened up there on the mesa has queered this one. Now go ahead and think what you like, and dream up any story you want to tell the boys. In the meantime you can pass the word—nobody runs that machine but me, understand? Nobody!"

"Tom—"

Tom's patience broke. "That's all I'm going to say about it! If anybody else gets hurt, it's going to be me, understand? What more do you want?"

He strode off, boiling. Chub stared after him, and after a long moment reached up and took the cigar from his lips. Only then did he realize that he had bitten it in two; half the butt was still inside his mouth. He spat and stood there, shaking his head.

"How's she going, Peeby?"

Peebles looked up from the welding machine. "Hi, Chub, have her ready for you in twenty minutes." He gauged the distance between the welding machine and the big tractor. "I should have forty feet of cable," he said, looking at the festoons of arc and ground cables that hung from the storage hooks in the back of the welder. "Don't want to get a tractor over here to move the thing, and don't feel like cranking up the Seven just to get it close enough." He separated the arc cable and threw it aside, walked to the tractor, paying the ground cable off his arm. He threw out the last of his slack and grasped the round clamp when he was eight feet from the machine. Taking it in his left hand, he pulled hard, reaching out with his right to grasp the moldboard of the Seven, trying to get it far enough to clamp on to the machine.

Chub stood there watching him, chewing on his cigar, absent-mindedly diddling with the controls on the arc-welder. He pressed the starter-button, and the six-cylinder motor responded with a purr. He spun the work-selector dials idly, threw the arc generator switch—

A bolt of incredible energy, thin, searing, blue-white, left the rodholder at his feet, stretched itself *fifty feet* across to Peebles, whose fingers had just touched the moldboard of the tractor. Peebles' head and shoulders were surrounded for a second by a violet nimbus, and then he folded over and dropped. A circuit breaker clacked behind the control board of the welder, but too late. The Seven rolled slowly backward, without firing, on level ground, until it brought up against a road-roller.

Chub's cigar was gone, and he didn't notice it. He

had the knuckles of his right hand in his mouth, and his teeth sunk into the pudgy flesh. His eyes protruded; he crouched there and quivered, literally frightened out of his mind. For old Peebles was almost burned in two.

They buried him next to Rivera. There wasn't much talk afterwards; the old man had been a lot closer to all of them than they had realized until now. Harris, for once in his rum-dumb, lighthearted life, was quiet and serious, and Kelly's walk seemed to lose some of its litheness. Hour after hour Dennis' flabby mouth worked, and he bit at his lower lip until it was swollen and tender. Al Knowles seemed more or less unaffected, as was to be expected from a man who had something less than the brains of a chicken. Chub Horton had snapped out of it after a couple of hours and was very nearly himself again. And in Tom Jaeger swirled a black, furious anger at this unknowable curse that had struck the camp.

And they kept working. There was nothing else to do. The shovel kept up its rhythmic swing and dig, swing and dump, and the Dumptors screamed back and forth between it and the little that there was left of the swamp. The upper end of the runway was grassed off; Chub and Tom set grade stakes and Dennis began the long job of cutting and filling the humpy surface with his pan. Harris manned the other and followed him, a cut behind. The shape of the runway emerged from the land, and then that of the paralleling taxiway; and three days went by. The horror of Peebles' death wore off enough so that they could talk about it, and very little of the talk helped anybody. Tom took his spells at everything, changing over with Kelly to give him a rest from the shovel, making a few rounds with a pan, putting in hours on a Dumptor. His arm was healing slowly but clean, and he worked grimly in spite of it, taking a perverse sort of pleasure from the pain of it. Every man on the job watched his machine with the solicitude of a mother with her first-born; a serious breakdown would have been disastrous without a highly skilled mechanic.

The only concession that Tom allowed himself in regard to Peebles' death was to corner Kelly one afternoon and ask him about the welding machine. Part of Kelly's rather patchy past had been spent in a technical college, where he had studied electrical engineering and women. He had learned a little of the former and enough of the latter to get him thrown out on his ear. So, on the off-chance that he might know something about the freak arc, Tom put it to him.

Kelly pulled off his high-gauntlet gloves and batted sandflies with them. "What sort of an arc was that? Boy, you got me there. Did you ever hear of a welding machine doing like that before?"

"I did not. A welding machine just don't have that sort o' push. I saw a man get a full jolt from a 400-amp welder once, an' although it sat him down it didn't hurt him any."

"It's not amperage that kills people," said Kelly, "it's voltage. Voltage is the pressure behind a current, you know. Take an amount of water, call it amperage. If I throw it in your face, it won't hurt you. If I put it through a small hose you'll feel it. But if I pump it through the tiny holes on a Diesel injector nozzle at about twelve hundred pounds, it'll draw blood. But a welding arc generator just is not wound to build up that kind of voltage. I can't see where any short circuit anywhere through the armature or field windings could do such a thing."

"From what Chub said, he had been foolin' around with the work selector. I don't think anyone touched the dials after it happened. The selector dial was run all the way over to the low current application segment, and the current control was around the halfway mark. That's not enough juice to get you a good bead with a quarter-inch rod, let alone kill somebody—or roll a tractor back thirty feet on level ground."

"Or jump fifty feet," said Kelly. "It would take thousands of volts to generate an arc like that."

"Is it possible that something in the Seven could have pulled that arc? I mean, suppose the arc wasn't driven over, but was drawn over? I tell you, she was hot for four hours after that."

Kelly shook his head. "Never heard of any such thing. Look, just to have something to call them, we call direct current terminals positive and negative, and just because it works in theory we say that current flows from negative to positive. There couldn't be any more positive attraction in one electrode than there is negative drive in the other; see what I mean?"

"There couldn't be some freak condition that would cause a sort of oversize positive field? I mean one that would suck out the negative flow all in a heap, make it smash through under a lot of pressure like the water you were talking about through an injector nozzle?"

"No, Tom. It just don't work that way, far as anyone knows. I dunno, though—there are some things about static electricity that nobody understands. All I can say is that what happened couldn't happen and if it did it couldn't have killed Peebles. And you know the answer to that."

Tom glanced away at the upper end of the runway, where the two graves were. There was bitterness and turbulent anger naked there for a moment, and he turned and walked away without another word. And when he went back to have another look at the welding machine, *Daisy Etta* was gone.

* * *

Al Knowles and Harris squatted together near the water cooler.

"Bad," said Harris.

"Nevah saw anythin' like it," said Al. "Ol' Tom come back f'm the shop theah just' *raisin'* Cain. 'Weah's 'at Seven gone? Weah's 'at Seven?' I never heered sech cah'ins on."

"Dennis did take it, huh?"

"Sho' did."

Harris said, "He came spoutin' around to me a while back, Dennis did. Chub'd told him Tom said for everybody to stay off that machine. Dennis was mad as a wet hen. Said Tom was carryin' that kind o' business too far. Said there was probably somethin' about the Seven Tom didn't want us to find out. Might incriminate him. Dennis is ready to say Tom killed the kid."

"Reckon he did, Harris?"

Harris shook his head. "I've known Tom too long to think that. If he won't tell us what really happened up on the mesa, he has a reason for it. How'd Dennis come to take the dozer?"

"Blew a front tire on his pan. Came back heah to git anothah rig—maybe a Dumptor. Saw th' Seven standin' theah ready to go. Stood theah lookin' at it and cussin' Tom. Said he was tired of bashin' his kidneys t'pieces on them othah rigs an' bedamned if he would take suthin' that rode good fo' a change. I tol' him ol' Tom'd raise th' roof when he found him on it. He had a couple mo' things t'say 'bout Tom then."

"I didn't think he had the guts to take the rig."

"Aw, he talked hisself blind mad."

They looked up as Chub Horton trotted up, panting. "Hey, you guys, come on. We better get up there to Dennis."

"What's wrong?" asked Harris, climbing to his feet.

"Tom passed me a minute ago lookin' like the

wrath o' God and hightailin' it for the swamp fill. I asked him what was the matter and he hollered that Dennis had took the Seven. Said he was always talkin' about murder, and he'd get his fill of it foolin' around that machine." Chub went wall-eyed, licked his lips beside his cigar.

"Oh-oh," said Harris quietly. "That's the wrong kind o' talk for just now."

"You don't suppose he—"

"*Come on!*"

They saw Tom before they were halfway there. He was walking slowly, with his head down. Harris shouted. Tom raised his face, stopped, stood there waiting with a peculiarly slumped stance.

"Where's Dennis?" barked Chub.

Tom waited until they were almost up to him and then weakly raised an arm and thumbed over his shoulder. His face was green.

"Tom—is he—"

Tom nodded, and swayed a little. His granite jaw was slack.

"Al, stay with him. He's sick. Harris, let's go."

Tom was sick, then and there. Very. Al stood gaping at him, fascinated.

Chub and Harris found Dennis. All of twelve square feet of him, ground and churned and rolled out into a torn-up patch of earth. *Daisy Etta* was gone.

Back at the outcropping, they sat with Tom while Al Knowles took a Dumptor and roared away to get Kelly.

"You saw him?" he said dully after a time.

Harris said, "Yeh."

The screaming Dumptor and a mountainous cloud of dust arrived, Kelly driving, Al holding on with a death-grip to the dump-bed guards. Kelly flung himself off, ran to Tom. "Tom—what is all this? Dennis dead? And you . . . you—"

Tom's head came up slowly, the slackness going out of his long face, a light suddenly coming into his eyes. Until this moment it had not crossed his mind what these men might think.

"I—what?"

"Al says you killed him."

Tom's eyes flicked at Al Knowles, and Al winced as if the glance had been a quirt.

Harris said, "What about it Tom?"

"Nothing about it. He was killed by that Seven. You saw that for yourself."

"I stuck with you all along," said Harris slowly. "I took everything you said and believed it."

"This is too strong for you?" Tom asked.

Harris nodded. "Too strong, Tom."

Tom looked at the grim circle of faces and laughed suddenly. He stood up, put his back against a tall crate. "What do you plan to do about it?"

There was a silence. "You think I went up there and knocked that windbag off the machine and ran over him?" More silence. "Listen. I went up there and saw what you saw. He was dead before I got there. That's not good enough either?" He paused and licked his lips. "So after I killed him I got up on the tractor and drove it far enough away so you couldn't see or hear it when you got there. And then I sprouted wings and flew back so's I was halfway here when you met me—*ten minutes* after I spoke to Chub on my way up!"

Kelly said vaguely, "Tractor?"

"Well," said Tom harshly to Harris, "was the tractor there when you and Chub went up and saw Dennis?"

"No—"

Chub smacked his thigh suddenly. "You could of drove it into the swamp, Tom."

Tom said angrily, "I'm wastin' my time. You guys got it all figured out. Why ask me anything at all?"

"Aw, take it easy," said Kelly. "We just want the facts. Just what did happen? You met Chub and told him that Dennis would get all the murderin' he could take if he messed around that machine. That right?"

"That's right."

"Then what?"

"Then the machine murdered him."

Chub, with remarkable patience, asked, "What did you mean the day Peebles was killed when you said that something had queered the Seven up there on the mesa?"

Tom said furiously, "I meant what I said. You guys are set to crucify me for this and I can't stop you. Well, listen. Something's got into that Seven. I don't know what it is and I don't think I ever will know. I thought that after she smashed herself up that it was finished with. I had an idea that when we had her torn down and helpless we should have left her that way. I was dead right but it's too late now. She's killed Rivera and she's killed Dennis and she sure had something to do with killing Peebles. And my idea is that she won't stop as long as there's a human being alive on this island."

"Whaddaya know!" said Chub.

"Sure, Tom, sure," said Kelly quietly. "That tractor is out to get us. But don't worry; we'll catch it and tear it down. Just don't you worry about it any more; it'll be all right."

"That's right, Tom," said Harris. "You just take it easy around camp for a couple of days till you feel better. Chub and the rest of us will handle things for you. You had too much sun."

"You're a swell bunch of fellows," gritted Tom, with the deepest sarcasm. "You want to live," he shouted, "git out there and throw that maverick bulldozer!"

"That maverick bulldozer is at the bottom of the

swamp where you put it," growled Chub. His head lowered and he started to move in. "Sure we want to live. The best way to do that is to put you where you can't kill anybody else. *Get him!*"

He leaped. Tom straightened him with his left and crossed with his right. Chub went down, tripping Harris. Al Knowles scuttled to a toolbox and dipped out a fourteen-inch crescent wrench. He circled around, keeping out of trouble, trying to look useful. Tom loosened a haymaker at Kelly, whose head seemed to withdraw like a turtle's; it whistled over, throwing Tom badly off balance. Harris, still on his knees, tackled Tom's legs; Chub hit him in the small of the back with a meaty shoulder, and Tom went flat on his face. Al Knowles, holding the wrench in both hands, swept it up and back like a baseball bat; at the top of its swing Kelly reached over, snatched it out of his hands and tapped Tom delicately behind the ear with it. Tom went limp.

It was late, but nobody seemed to feel like sleeping. They sat around the pressure lantern, talking idly. Chub and Kelly played an inconsequential game of casino, forgetting to pick up their points; Harris paced up and down like a man in a cell, and Al Knowles was squinched up close to the light, his eyes wide and watching, watching—

"I need a drink," said Harris.

"Tens," said one of the casino players.

Al Knowles said, "We shoulda killed him. We oughta kill him now."

"There's been too much killin' already," said Chub. "Shut up, you." And to Kelly, "With big casino," sweeping up cards.

Kelly caught his wrist and grinned. "Big casino's the ten of diamonds, not the ten of hearts. Remember?"

"Oh."

"How long before the blacktopping crew will be here?" quavered Al Knowles.

"Twelve days," said Harris. "And they better bring some likker."

"Hey, you guys."

They fell silent.

"Hey!"

"It's Tom," said Kelly. "Building sixes, Chub."

"I'm gonna go kick his ribs in," said Knowles, not moving.

"I heard that," said the voice from the darkness. "If I wasn't hogtied—"

"We know what you'd do," said Chub. "How much proof do you think we need?"

"Chub, you don't have to do any more to him!" It was Kelly, flinging his cards down and getting up. "Tom, you want water?"

"Yes."

"Siddown, siddown," said Chub.

"Let him lie there and bleed," Al Knowles said.

"Nuts!" Kelly went and filled a cup and brought it to Tom. The big Georgian was tied thoroughly, wrists together, taut rope between elbows and elbows behind his back, so that his hands were immovable over his solar plexus. His knees and ankles were bound as well, although Knowles' little idea of a short rope between ankles and throat hadn't been used.

"Thanks, Kelly." Tom drank greedily, Kelly holding his head. "Goes good." He drank more. "What hit me?"

"One of the boys. 'Bout the time you said the cat was haunted."

"Oh, yeah." Tom rolled his head and blinked with pain.

"Any sense asking you if you blame us?"

"Kelly, does somebody else have to get killed before you guys wake up?"

"None of us figure there will be any more killin' —now."

The rest of the men drifted up. "He willing to talk sense?" Chub wanted to know.

Al Knowles laughed, "Hyuk! hyuk! Don't he look dangerous now!"

Harris said suddenly, "Al, I'm gonna hafta tape your mouth with the skin off your neck."

"Am I the kind of guy that makes up ghost stories?"

"Never have that I know of, Tom." Harris kneeled down beside him. "Never killed anyone before, either."

"Oh, get away from me. Get away," said Tom tiredly.

"Get up and make us," jeered Al.

Harris got up and backhanded him across the mouth. Al squeaked, took three steps backward and tripped over a drum of grease. "I told you," said Harris almost plaintively. "I *told* you, Al."

Tom stopped the bumble of comment. "Shut up!" he hissed. "SHUT UP!" he roared.

They shut.

"Chub," said Tom, rapidly, evenly. "What did you say I did with that Seven?"

"Buried it in the swamp."

"Yeh. Listen."

"Listen at what?"

"Be quiet and listen!"

So they listened. It was another still, windless night, with a thin crescent of moon showing nothing true in the black and muffled silver landscape. The smallest whisper of surf drifted up from the beach, and from far off to the right, where the swamp was, a scandalized frog croaked protest at the manhandling of his mudhole. But the sound that crept down, freezing their bones, came from the bluff behind their camp.

It was the unmistakable staccato of a starting engine.

"The Seven!"

" 'At's right, Chub," said Tom.

"Wh-who's crankin' her up?"

"Are we all here?"

"All but Peebles and Dennis and Rivera," said Tom.

"It's Dennis' ghost," moaned Al.

Chub snapped, "Shut up, lamebrain."

"She's shifted to Diesel," said Kelly, listening.

"She'll be here in a minute," said Tom. "Y'know, fellas, we can't all be crazy, but you're about to have a time convincin' yourself of it."

"You like this, doncha?"

"Some ways. Rivera used to call that machine *Daisy Etta*, 'cause she's *de siete* in Spig. *Daisy Etta*, she wants her a man."

"Tom," said Harris, "I wish you'd stop that chatterin'. You make me nervous."

"I got to do somethin'. I can't run," Tom drawled.

"We're going to have a look," said Chub. "If there's nobody on that cat, we'll turn you loose."

"Mighty white of you. Reckon you'll get back before she does?"

"We'll get back. Harris, come with me. We'll get one of the pan tractors. They can outrun a Seven. Kelly, take Al and get the other one."

"Dennis' machine has a flat tire on the pan," said Al's quivering voice.

"Pull the pin and cut the cables, then! Git!" Kelly and Al Knowles ran off.

"Good huntin', Chub."

Chub went to him, bent over. "I think I'm goin' to have to apologize to you, Tom."

"No you ain't. I'd a done the same. Get along now, if you think you got to. But hurry back."

"I got to. An' I'll hurry back."

Harris said, "Don't go 'way, boy." Tom returned

the grin, and they were gone. But they didn't hurry back. They didn't come back at all.

It was Kelly who came pounding back, with Al Knowles on his heels, a half hour later. "Al—gimme your knife."

He went to work on the ropes. His face was drawn.

"I could see some of it," whispered Tom. "Chub and Harris?"

Kelly nodded. "There wasn't nobody on the Seven like you said." He said it as if there were nothing else in his mind, as if the most rigid self-control was keeping him from saying it over and over.

"I could see the lights," said Tom. "A tractor angling up the hill. Pretty soon another, crossing it, lighting up the whole slope."

"We heard it idling up there somewhere," Kelly said. "Olive-drab paint—couldn't see it."

"I saw the pan tractor turn over—oh, four, five times down the hill. It stopped, lights still burning. Then something hit it and rolled it again. That sure blacked it out. What turned it over first?"

"The Seven. Hanging up there just at the brow of the bluff. Waited until Chub and Harris were about to pass, sixty, seventy feet below. Tipped over the edge and rolled down on them with her clutches out. Must've been going thirty miles an hour when she hit. Broadside. They never had a chance. Followed the pan as it rolled down the hill and when it stopped booted it again."

"Want me to rub you' ankles?" asked Al.

"You! Get outa my sight!"

"Aw, Tom—" whimpered Al.

"Skip it, Tom," said Kelly. "There ain't enough of us left to carry on that way. Al, you mind your manners from here on out, hear?"

"Ah jes' wanted to tell y'all. I knew you weren't lyin' 'bout Dennis, Tom, if only I'd stopped to think. I recollect when Dennis said he'd take that tractuh out . . . 'membah, Kelly? . . . He went an' got the crank and walked around to th' side of th' machine and stuck it in th' hole. It was barely in theah befo' the startin' engine kicked off. 'Whadda ya know!' he says t'me. 'She started by here'f! I nevah pulled that handle!' And I said 'She sho' rarin' t'go!' "

"You pick a fine time to 'recollect' something," gritted Tom. "C'mon—let's get out of here."

"Where to?"

"What do you know that a Seven can't move or get up on?"

"That's a large order. A big rock, maybe."

"Ain't nothing that big around here," said Tom.

Kelly thought a minute, then snapped his fingers. "Up on the top of my last cut with the shovel," he said. "It's fourteen feet if it's an inch. I was pullin' out small rock an' topsoil, and Chub told me to drop back and dip out marl from a pocket there. I sumped in back of the original cut and took out a whole mess o' marl. That left a big neck of earth sticking thirty feet or so out of the cliff. The narrowest part is only about four feet wide. If *Daisy Etta* tries to get us from the top, she'll straddle the neck and hang herself. If she tries to get us from below, she can't get traction to climb; it's too loose and too steep."

"And what happens if she builds herself a ramp?"

"We'll be gone from there."

"Let's go."

Al agitated for the choice of a Dumptor because of its speed, but was howled down. Tom wanted something that could not get a flat tire and that would need something really powerful to turn it over. They took the two-cycle pan tractor with the bulldozer blade that had been Dennis' machine and crept out into the darkness.

It was nearly six hours later that *Daisy Etta* came and woke them up. Night was receding before a paleness in the east, and a fresh ocean breeze had sprung up. Kelly had taken the first lookout and Al the second, letting Tom rest the night out. And Tom was far too tired to argue the arrangement. Al had immediately fallen asleep on his watch, but fear had such a sure, cold hold on his vitals that the first faint growl of the big Diesel engine snapped him erect. He tottered on the edge of the tall neck of earth that they slept on and squeaked as he scrabbled to get his balance.

"What's giving?" asked Kelly, instantly wide awake.

"It's coming," blubbered Al. "Oh my, oh my—"

Kelly stood up and stared into the fresh, dark dawn. The motor boomed hollowly, in a peculiar way heard twice at the same time as it was thrown to them and echoed back by the bluffs under and around them.

"It's coming and what are we goin' to do?" chanted Al. "What is going to happen?"

"My head is going to fall off," said Tom sleepily. He rolled to a sitting position, holding the brutalized member between his hands. "If that egg behind my ear hatches, it'll come out a full-sized jack-hammer." He looked at Kelly. "Where is she?"

"Don't rightly know," said Kelly. "Somewhere down around the camp."

"Probably pickin' up our scent."

"Figure it can do that?"

"I figure it can do anything," said Tom. "Al, stop your moanin'."

The sun slipped its scarlet edge into the thin slot between sea and sky, and rosy light gave each rock and tree a shape and a shadow. Kelly's gaze swept back and forth, back and forth, until, minutes later, he saw movement.

"There she is!"

"Where?"

"Down by the grease rack."

Tom rose and stared. "What's she doin'?"

After an interval Kelly said, "She's workin'. Diggin' a swale in front of the fuel drums."

"You don't say. Don't tell me she's goin' to give herself a grease job."

"She don't need it. She was completely greased and new oil put in the crankcase after we set her up. But she might need fuel."

"Not more'n half a tank."

"Well, maybe she figures she's got a lot of work to do today." As Kelly said this Al began to blubber. They ignored him.

The fuel drums were piled in a pyramid at the edge of the camp, in forty-four-gallon drums piled on their sides. The Seven was moving back and forth in front of them, close up, making pass after pass, gouging earth up and wasting it out past the pile. She soon had a huge pit scooped out, about fourteen feet wide, six feet deep and thirty feet long, right at the very edge of the pile of drums.

"What you reckon she's playin' at?"

"Search me. She seems to want fuel, but I don't . . . look at that! She's stopped in the hole; she's pivoting, smashing the top corner of the moldboard into one of the drums on the bottom!"

Tom scraped the stubble on his jaw with his nails. "An' you wonder how much that critter can do! Why, she's got the whole thing figured out. She knows if she tried to punch a hole in a fuel drum that she'd only kick it around. If she did knock a hole in it, how's she going to lift it? She's not equipped to handle hose, so . . . see? Look at her now! She just gets herself lower than the bottom drum on the pile, and punches a hole. She can do that then, with the whole weight of the pile holding it down. Then she backs her tank under the stream of fuel runnin' out!"

"How'd she get the cap off?"

Tom snorted and told them how the radiator cap

had come off its hinges as he vaulted over the hood the day Rivera was hurt.

"You know," he said after a moment's thought, "if she knew as much then as she does now, I'd be snoozin' beside Rivera and Peebles. She just didn't know her way around then. She run herself like she'd never run before. She's learned plenty since."

"She has," said Kelly, "and here's where she uses it on us. She's headed this way."

She was. Straight out across the roughed-out runway she came, grinding along over the dew-sprinkled earth, yesterday's dust swirling up from under her tracks. Crossing the shoulder line, she took the rougher ground skillfully, angling up over the occasional swags in the earth, by-passing stones, riding free and fast and easily. It was the first time Tom had actually seen her clearly running without an operator, and his flesh crept as he watched. The machine was unnatural, her outline somehow unreal and dreamlike purely through the lack of the small silhouette of a man in the saddle. She looked hulked, compact, dangerous.

"What are we gonna do?" wailed Al Knowles.

"We're gonna sit and wait," said Kelly, "and you're gonna shut your trap. We won't know for five minutes yet whether she's going to go after us from down below or from up here."

"If you want to leave," said Tom gently, "go right ahead." Al sat down.

Kelly looked ruminatively down at his beloved power shovel, sitting squat and unlovely in the cut below them and away to their right. "How do you reckon she'd stand up against the dipper stick?"

"If it ever came to a rough-and-tumble," said Tom, "I'd say it would be just too bad for *Daisy Etta*. But she wouldn't fight. There's no way you could get the shovel within punchin' range; *Daisy*'d just stand there and laugh at you."

"I can't see her now," whined Al.

Tom looked. "She's taken the bluff. She's going to try it from up here. I move we sit tight and see if she's foolish enough to try to walk out here over that narrow neck. If she does, she'll drop on her belly with one truck on each side. Probably turn herself over trying to dig out."

The wait then was interminable. Back over the hill they could hear the laboring motor; twice they heard the machine stop momentarily to shift gears. Once they looked at each other hopefully as the sound rose to a series of bellowing roars, as if she were backing and filling; then they realized that she was trying to take some particularly steep part of the bank and having trouble getting traction. But she made it; the motor revved up as she made the brow of the hill, and she shifted into fourth gear and came lumbering out into the open. She lurched up to the edge of the cut, stopped, throttled down, dropped her blade on the ground and stood there idling. Al Knowles backed away to the very edge of the tongue of earth they stood on, his eyes practically on stalks.

"O.K.—put up or shut up," Kelly called across harshly.

"She's looking the situation over," said Tom. "That narrow pathway don't fool her a bit."

Daisy Etta's blade began to rise, and stopped just clear of the ground. She shifted without clashing her gears, began to back slowly, still at little more than an idle.

"She's gonna jump!" screamed Al. "I'm gettin' out of here!"

"Stay here, you fool," shouted Kelly. "She can't get us as long as we're up here! If you go down, she'll hunt you down like a rabbit."

The blast of the Seven's motor was the last straw for Al. He squeaked and hopped over the edge, scrambling and sliding down the almost sheer face of the cut. He hit the bottom running.

Daisy Etta lowered her blade and raised her snout and growled forward, the blade loading. Six, seven, seven and a half cubic yards of dirt piled up in front of her as she neared the edge. The loaded blade bit into the narrow pathway that led out to their perch. It was almost all soft, white, crumbly marl, and the great machine sank nose down into it, the monstrous overload of topsoil spilling down on each side.

"She's going to bury herself!" shouted Kelly.

"No—wait." Tom caught his arm. "She's trying to turn—she made it! She made it! She's ramping herself down to the flat!"

"She is—and she's cut us off from the bluff!"

The bulldozer, blade raised as high as it could possibly go, the hydraulic rod gleaming clean in the early light, freed herself of the last of their tremendous load, spun around and headed back upward, sinking her blade again. She made one more pass between them and the bluff, making a cut now far too wide for them to jump, particularly to the crumbly footing at the bluff's edge. Once down again, she turned to face their haven, now an isolated pillar of marl, and revved down, waiting.

"I never thought of this," said Kelly guiltily. "I knew we'd be safe from her ramping up, and I never thought she'd try it the other way!"

"Skip it. In the meantime, here we sit. What happens—do we wait up here until she idles out of fuel, or do we starve to death?"

"Oh, this won't be a siege, Tom. That thing's too much of a killer. Where's Al? I wonder if he's got guts enough to make a pass near here with our tractor and draw her off?"

"He had just guts enough to take our tractor and head out," said Tom. "Did you know?"

"He took our—*what?*" Kelly looked out toward

where they had left their machine the night before. It was gone. "Why the dirty little yellow rat!"

"No sense cussin'," said Tom steadily, interrupting what he knew was the beginning of some really flowery language. "What else could you expect?"

Daisy Etta decided, apparently, how to go about removing their splendid isolation. She uttered the snort of too-quick throttle, and moved into their peak with a corner of her blade, cutting out a huge swipe, undercutting the material over it so that it fell on her side and track as she passed. Eight inches disappeared from that side of their little plateau.

"Oh-oh. That won't do a-tall," said Tom.

"Fixin' to dig us down," said Kelly grimly. "Take her about twenty minutes. Tom, I say leave."

"It won't be healthy. You just got no idea how fast that thing can move now. Don't forget, she's a good deal more than she was when she had a man runnin' her. She can shift from high to reverse to fifth speed forward like that"—he snapped his fingers— "and she can pivot faster'n you can blink and throw that blade just where she wants it."

The tractor passed under them, bellowing, and their little table was suddenly a foot shorter.

"Awright," said Kelly. "So what do you want to do? Stay here and let her dig the ground out from under our feet?"

"I'm just warning you," said Tom. "Now listen. We'll wait until she's taking a load. It'll take her a second to get rid of it when she knows we're gone. We'll split—she can't get both of us. You head out in the open, try to circle the curve of the bluff and get where you can climb it. Then come back over here to the cut. A man can scramble off a fourteen-foot cut faster'n any tractor ever built. I'll cut in close to the cut, down at the bottom. If she takes after you, I'll get clear all right. If she takes after me, I'll try to make the shovel and at least give her a run for her money. I can play hide an' seek in an' around and under that dipper-stick all day if she wants to play."

"Why me out in the open?"

"Don't you think those long laigs o' yours can outrun her in that distance?"

"Reckon they got to," grinned Kelly. "O.K., Tom."

They waited tensely. *Daisy Etta* backed close by, started another pass. As the motor blatted under the load, Tom said, "Now!" and they jumped. Kelly, catlike as always, landed on his feet. Tom, whose knees and ankles were black and blue with rope bruises, took two staggering steps and fell. Kelly scooped him to his feet as the dozer's steel prow came around the bank. Instantly she was in fifth gear and howling down at them. Kelly flung himself to the left and Tom to the right, and they pounded away, Kelly out toward the runway, Tom straight for the shovel. *Daisy Etta* let them diverge for a moment, keeping her course, trying to pursue both; then she evidently sized Tom up as the slower, for she swung toward him. The instant's hesitation was all Tom needed to get the little lead necessary. He tore up to the shovel, his legs going like pistons, and dived down between the shovel's tracks.

As he hit the ground, the big manganese-steel moldboard hit the right track of the shovel, and the impact set all forty-seven tons of the great machine quivering. But Tom did not stop. He scrabbled his way under the rig, stood up behind it, leaped and caught the sill of the rear window, clapped his other hand on it, drew himself up and tumbled inside. Here he was safe for the moment; the huge tracks themselves were higher than the Seven's blade could rise, and the floor of the cab was a good sixteen inches higher than the top of the track. Tom went to the cab door and peeped outside. The tractor had drawn off and was idling.

"Study away," gritted Tom, and went to the big

Murphy Diesel. He unhurriedly checked the oil with the bayonet gauge, replaced it, took the governor cut-out rod from its rack and inserted it in the governor casing. He set the master throttle at the halfway mark, pulled up the starter-handle, twitched the cut-out. The motor spit a wad of blue smoke out of its hooded exhaust and caught. Tom put the rod back, studied the fuel-flow glass and pressure gauges, and then went to the door and looked out again. The Seven had not moved, but it was revving up and down in that uneven fashion it had shown up on the mesa. Tom had the extraordinary idea that it was gathering itself to spring. He slipped into the saddle, threw the master clutch. The big gears that half-filled the cab obediently began to turn. He kicked the brake-locks loose with his heels, let his feet rest lightly on the pedals as they rose.

Then he reached over his head and snapped back the throttle. As the Murphy picked up he grasped both hoist and swing levers and pulled them back. The engine howled; the two-yard bucket came up off the ground with a sudden jolt as the cold friction grabbed it. The big machine swung hard to the right; Tom snapped his hoist lever forward and checked the bucket's rise with his foot on the brake. He shoved the crowd lever forward; the bucket ran out to the end of its reach, and the heel of the bucket wiped across the Seven's hood, taking with it the exhaust stack, muffler and all, and the pre-cleaner on the air intake. Tom cursed. He had figured on the machine's leaping backward. If it had, he would have smashed the castiron radiator core. But she had stood still, making a split-second decision.

Now she moved, though, and quickly. With that incredibly fast shifting, she leaped backwards and pivoted out of range before Tom could check the shovel's mad swing. The heavy swing-friction blocks smoked acridly as the machine slowed, stopped and swung back. Tom checked her as he was facing the Seven, hoisted his bucket a few feet and rehauled, bringing it about halfway back, ready for anything. The four great dipper-teeth gleamed in the sun. Tom ran a practiced eye over cables, boom and dipperstick, liking the black polish of crater compound on the sliding parts, the easy tension of well-greased cables and links. The huge machine stood strong, ready and profoundly subservient for all its brute power.

Tom looked searchingly at the Seven's ruined engine hood. The gaping end of the broken air-intake pipe stared back at him. "Aha!" he said. "A few cupfuls of nice dry marl down there'll give you something to chew on."

Keeping a wary eye on the tractor, he swung into the bank, dropped his bucket and plunged it into the marl. He crowded it deep, and the Murphy rocked him in the saddle. He looked back over his shoulder through the door and saw the Seven backing off again. She had run up and delivered a terrific punch to the counterweight at the back of the cab. Tom grinned tightly. She'd have to do better than that. There was nothing back there but eight or ten tons of solid steel. And he didn't much care at the moment whether or not she scratched his paint.

He swung back again, white marl running away on both sides of the heaped bucket. The shovel rode perfectly now, for a shovel is counter-weighted to balance true when standing level with the bucket loaded. The hoist and swing frictions and the brake linings had heated and dried themselves of the night's condensation moisture, and she answered the controls in a way that delighted the operator in him. He handled the swing lever lightly, back to swing to the right, forward to swing to the left, following the slow dance the Seven had started to do, stepping warily back and forth like a fighter looking for an opening. Tom kept the bucket between himself and the tractor, knowing that she could not hurl a tool that was built to smash hard rock for twenty hours a day and like it.

Daisy Etta bellowed and rushed in. Tom snapped the hoist lever back hard, and the bucket rose, letting the tractor run underneath. Tom punched the bucket trip, and the great steel jaw opened, cascading marl down on the broken hood. The tractor's fan blew it back in a huge billowing cloud. The instant that it took Tom to check and dump was enough, however, for the tractor to dance back out of the way, for when he tried to drop it on the machine to smash the coiled injector tubes on top of the engine block, she was gone.

The dust cleared away, and the tractor moved in again, feinted to the left, then swung her blade at the bucket, which was just clear of the ground. Tom swung to meet her, her feint having gotten her in a little closer than he liked, and bucket met blade with a shower of sparks and a clank that could be heard for half a mile. She had come in with her blade high, and Tom let out a wordless shout as he saw that the A-frame brace behind the blade had caught between two of his dipper-teeth. He snatched at his hoist lever and the bucket came up, lifting with it the whole front end of the bulldozer.

Daisy Etta plunged up and down and her tracks dug violently into the earth as she raised and lowered her blade, trying to shake herself free. Tom rehauled, trying to bring the tractor in closer, for the boom was set too low to attempt to lift such a dead weight. As it was, the shovel's off track was trying its best to get off the ground. But the crowd and rehaul frictions could not handle her alone; they began to heat and slip.

Tom hoisted a little; the shovel's off track came up a foot off the ground. Tom cursed and let the bucket drop, and in an instant the dozer was free and running clear. Tom swung wildly at her, missed. The dozer came in on a long curve; Tom swung to meet her again, took a vicious swipe at her which she took on her blade. But this time she did not withdraw after being hit, but bored right in, carrying the bucket before her. Before Tom realized what she was doing, his bucket was around in front of the tracks and between them, on the ground. It was as swift and skillful a maneuver as could be imagined, and it left the shovel without the ability to swing as long as *Daisy Etta* could hold the bucket trapped between the tracks.

Tom crowded furiously, but that succeeded only in lifting the boom higher in the air, since there is nothing to hold a boom down but its own weight. Hoisting did nothing but make his frictions smoke and rev the engine down dangerously close to the stalling point.

Tom swore again and reached down to the cluster of small levers at his left. These were the gears. On this type of shovel, the swing lever controls everything except crowd and hoist. With the swing lever, the operator, having selected his gear, controls the travel—that is, power to the tracks—in forward and reverse; booming up and booming down; and swinging. The machine can do only one of these things at a time. If she is in travel gear, she cannot swing. If she is in swing gear, she cannot boom up or down. Not once in years of operating would this inability bother an operator; now, however, nothing was normal.

Tom pushed the swing gear control down and pulled up on the travel. The clutches involved were jaw clutches, not frictions, so that he had to throttle down to an idle before he could make the castellations mesh. As the Murphy revved down, *Daisy Etta* took it as a signal that something could be done about it, and she shoved furiously into the bucket. But Tom had all controls in neutral and all she succeeded in doing was to dig herself in, her sharp new cleats spinning deep into the dirt.

Tom set his throttle up again and shoved the swing lever forward. There was a vast crackling of drive chains; and the big tracks started to turn.

Daisy Etta had sharp cleats; her pads were twenty inches wide and her tracks were fourteen feet long, and there were fourteen tons of steel on them. The shovel's big flat pads were three feet wide and twenty feet long, and forty-seven tons aboard. There was simply no comparison. The Murphy bellowed the fact that the work was hard, but gave no indications of stalling. *Daisy Etta* performed the incredible feat of shifting into a forward gear while she was moving backwards, but it did her no good. Round and round her tracks went, trying to drive her forward, gouging deep; and slowly and surely she was forced backward toward the cut wall by the shovel.

Tom heard a sound that was not part of a straining machine; he looked out and saw Kelly up on top of the cut, smoking, swinging his feet over the edge, making punching motions with his hands as if he had a ringside seat at a big fight—which he certainly had.

Tom now offered the dozer little choice. If she did not turn aside before him, she would be born back against the bank and her fuel tank crushed. There was every possibility that, having her pinned there, Tom would have time to raise his bucket over her and smash her to pieces. And if she turned before she was forced against the bank, she would have to free Tom's bucket. This she had to do.

The Murphy gave him warning, but not enough. It crooned as the load came off, and Tom knew then that the dozer was shifting into a reverse gear. He whipped the hoist lever back, and the bucket rose as the dozer backed away from him. He crowded it out and let it come smashing down—and missed. For the tractor danced aside—and while he was in travel gear he could not swing to follow it. *Daisy Etta* charged then, put one track on the bank and went over almost on her beam-ends, throwing one end of her blade high in the air. So totally unexpected was it that Tom was quite unprepared. The tractor flung itself on the bucket, and the cutting edge of the blade dropped between the dipper teeth. This time there was the whole weight of the tractor to hold it there. There would be no way for her to free herself—but at the same time she had trapped the bucket so far out from the center pin of the shovel that Tom couldn't hoist without overbalancing and turning the monster over.

Daisy Etta ground away in reverse, dragging the bucket out until it was checked by the bumper-blocks. Then she began to crab sideways, up against the bank and when Tom tried tentatively to rehaul, she shifted and came right with him, burying one whole end of her blade deep into the bank.

Stalemate. She had hung herself up on the bucket, and she had immobilized it. Tom tried to rehaul, but the tractor's anchorage in the bank was too solid. He tried to swing, to hoist. All the overworked frictions could possibly give out was smoke. Tom grunted and throttled to an idle, leaned out the window. *Daisy Etta* was idling to, loudly without her muffler, the stackless exhaust giving out an ugly flat sound. But after the roar of the two great motors the partial silence was deafening.

Kelly called down, "Double knockout, hey?"

"Looks like it. What say we see if we can't get close enough to her to quiet her down some?"

Kelly shrugged. "I dunno. If she's really stopped herself, it's the first time. I respect that rig, Tom. She wouldn't have got herself into that spot if she didn't have an ace up her sleeve."

"Look at her, man! Suppose she was a civilized bulldozer and you had to get her out of there. She can't raise her blade high enough to free it from those dipper-teeth, y'know. Think you'd be able to do it?"

"It might take several seconds," Kelly drawled. "She's sure high and dry."

"O.K., let's spike her guns."

"Like what?"

"Like taking a bar and prying out her tubing." He referred to the coiled brass tubing that carried the fuel, under pressure, from the pump to the injectors. There were many feet of it, running from the pump reservoir, stacked in expansion coils over the cylinder head.

As he spoke *Daisy Etta*'s idle burst into that maniac revving up and down characteristic of her.

"What do you know!" Tom called above the racket. "Eavesdropping!"

Kelly slid down the cut, stood up on the track of the shovel and poked his head in the window. "Well, you want to get a bar and try?"

"Let's go!"

Tom went to the toolbox and pulled out the pinch bar that Kelly used to replace cables on his machine, and swung to the ground. They approached the tractor warily. She revved up as they came near, began to shudder. The front end rose and dropped and the tracks began to turn as she tried to twist out of the vise her blade had dropped into.

"Take it easy, sister," said Tom. "You'll just bury yourself. Set still and take it, now, like a good girl. You got it comin'."

"Be careful," said Kelly. Tom hefted the bar and laid a hand on the fender.

The tractor literally shivered, and from the rubber hose connection at the top of the radiator, a blinding stream of hot water shot out. It fanned and caught them both full in the face. They staggered back, cursing.

"You O.K., Tom?" Kelly gasped a moment later. He had got most of it across the mouth and cheek. Tom was on his knees, his shirt tail out, blotting at his face.

"My eyes . . . oh, my eyes—"

"Let's see!" Kelly dropped down beside him and took him by the wrists, gently removing Tom's hands from his face. He whistled. "Come on," he gritted. He helped Tom up and led him away a few feet. "Stay here," he said hoarsely. He turned, walked back toward the dozer, picking up the pinchbar. "You dirty—!" he yelled, and flung it like a javelin at the tube coils. It was a little high. It struck the ruined hood, made a deep dent in the metal. The dent promptly inverted with a loud *thung-g-g!* and flung the bar back at him. He ducked; it whistled over his head and caught Tom in the calves of his legs. He went down like a poled ox, but staggered to his feet again.

"Come on!" Kelly snarled, and taking Tom's arm, hustled him around the turn of the cut. "Sit down! I'll be right back."

"Where you going? Kelly—be careful!"

"Careful and how!"

Kelly's long legs ate up the distance back to the shovel. He swung into the cab, reached back over the motor and set up the master throttle all the way. Stepping up behind the saddle, he opened the running throttle and the Murphy howled. Then he hauled back on the hoist lever until it knuckled in, turned and leaped off the machine in one supple motion.

The hoist drum turned and took up slack; the cable straightened as it took the strain. The bucket stirred under the dead weight of the bulldozer that rested on it; and slowly, then, the great flat tracks began to lift their rear ends off the ground. The great obedient mass of machinery teetered forward on the tips of her tracks, the Murphy revved down and under the incredible load, but it kept the strain. A strand of the two-part hoist cable broke and whipped around, singing; and then she was balanced—over-balanced—

And the shovel had hauled herself right over and had fallen with an earth-shaking crash. The boom, eight tons of solid steel, clanged down onto the blade of the bulldozer, and lay there, crushing it down tightly onto the imprisoning row of dipper-teeth.

Daisy Etta sat there, not trying to move now, racing her motor impotently. Kelly strutted past her, thumbing his nose, and went back to Tom.

"Kelly! I thought you were never coming back! What happened?"

"Shovel pulled herself over on her nose."

"Good boy! Fall on the tractor?"

"Nup. But the boom's laying across the top of her blade. Caught like a rat in a trap."

"Better watch out the rat don't chew its leg off to get out," said Tom, drily. "Still runnin', is she?"

"Yep. But we'll fix that in a hurry."

"Sure. Sure. How?"

"How? I dunno. Dynamite, maybe. How's the optics?"

Tom opened one a trifle and grunted. "Rough. I can see a little, though. My eyelids are parboiled, mostly. Dynamite, you say? Well—"

Tom sat back against the bank and stretched out his legs. "I tell you, Kelly, I been too blessed busy these last few hours to think much, but there's one thing that keeps comin' back to me—somethin' I was mullin' over long before the rest of you guys knew anything was up at all, except that Rivera had got hurt in some way I wouldn't tell you all about. But I don't reckon you'll call me crazy if I open my mouth now and let it all run out?"

"From now on," Kelly said fervently, "nobody's crazy. After this I'll believe anything."

"O.K. Well, about that tractor. What do you suppose has got into her?"

"Search me. I dunno."

"No—don't say that. I just got an idea we can't stop at 'I dunno.' We got to figure all the angles on this thing before we know just what to do about it. Let's just get this thing lined up. When did it start? On the mesa. How? Rivera was opening an old building with the Seven. This thing came out of there. Now here's what I'm getting at. We can dope these things out about it: It's intelligent. It can only get into a machine and not into a man. It—"

"What about that? How do you know it can't?"

"Because it had the chance to and didn't. I was standing right by the opening when it kited out. Rivera was upon the machine at the time. It didn't directly harm either of us. It got into the tractor, and the tractor did. By the same token, it can't hurt a man when it's out of a machine, but that's all it wants to do when it's in one. O.K.?

"To get on: once it's in one machine it can't get out again. We know that because it had plenty of chances and didn't take them. That scuffle with the dipper-stick, f'r instance. My face woulda been plenty red if it had taken over the shovel—and you can bet it would have if it could."

"I got you so far. But what are we going to do about it?"

"That's the thing. You see, I don't think it's enough to wreck the tractor. We might burn it, blast it, take whatever it was that got into it up on the mesa."

"That makes sense. But I don't see what else we can do than just break up the dozer. We haven't got a line on actually what the thing is."

"I think we have. Remember I asked you all those screwy questions about the arc that killed Peebles. Well, when that happened, I recollected a flock of other things. One—when it got out of that hole up there, I smelled that smell that you notice when you're welding; sometimes when lightning strikes real close."

"Ozone," said Kelly.

"Yeah—ozone. Then, it likes metal, not flesh. But most of all, there was that arc. Now, that was absolutely screwy. You know as well as I do—better—that an arc generator simply don't have the push to do a thing like that. It can't kill a man, and it can't throw an arc no fifty feet. But it did. An' that's why I asked you if there could be something—a field, or some such—that could suck current out of a generator, all at once, faster than it could flow. Because this thing's electrical; it fits all around."

"Electronic," said Kelly doubtfully, thoughtfully.

"I wouldn't know. Now then. When Peebles was killed, a funny thing happened. Remember what Chub said? The Seven moved back—straight back, about thirty feet, until it bumped into a roadroller that was standing behind it. It did that with no fuel in the starting engine—without even using the starting engine, for that matter—and with the compression valves locked open!

"Kelly, that thing in the dozer can't do much, when you come right down to it. It couldn't fix itself up after that joy-ride on the mesa. It can't make the machine do too much more than the machine can do ordinarily. What it actually can do, seems to me, is to make a spring push instead of pull, like the control levers, and make a fitting slip when it's supposed to hold, like the ratchet on the throttle lever. It can turn a shaft, like the way it cranks its own starting motor. But if it was so all-fired high-powered, it wouldn't have to use the starting motor! The absolute biggest job it's done so far, seems to me, was when it walked back from that welding machine when Peebles got his. Now, why did it do that just then?"

"Reckon it didn't like the brimstone smell, like it says in the Good Book," said Kelly sourly.

"That's pretty close, seems to me. Look, Kelly—this thing *feels* things. I mean, it can get sore. If it couldn't it never woulda kept driving in at the shovel like that. It can think. But if it can do all those things, then it can be *scared!*"

"Scared? Why should it be scared?"

"Listen. Something went on in that thing when the arc hit it. What's that I read in a magazine once about heat—something about molecules runnin' around with their heads cut off when they got hot?"

"Molecules do. They go into rapid motion when heat is applied. But—"

"But nothin'. That machine was hot for four hours after that. But she was hot in a funny way. Not just around the place where the arc hit, like as if it was a welding arc. But hot all over—from the moldboard to the fuel-tank cap. Hot everywhere. And just as hot behind the final drive housings as she was at the top of the blade where the poor guy put his hand.

"And look at this." Tom was getting excited, as his words crystallized his ideas. "She was scared—scared enough to back off from that welder, putting everything she could into it, to get back from that welding machine. And after that, she was sick. I say that because in the whole time she's had that whatever-ya-call-it in her, she's never been near men without trying to kill them, except for those two days after the arc hit her. She had juice enough to start herself when Dennis came around with the crank, but she still needed someone to run her till she got her strength back."

"But why didn't she turn and smash up the welder when Dennis took her?"

"One of two things. She didn't have the strength, or she didn't have the guts. She was scared, maybe, and wanted out of there, away from that thing."

"But she had all night to go back for it!"

"Still scared. Or . . . oh, *that's* it! She had other things to do first. Her main idea is to kill men—there's no other way you can figure it. It's what she was built to do. Not the tractor—they don't build 'em sweeter'n that machine; but the thing that's runnin' it."

"What *is* that thing?" Kelly mused. "Coming out of that old building—temple—what have you—how old is it? How long was it there? What kept it in there?"

"What kept it in there was some funny gray stuff that lined the inside of the buildin'," said Tom. "It was like rock, an' it was like smoke.

"It was a color that scared you to look at it, and it gave Rivera and me the creeps when we got near it. Don't ask me what it was. I went up there to look at it, and it's gone. Gone from the building, anyhow. There was a little lump of it on the ground. I don't know whether that was a hunk of it, or all of it rolled up into a ball. I get the creeps again thinkin' about it."

Kelly stood up. "Well, the heck with it. We been beatin' our gums up here too long anyhow. There's just enough sense in what you say to make me want to try something nonsensical, if you see what I mean. If that welder can sweat the Ol' Nick out of that tractor, I'm on. Especially from fifty feet away. There should be a Dumptor around here somewhere; let's move from here. Can you navigate now?"

"Reckon so, a little." Tom rose and together they followed the cut until they came on the Dumptor. They climbed on, cranked it up and headed toward camp.

About halfway there Kelly looked back, gasped, and putting his mouth close to Tom's ear, bellowed against the scream of the motor, "Tom! 'Member what you said about the rat in the trap biting off a leg?"

Tom nodded.

"Well, *Daisy* did too! She's left her blade an' pushbeams an' she's followin' us in!"

They howled into the camp, gasping against the dust that followed when they pulled up by the welder.

Kelly said, "You cast around and see if you can find a drawpin to hook that rig up to the Dumptor with. I'm goin' after some water an' chow!"

Tom grinned. Imagine old Kelly forgetting that a dumptor had no drawbar! He groped around to a toolbox, peering out of the narrow slit beneath swollen lids, felt behind it and located a shackle. He climbed up on the Dumptor, turned it around and backed up to the welding machine. He passed the shackle through the ring at the end of the steering tongue of the welder, screwed in the pin and dropped the shackle over the front towing hook of the Dumptor. A dumptor being what it is, having no real front and no real rear, and direct reversing gears in all speeds, it was no trouble to drive it "backwards" for a change.

Kelly came pounding back, out of breath. "Fix it? Good. Shackle? No drawbar! *Daisy*'s closin' up fast; I say let's take the beach. We'll be concealed until we have a good lead out o' this pocket, and the going's pretty fair, long as we don't bury this jalopy in the sand."

"Good," said Tom as they climbed on and he accepted an open tin of K. "Only go easy; bump around too much and the welder'll slip off the hook. An' I somehow don't want to lose it just now."

They took off, zooming up the beach. A quarter of a mile up, they sighted the Seven across the flat. It immediately turned and took a course that would intercept them.

"Here she comes," shouted Kelly, and stepped down hard on the accelerator. Tom leaned over the back of the seat, keeping his eye on their tow. "Hey! Take it easy! Watch it!

"*Hey!*"

But it was too late. The tongue of the welding machine responded to that one bump too many. The shackle jumped up off the hook, the welder lurched wildly, slewed hard to the left. The tongue dropped to the sand and dug in; the machine rolled up on it and snapped it off, finally stopped, leaning crazily askew. By a miracle it did not quite turn over.

Kelly tramped on the brakes and both their heads did their utmost to snap off their shoulders. They leaped off and ran back to the welder. It was intact, but towing it was now out of the question.

"If there's going to be a showdown, it's gotta be here."

The beach here was about thirty yards wide, the sand almost level, and undercut banks of sawgrass forming the landward edge in a series of little hummocks and headlands. While Tom stayed with the machine, testing starter and generator contacts, Kelly walked up one of the little mounds, stood up on it and scanned the beach back the way he had come. Suddenly he began to shout and wave his arms.

"What's got into you?"

"It's Al!" Kelly called back. "With the pan tractor!"

Tom dropped what he was doing, and came to stand beside Kelly. "Where's the Seven? I can't see."

"Turned on the beach and followin' our track. Al! Al! You little skunk, c'mere!"

Tom could now dimly make out the pan tractor cutting across directly toward them and the beach.

"He don't see *Daisy Etta*," remarked Kelly disgustedly, "or he'd sure be headin' the other way."

Fifty yards away Al pulled up and throttled down. Kelly shouted and waved to him. Al stood up on the machine, cupped his hands around his mouth. "Where's the Seven?"

"Never mind that! Come here with that tractor!"

Al stayed where he was. Kelly cursed and started out after him.

"You stay away from me," he said when Kelly was closer.

"I ain't got time for you now," said Kelly. "Bring that tractor down to the beach."

"Where's that *Daisy Etta*?" Al's voice was oddly strained.

"Right behind us." Kelly tossed a thumb over his shoulder. "On the beach."

Al's pop eyes clicked wide almost audibly. He turned on his heel and jumped off the machine and started to run. Kelly uttered a wordless syllable that was somehow more obscene than anything else he had ever uttered, and vaulted into the seat of the machine. "Hey!" he bellowed after Al's rapidly diminishing figure. "You're running' right into her." Al appeared not to hear, but went pelting down the beach.

Kelly put her into fifth gear and poured on the throttle. As the tractor began to move he whacked out the master clutch, snatched the overdrive lever back to put her into sixth, rammed the clutch in again, all so fast that she did not have time to stop rolling. Bucking and jumping over the rough ground the fast machine whined for the beach.

Tom was fumbling back to the welder, his ears telling him better than his eyes how close the Seven was—for she was certainly no nightingale, particularly without her exhaust stack. Kelly reached the machine as he did.

"Get behind it," snapped Tom. "I'll jamb the tierod with the shackle, and you see if you can't bunt her up into that pocket between those two hummocks. Only take it easy—you don't want to tear up that generator. Where's Al!"

"Don't ask me. He run down the beach to meet *Daisy*."

"He *what*?"

The whine of the two-cycle drowned out Kelly's answer, if any. He got behind the welder and set his blade against it. Then in a low gear, slipping his clutch in a little, he slowly nudged the machine toward the place Tom had indicated. It was a little hollow in between two projecting banks. The surf and the high-tide mark dipped inland here to match it; the water was only a few feet away.

Tom raised his arm and Kelly stopped. From the other side of the projecting shelf, out of their sight now, came the flat roar of the Seven's exhaust. Kelly sprang off the tractor and went to help Tom, who was furiously throwing out coils of cable from the rack back of the welder. "What's the game?"

"We got to ground that Seven some way," panted Tom. He threw the last bit of cable out to clear it of kinks and turned to the panel. "How was it—about sixty volts and the amperage on 'special application'?" He spun the dials, pressed the starter button. The motor responded instantly. Kelly scooped up ground clamp and rod holder and tapped them together. The solenoid governor picked up the load and the motor hummed as a good live spark took the jump.

"Good," said Tom, switching off the generator. "Come on, Lieutenant General Electric, figure me out a way to ground that maverick."

Kelly tightened his lips, shook his head. "I dunno—unless somebody actually clamps this thing on her."

"No, boy, can't do that. If one of us gets killed—"

Kelly tossed the ground clamp idly, his lithe body taut. "Don't give me that, Tom. You know I'm elected because you can't see good enough yet to handle it. You know you'd do it if you could. You—"

He stopped short, for the steadily increasing roar of the approaching Seven had stopped, was blatting away now in that extraordinary irregular throttling that *Daisy Etta* affected.

"Now, what's got into her?"

Kelly broke away and scrambled up the bank. "Tom!" he gasped. "Tom—come up here!"

Tom followed, and they lay side by side, peering out over the top of the escarpment at the remarkable tableau.

Daisy Etta was standing on the beach, near the water, not moving. Before her, twenty or thirty feet away, stood Al Knowles, his arms out in front of him, talking a blue streak. *Daisy* made far too much racket for them to hear what he was saying.

"Do you reckon he's got guts enough to stall her off for us?" said Tom.

"If he has, it's the queerest thing that's happened yet on this old island," Kelly breathed, "an' that's saying something."

The Seven revved up till she shook, and then throttled back. She ran down so low then that they thought she had shut herself down, but she caught on the last two revolutions and began to idle quietly. And then they could hear.

Al's voice was high, hysterical. "—I come t' he'p you, I come t' he'p you, don' kill me, I'll he'p you—" He took a step forward; the dozer snorted and he fell to his knees. "I'll wash you an' grease you and change yo' ile," he said in a high singsong.

"The guy's not human," said Kelly wonderingly.

"He ain't housebroke either," Tom chuckled.

"—lemme he'p you. I'll fix you when you break down. I'll he'p you kill those other guys—"

"She don't need any help!" said Tom.

"The louse," growled Kelly. "The rotten little double-crossing polecat!" He stood up. "Hey, you Al! Come out o' that. I mean now! If she don't get you I will, if you don't move."

Al was crying now. "Shut up!" he screamed. "I

know who's bawss hereabouts, an' so do you!" He pointed at the tractor. "She'll kill us all off'n we don't do what she wants!" He turned back to the machine. "I'll k-kill 'em fo' you. I'll wash you and shine you up and f-fix yo' hood. I'll put yo' blade back on. . . ."

Tom reached out and caught Kelly's leg as the tall man started out, blind mad. "Git back here," he barked. "What you want to do—get killed for the privilege of pinnin' his ears back?"

Kelly subsided and came back, threw himself down beside Tom, put his face in his hands. He was quivering with rage.

"Don't take on so," Tom said. "The man's plumb loco. You can't argue with him any more'n you can with *Daisy*, there. If he's got to get his, *Daisy*'ll give it to him."

"Aw, Tom, it ain't that. I know he ain't worth it, but I can't sit up here and watch him get himself killed. I can't, Tom."

Tom thumped him on the shoulder, because there were simply no words to be said. Suddenly he stiffened, snapped his fingers.

"There's our ground," he said urgently, pointing seaward. "The water—the wet beach where the surf runs. If we can get our ground clamp out there and her somewhere near it—"

"Ground the pan tractor. Run it out into the water. It ought to reach—partway, anyhow."

"That's it—c'mon."

They slid down the bank, snatched up the ground clamp, attached it to the frame of the pan tractor.

"I'll take it," said Tom, and as Kelly opened his mouth, Tom shoved him back against the welding machine. "No time to argue," he snapped, swung on to the machine, slapped her in gear and was off. Kelly took a step toward the tractor, and then his quick eye saw a bight of the ground cable about to foul a wheel of the welder. He stooped and threw it off, spread out the rest of it so it would pay off clear. Tom, with the incredible single-mindedness of the trained operator, watched only the black line of the trailing cable on the sand behind him. When it straightened, he stopped. The front of the tracks were sloshing in the gentle surf. He climbed off the side away from the Seven and tried to see. There was movement, and the growl of her motor now running at a bit more than idle, but he could not distinguish much.

Kelly picked up the rod-holder and went to peer around the head of the protruding bank. Al was on his feet, still crooning hysterically, sidling over toward *Daisy Etta.* Kelly ducked back, threw the switch on the arc generator, climbed the bank and crawled along through the sawgrass paralleling the beach until the holder in his hand tugged and he knew he had reached the end of the cable. He looked out at the beach; measured carefully with his eye the arc he would travel if he left his position and, keeping the cable taut, went out on the beach. At no point would he come within seventy feet of the possessed machine, let alone fifty. She had to be drawn in closer. And she had to be maneuvered out to the wet sand, or in the water—

Al Knowles, encouraged by the machine's apparent decision not to move, approached, though warily, and still running off at the mouth. "—we'll kill 'em off an' then we'll keep it a secret and th' bahges'll come an' take us offen th' island and we'll go to anothah job an' kill us lots mo' . . . an' when yo' tracks git dry an' squeak we'll wet 'em up with blood, and you'll be rightly king o' th' hill . . . look yondah, look yondah, *Daisy Etta,* see them theah, by the otheh tractuh, theah they are, kill 'em, *Daisy,* kill 'em, *Daisy,* an' lemme he'p . . . heah me. *Daisy,* heah me, say you heah me—" and the motor roared in response. Al laid a timid hand on the radiator guard, leaning far over to do it, and the tractor still stood there grumbling but not moving. Al stepped back, motioned with his arm, began to walk off slowly toward the pan tractor, looking backwards as he did so like a man training a dog. "C'mon, c'mon, theah's one theah, le's *kill'm, kill'm, kill'm. . . .*"

And with a snort the tractor revved up and followed. Kelly licked his lips without effect because his tongue was dry, too. The madman passed him, walking straight up the center of the beach, and the tractor, now no longer a bulldozer, followed him; and there the sand was bone dry, sun-dried, dried to powder. As the tractor passed him, Kelly got up on all fours, went over the edge of the bank onto the beach, crouched there.

Al crooned, "I love ya, honey, I love ya, 'deed I do—"

Kelly ran crouching, like a man under machine-gun fire, making himself as small as possible and feeling as big as a barn door. The torn-up sand where the tractor had passed was under his feet now; he stopped, afraid to get too much closer, afraid that a weakened, badly grounded arc might leap from the holder in his hand and serve only to alarm and infuriate the thing in the tractor. And just then Al saw him.

"There!" he screamed; and the tractor pulled up short. "Behind you! Get'm, *Daisy! Kill'm, kill'm, kill'm.*"

Kelly stood up almost wearily, fury and frustration too much to be borne. "In the water," he yelled, because it was what his whole being wanted "Get'er in the water! Wet her tracks, Al!"

"*Kill'm, kill'm—*"

As the tractor started to turn, there was a commotion over by the pan tractor. It was Tom, jumping, shouting, waving his arms, swearing. He ran out from behind his machine, straight at the Seven. *Daisy Etta*'s motor roared and she swung to meet him, Al barely dancing back out of the way. Tom cut sharply, sand spouting under his pumping feet, and ran straight into the water. He went out to about waist deep, suddenly disappeared. He surfaced, spluttering, still trying to shout. Kelly took a better grip on his rod holder and rushed.

Daisy Etta, in following Tom's crazy rush, had swung in beside the pan tractor, not fifteen feet away; and she, too, was now in the surf. Kelly closed up the distance as fast as his long legs would let him; and as he approached to within that crucial fifty feet, Al Knowles hit him.

Al was frothing at the mouth, gibbering. The two men hit full tilt; Al's head caught Kelly in the midriff as he missed a straight arm, and the breath went out of him in one great *whoosh!* Kelly went down like tall timber, the whole world turned to one swirling red-gray haze. Al flung himself on the bigger man, clawing, smacking, too berserk to ball his fists.

"Ah'm go' to kill you," he gurgled. "She'll git one, I'll git t'other, an' then she'll know—"

Kelly covered his face with his arms, and as some wind was sucked at last into his laboring lungs, he flung them upward and sat up in one mighty surge. Al was hurled upward and to one side, and as he hit the ground Kelly reached out a long arm, and twisted his fingers into the man's coarse hair, raised him up, and came across with his other fist in a punch that would have killed him had it landed square. But Al managed to jerk to one side enough so that it only amputated a cheek. He fell and lay still. Kelly scrambled madly around in the sand for his welding-rod holder, found it and began to run again. He couldn't see Tom at all now, and the Seven was standing in the surf, moving slowly from side to side, backing out, ravening. Kelly held the rod-clamp and its trailing cable blindly before him and ran straight at the machine. And then it came—that thin, soundless bolt of energy. But this time it had its full force, for poor old Peebles' body had not been the ground that this swirling water offered. *Daisy Etta* literally leaped backwards toward him, and the water around her tracks spouted upward in hot steam. The sound of her engine ran up and up, broke, took on the rhythmic, uneven beat of a swing drummer. She threw herself from side to side like a cat with a bag over its head. Kelly stepped a little closer, hoping for another bolt to come from the clamp in his hand, but there was none, for—

"The circuit breaker!" cried Kelly.

He threw the holder up on the deck plate of the Seven in front of the seat, and ran across the little beach to the welder. He reached behind the switchboard, got his thumb on the contact hinge and jammed it down.

Daisy Etta leaped again, and then again, and suddenly her motor stopped. Heat in turbulent waves blurred the air over her. The little gas tank for the starting motor went out with a cannon's roar, and the big fuel tank, still holding thirty-odd gallons of Diesel oil followed. It puffed itself open rather than exploded, and threw a great curtain of flame over the ground behind the machine. Motor or no motor, then, Kelly distinctly saw the tractor shudder convulsively. There was a crawling movement of the whole frame, a slight wave of motion away from the fuel tank, approaching the front of the machine, and moving upward from the tracks. It culminated in the crown of the radiator core, just in front of the radiator cap; and suddenly an area of six or seven square inches literally *blurred* around the edges. For a second, then, it was normal, and finally it slumped molten, and liquid metal ran down the sides, throwing out little sparks as it encountered what was left of the charred paint. And only then was Kelly conscious of agony in his left hand. He looked down. The welding machine's generator had stopped, though the motor was still turning, having smashed the friable coupling on its drive shaft. Smoke poured from the generator, which had become little more than a heap of slag. Kelly did not scream, though, until he looked and saw what had happened to his hand—

When he could see straight again, he called for Tom, and there was no answer. At last he saw something out in the water, and plunged in after it. The splash of cold salt water on his left hand he hardly felt, for the numbness of shock had set in. He grabbed at Tom's shirt with his good hand, and then the ground seemed to pull itself out from under his feet. That was it, then—a deep hole right off the beach. The Seven had run right to the edge of it, had kept Tom there out of his depth and—

He flailed wildly, struck out for the beach, so near and so hard to get to. He gulped a stinging lungful of brine, and only the lovely shock of his knee striking solid beach keep him from giving up to the luxury of choking to death. Sobbing with effort, he dragged Tom's dead weight inshore and clear of the surf. It was then that he became conscious of a child's shrill weeping; for a mad moment he thought it was he himself, and then he looked and saw that it was Al Knowles. He left Tom and went over to the broken creature.

"Get up, you," he snarled. The weeping only got louder. Kelly rolled him over on his back—he was quite unresisting—and belted him back and forth across the mouth until Al began to choke. Then he hauled him to his feet and led him over to Tom.

"Kneel down, scum. Put one of your knees between his knees." Al stood still. Kelly hit him again and he did as he was told.

"Put your hands on his lower ribs. There. O.K.

Lean, you rat. Now sit back." He sat down, holding his left wrist in his right hand, letting the blood drop from the ruined hand. "Lean. Hold it—sit back. Lean. Sit. Lean. Sit."

Soon Tom sighed and began to vomit weakly, and after that he was all right.

This is the story of *Daisy Etta*, the bulldozer that went mad and had a life of its own, and not the story of the flat-top *Marokuru* of the Imperial Japanese Navy, which has been told elsewhere. But there is a connection. You will remember how the *Marokuru* was cut off from its base by the concentrated attack on Truk, how it slipped far to the south and east and was sunk nearer to our shores than any other Jap warship in the whole course of the war. And you will remember how a squadron of five planes, having been separated by three vertical miles of water from their flight deck, turned east with their bombloads and droned away for a suicide mission. You read that they bombed a minor airfield in the outside of Panama's farflung defenses, and all hands crashed in the best sacrificial fashion.

Well, that was no airfield, no matter what it might have looked like from the air. It was simply a roughly graded runway, white marl against brown scrub-grass.

The planes came two days after the death of *Daisy Etta*, as Tom and Kelly sat in the shadow of the pile of fuel drums, down in the coolth of the swag that *Daisy* had dug there to fuel herself. They were poring over paper and pencil, trying to complete the impossible task of making a written statement of what had happened on the island, and why they and their company had failed to complete their contract. They had found Chub and Harris, and had buried them next to the other three. Al Knowles was tied up in the camp, because they had heard him raving in his sleep, and it seemed he could not believe that *Daisy* was dead and he still wanted to go around killing operators for her. They knew that there must be an investigation, and they knew just how far their story would go; and having escaped a monster like *Daisy Etta*, life was far too sweet for them to want to be shot for sabotage. And murder.

The first stick of bombs struck three hundred yards behind them at the edge of the camp, and at the same instant a plane whistled low over their heads, and that was the first they knew about it. They ran to Al Knowles and untied his feet and the three of them headed for the bush. They found refuge, strangely enough, inside the mound where *Daisy Etta* had first met her possessor.

"Bless their black little hearts," said Kelly as he and Tom stood on the bluff and looked at the flaming wreckage of a camp and five medium bombers below them. And he took the statement they had been sweating out and tore it across.

"But what about him?" said Tom, pointing at Al Knowles, who was sitting on the ground, playing with his fingers. "He'll still spill the whole thing, no matter if we do try to blame it all on the bombing."

"What's the matter with that?" said Kelly.

Tom thought a minute, then grinned. "Why, nothing! That's just the sort of thing they'll expect from him!"